"HERR... H[ERR]...
PLEASE [...]"

Wolff made no re[ply ...]
him by means of a painful grip on the elbow.

Weber didn't struggle, though he was young and strong—it would have done him no good, not against Wolff. He continued to beg, stumbling in the dark on the rough uneven path. He hadn't meant to say anything against the Führer, would never do it again, his mother was a widow and his only brother had been killed at Stalingrad. Terror radiated from him like heat.

Wolff put away the gun and took the thin-bladed knife in his hand. He stopped next to a large rock and pressed the knife tip against the soft pulsing flesh of Weber's throat.

"Turn around," he whispered.

Weber whimpered. He couldn't make himself do it. Wolff spun him around, slamming him back up against the rock. He bent over him, letting him see his face as clearly as possible in the dark, letting him see death.

It was too much for Weber. With the knife at his throat, he started to sob, uttering inarticulate choking sounds.

Wolff plunged the blade in, then drank long and deep, filling himself with the warmth of lifeblood. It was interesting how Weber kept whimpering while he died, much longer than usual. At the very peak of sensation, Wolff shuddered and let the body fall into the snow. The Arctic wind blew into his face, and Wolff suddenly felt as if he could sweep the storm away, or fly with it, far out onto the sea . . .

PINNACLE BOOKS HAS SOMETHING FOR EVERYONE—

MAGICIANS, EXPLORERS, WITCHES AND CATS

THE HANDYMAN (377-3, $3.95/$4.95)
He is a magician who likes hands. He likes their comfortable shape and weight and size. He likes the portability of the hands once they are severed from the rest of the ponderous body. Detective Lanark must discover who The Handyman is before more handless bodies appear.

PASSAGE TO EDEN (538-5, $4.95/$5.95)
Set in a world of prehistoric beauty, here is the epic story of a courageous seafarer whose wanderings lead him to the ends of the old world—and to the discovery of a new world in the rugged, untamed wilderness of northwestern America.

BLACK BODY (505-9, $5.95/$6.95)
An extraordinary chronicle, this is the diary of a witch, a journal of the secrets of her race kept in return for not being burned for her "sin." It is the story of Alba, that rarest of creatures, a white witch: beautiful and able to walk in the human world undetected.

THE WHITE PUMA (532-6, $4.95/NCR)
The white puma has recognized the men who deprived him of his family. Now, like other predators before him, he has become a man-hater. This story is a fitting tribute to this magnificent animal that stands for all living creatures that have become, through man's carelessness, close to disappearing forever from the face of the earth.

Available wherever paperbacks are sold, or order direct from the Publisher. Send cover price plus 50¢ per copy for mailing and handling to Pinnacle Books, Dept. 687, 475 Park Avenue South, New York, N.Y. 10016. Residents of New York and Tennessee must include sales tax. DO NOT SEND CASH. For a free Zebra/ Pinnacle catalog please write to the above address.

DARKNESS ON THE ICE

LOIS TILTON

PINNACLE BOOKS
WINDSOR PUBLISHING CORP.

Thanks to the guys on the Military RT

PINNACLE BOOKS

are published by

Windsor Publishing Corp.
475 Park Avenue South
New York, NY 10016

Copyright © 1993 by Lois Tilton

All rights reserved. No part of this book may be reproduced in any form or by any means without the prior written consent of the Publisher, excepting brief quotes used in reviews.

Pinnacle and the P logo are trademarks of Windsor Publishing Corp.

If you purchased this book without a cover you should be aware that this book is stolen property. It was reported as "unsold and destroyed" to the Publisher and neither the Author nor the Publisher has received any payment for this "stripped book."

First Printing: February, 1993

Printed in the United States of America

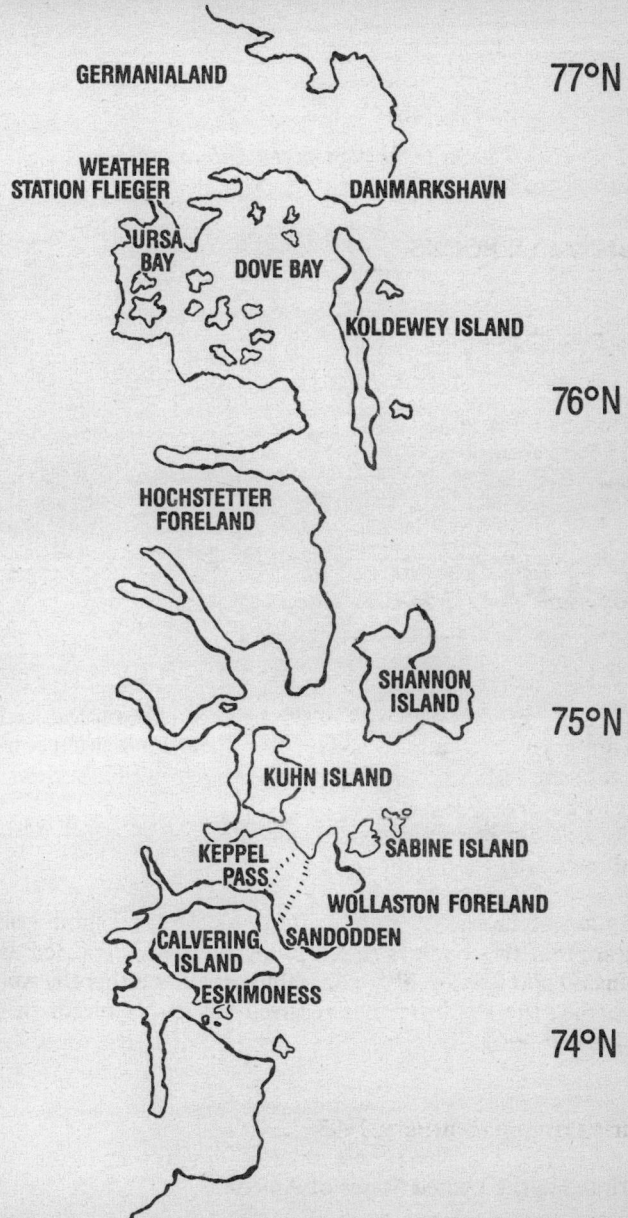

Prologue

1995

The midnight sun moved low on the horizon across the northern sky. Never setting, its path traced an irregular halo, rising highest in the south at azure noon and lowest in the north when the sky darkened to indigo at midnight.

This was July on Greenland far above the Arctic Circle, beginning the brief, rushed summer when the pack ice released its grip on the eastern coast. It was a season of light and life, the sky full of sea birds — gulls, gannets, terns — racing to incubate their eggs and bring the young to adulthood in the few weeks before winter closed in again.

Icebergs floated in the deep blue water of Dove Bay, with an occasional polar bear basking on the ice. Most of the bergs had been brought south from the polar pack ice by the Greenland Current, but a few had calved off the glaciers that extended from an arm of the vast continental ice cap to this eastern shoreline of Greenland. There were no native settlements along the northeastern coast. The grip of the ice was too harsh for humans to survive without technology. A hundred years ago caribou herds had roamed the coastal valleys, but they had long since disappeared, leaving only seals, and an occasional bear or fox for the hunter who might come this way.

But there were weather stations along the coast, and in July a small party of glaciologists landed at Danmarkshavn station near the northeast shore of Dove Bay. To the west, the bay was indented with fjords, the long, deep sea-canyons cutting into the coast. The scientists brought their boat to the mouth of the fjord named Ursa Bay, then camped there overnight on the narrow beach below the headland, while the midnight sun dipped low toward the horizon.

There were three of them. For McIvery and Newcomb the trip to the Greenland ice field had been an annual holiday for the last four years, coming conveniently during the summer vacation from their universities. For Sharon Feldman it was her first visit to Greenland; she was just beginning the fieldwork she hoped would earn her the Ph.D.

The landscape here could only be described as austere: rock and ice, sea and sky overhead. But the site was almost pristine. The annual expeditions had made it a point to pack the trash from their camps out with them. They deplored the threatened coming of petroleum geologists to the empty coast, the threat of oil spills ruining the lichens and the nesting sites of the birds that flew over their heads, screaming at the disturbance of the Arctic peace.

"It's so empty, so wild!" Feldman sighed, exhilarated by the crisp, fresh air.

Not always empty, McIvery pointed out. Hunters had been coming here for decades. "And you can see the remains of a World War II German outpost near the top of the headland."

"Here? On Greenland?"

"Oh, yes. A German weather reporting station. Of course, there's not much left to see. Jay and I have been up before. There's a path. We could show you tomorrow."

She shuddered. "Nazis? No, *thanks*."

In the brighter light of morning they proceeded up the fjord, into the shadows cast by the mountains rising on both sides. At the head of the fjord the sunlight was reflected—so blinding white it hurt their eyes—from a glacier, a finger of the ice cap flowing down through the pass toward the sea. They beached the boat and climbed out, armed with instruments and probes for drilling and measuring the ice. Since the beginning of the study eight years ago, Ursa glacier had been retreating back from the bay at the rate of six to twelve inches per year, though their measurements showed it had been advancing recently, as glacial time went — as late as the middle of this century.

Metal rods, driven into the rocky ground, marked the limits of the glacier in successive years. It was clear as they climbed up, slipping on the scree — loose rock on the slope — that the ice flow was still retreating. Feldman stopped now and then just to breathe in the air as she set up her surveying equipment. The sky was as clear as a flawless blue sapphire.

At first she thought it was the pelt of an animal lying buried at the edge of the receding ice. Probably a sled dog, from the dark gray color of the fur. Curiosity brought her a couple of steps closer. There was something . . .

She knelt to brush away a thin layer of half-melted ice, exposing —

Feldman gasped soundlessly, a choked-off scream. The pelt had been the fur edging the hood of a parka. And inside it . . . With hands that trembled from the shock, she brushed away more of the mixture of slush and stone. Yes, it was a man's face. The skin of the forehead under the hood was pale as wax, and the eyes — she jerked her hand away. The eye she had just exposed was open, a light blue, with the melted snow running from it like tears.

McIvery and Newcomb stood over the body. Jay Newcomb whistled in awe. "He's *perfectly* preserved. You almost think he's looking right up at you."

"Best thing to do is leave him here like this, contact the authorities," McIvery said, kneeling down. "Don't want him to thaw before they can get him out." In contradiction of his own advice, he scraped off a little more of the ice, loosening the neck of the parka. It wasn't unusual to find bodies preserved in the ice. Hikers, climbers died on the glaciers by the dozens every year, buried in an avalanche, fallen into a crevasse. Remains had even been found from as far back as the stone age.

But this one was fairly recent. The pale Caucasian features alone were proof of that. No Vikings on Greenland had ever gone this far up the east coast. Although, he speculated, it would be quite a find to suddenly discover that they had, after all. But this parka was modern. He pulled again at it. There was something underneath, a coat—the collar. Suddenly he tugged harder, making Newcomb say, "Hey, wait a minute, Ian!"

But McIvery looked up with discovery in his voice, "Look at that! Goddamn, look at that!"

The others bent closer. "See it? The collar patch? This is a German officer! He must have been here since the war!"

It was several days before the experts had gathered at the glacier to remove the body from the imprisoning ice and fly it to the medical facilities of the US Air Force base at Thule. A party of reporters descended to film and photograph the grave and the ruins of the weather station, then departed the next day, leaving the locations now somewhat less than pristine.

At the Thule base, delivery of the body was an event of some interest, but the medical officer assumed that as a matter of course the remains would be kept frozen until arrangements had been made with the proper authorities to have them shipped back to Germany. Strangely, there was no identification on the body, so he had fingerprints taken to send to the German Embassy. It was assumed that the dead man had been one of the members of the weather party stationed near the mouth of Ursa Bay during the war.

Then a special flight came in from Washington, two high-ranking officers with orders to thaw and examine the remains before they could be released. The doctor's first reaction was to protest. Thawing the body would only accelerate the process of decomposition. And an autopsy—why?

But the orders allowed no latitude for protest. The full colonel was clear on that point. As to the autopsy, the doctor was to proceed to that step only upon authorization. First he was to conduct a complete—a very complete—examination of the remains. There was a list of tests to be performed. Those that couldn't be processed in the lab on Thule would be sent to the US.

The doctor looked up from the list of blood tests in dismay and confusion. What was he supposed to be looking for? Some rare disease? Something to do with secret Nazi germ warfare? Was there a biohazard?

The colonel frowned. There was a possible biohazard, yes. All due precautions should be taken. As to what they were looking for, all he could say was that any anomalies should be reported to him immediately.

Later, considerably subdued, the doctor stood over the body on the operating table and cleared his throat for the microphone. The remains were those of an adult male, aged about thirty. Thawed, the corpse exhibited no rigor. There was no lividity, and the color of the skin was very pale. Altogether, the signs suggested exsanguination, but there was no obvious wound. Perhaps the body had frozen very quickly after death.

Finished with his observations, he took a syringe to draw a sample of blood. It would have to be a large sample, considering the number of tests the Army had ordered. Judging from the extreme pallor, the absence of lividity, he wondered if the corpse would even have enough blood left in it to satisfy the lab's demands.

He hesitated. The corpse lay white and flaccid under the harsh operating room lights that mercilessly revealed the emaciated ribcage, the various scars, some long-healed and others fairly recent. This wasn't exactly his line of work. He was an internist, not a pathologist. Finally he inserted the needle through the chest, directly into the heart muscle.

For a moment the tube was empty, then a dark red fluid rose up part of the way into it. The doctor stared. It looked more like fresh blood than the blackish substance he'd expected to find in a body this old. Could it be the freezing?

There was another pulse of blood, raising the level.

"What the—"

A third pulse filled the tube.

"Good God!"

It was a heartbeat. Slow, faint—but after fifty years buried under the ice, this man was alive!

Immediately, the doctor began resuscitation procedures, shouting orders for a crash cart, for nurses and technicians. The blood sample was sent for type and cross-match. He didn't really stop to question what he was doing, quite forgetting the colonel's instructions. There must have been a mistake, that was all.

The medical staff at Thule base was experienced at reviving cases of near freezing. The doctor was still hard at work bringing this latest victim back to life when the senior lab technician came into the operating room.

"Doctor, I think you should see—"

"You have the blood typed yet? Dammit, what's the delay?"

"Uh, Doctor, this sample . . ." The technician held out a printout from the lab. "I did the test twice over. This sample—I don't know what it is, but this just isn't human blood!"

Chapter One

1944

The beast of war had paused for a moment to draw its breath, to lick its wounds. Along the western front the exhausted armies rested while their generals rushed men and materiel forward to replace what they had wasted in the bitter fighting that had driven the Germans back behind the Westwall, desperately prepared to defend their own soil.

Even as the Allied armies advanced, the few remaining days of Hitler's Reich were growing shorter. Lengthening shadows filled the deep forested valleys of the Ardennes and the dark, fir-covered slopes of the Eifel hills on the eastern side of the river Our. The armies on both sides of the river regarded each other warily, too weary to do much more than hold their respective positions. The great battles were taking place elsewhere now. At night a few patrols might set out, probing, testing the readiness of the enemy, but otherwise the forces waited, relieved to be out of the worst of the fighting for the moment, wondering how long their respite could last.

But the figure that moved through the darkness of the forested hills one night in late September wore the uniform of no army, bore no visible weapons. In unrelieved black, he came out from behind the German lines, past the concrete barrier of the Westwall, through the deepest woods, a moving shadow among the tall black fir trunks. His pace was a tireless jog that carried him west through the silence of the forest, past the uneasy sleep of farmsteads and villages, into the deserted land that lay between the armies.

Once he paused, motionless, invisible in the night. Above him the wind hissed through the fir branches, but he stood still, waiting, listening for the distant footsteps approaching. A German patrol came into sight one by one, the tread of their boots soft on the thick forest floor. The scent of the soldiers was familiar: sweat and leather and harsh tobacco and gun oil.

Their scent, their body warmth, the steady pulse of their hearts, each intake and exhalation of breath — Wolff's senses tingled as he stood unseen in the dark and waited for them to pass, untouched, unharmed. Another time, perhaps, it would be otherwise. But tonight he had a different purpose.

Once the patrol had gone its own way, he began the descent from the heights, into the steep narrow valley of the Our. He could hear the water running over its bed, the lap of its waves against the ruins of the bridge blown up by the retreating German forces. He frowned, confronting the stretch of water, then after a moment he waded into the dark current. The river at this point was not much higher than his waist, and shortly he emerged on the American-held bank.

By now a light rain was beginning to fall, blown by the wind, but Wolff ignored it, moving quickly toward the high ridge on the western side of the river. His pace was still tireless. He didn't seem to breathe as he loped towards the cleared farmland beyond the trees. Then, catching sight of the American sentry, he paused.

Stalking with a predator's silent footsteps, he came up behind the soldier, a shadow in motion, part of the night. The American was less than fully alert. Miserable in the chilly, windswept rain, he had hunched his shoulders down into the turned-up collar of his field jacket and was lingering longer than he should have in the dark shelter of the trees.

A slow, feral smile appeared briefly on Wolff's pale face. His hungry senses almost reeled from the nearness of the man's blood-warmth, the scent of him, the sound of his heartbeat.

The steel helmet protected the back of the soldier's neck, but it was less of an impediment than the coal-scuttle German model had been on more than one other occasion. It took only an instant. The American felt his neck bend backward, as if it were going to break. His rifle fell to the ground. He couldn't breathe, couldn't cry out for help. The grip was unbreakable, inhumanly strong. He struggled, choking, helpless.

Wolff drank in all of his victim's terror, keeping up the pressure until the man's vision began to darken. Then, with a quick, sure thrust, he plunged the steel of his dagger into the soldier's exposed throat. Just as quickly, he withdrew the blade and brought his lips to the spurting wound. He could hear the pulse of heart valves opening and closing as the rich hot flow surged through the arteries, burst into his mouth. Oh, it was good!

It took too long, but Wolff couldn't let go until the heartbeat had stuttered to a halt. He always tried to make the effort to discipline his hunger, but the bloodlust, once released, was overwhelming—intense and utterly primal. He wanted to throw back his head and howl at the invisible moon, like the wolf from which he had taken his name.

But his will mastered the impulse, and a moment later he was back in control. He carefully wiped the narrow blade of his knife on the sleeve of the dead soldier's field jacket and slid it into its sheath. Then he lifted the loose-limbed body and carried it deeper into the trees. Time was getting short.

The US Army battalion had its headquarters at the farm just ahead. Free now from the pangs of his need, Wolff passed more sentries, eluding them easily in the dark, moving from one outbuilding to the next, past the barns and sheds filled with sleeping soldiers.

He paused to quickly survey the farmhouse. This was where it should be—the battalion S-2, intelligence headquarters. Most of the rooms were dark, except for two on the ground floor. Sentries at every door. Not good. No open windows, no entrance from a cellar.

His hand went to the inside of his black pullover sweater, to the silenced Walther PPK strapped to his waist, next to the packet of documents. He hated to use a gun, but it might well come to that, tonight.

He chose the back door, coming around the corner behind the sentry. A quick snap of the neck eliminated him. Wolff dropped the corpse next to the stairs, into the shadow, counting the minutes now, the odds of getting in and out before someone spotted the soldier missing from his post. He pulled out the Walther, slipped inside the door.

He was in the kitchen, a large square room with a tiled floor, filled now with the equipment of soldiers, not cooks. A dozen of them were asleep wherever they had managed to find the space—on the wooden chairs, rolled in blankets on the floor. A few snored, one twitched and cried out in a dream. The room was thick with the warmth and scent of them.

Wolff passed through into a hallway. Ahead was light and the sound of low voices. Another sentry at one door. Wolff tensed, cursing silently. His hand closed around the grip of the gun, well aware how much noise a shot would make, even with the silencer. They'd be able to hear it—inside the room, even back in the kitchen.

The hall was half dark, the only light coming from the far end where the guard stood, bored, shifting from one foot to the other. Wolff tensed his muscles, thinking of time and the dead sentry outside, bound to be discovered soon.

The guard yawned, closing his eyes for one moment, and that was all Wolff needed. He rushed in silence, struck, and snatched up the dead man's rifle before it could hit the floor.

Quickly now, through the door, gun ready. Two men, backs to the door, looked up, startled—the radioman and an officer. Two shots, and they fell back, first one, then the other. Wolff had always been an excellent shot with a pistol. There was the sharp strong scent of cordite, blood and pulped brain matter, but he ignored it, dragged the guard inside, shut the door.

Papers now. Wolff ransacked the room, pulling open files, strewing their contents on the tables and chairs. From inside his sweater he took the folder of documents, tossed the papers in with the rest. Then he filled the folder almost at random, pulling documents from the American files, only glancing quickly to see the headings: SECRET and TOP SECRET.

Finished. Mission accomplished. Wolff straightened, tucked the folder back inside his sweater, and listened carefully for some sign that his infiltration might have been discovered. Again, briefly, the cruel grin, then he holstered the gun and left the farmhouse the way he had come, the US battalion still sleeping undisturbed.

Time to meet his contact before dawn, back on the German side of the river, behind the fortified line. As he moved quickly through the night, Wolff didn't speculate concerning the military secrets that might be in the papers he was carrying. The point of this operation had been the documents he had left behind, seemingly discarded as he ransacked the American files. These had been very carefully prepared, and if all went well, they would soon cause the Allies to believe that certain SS Panzer divisions had been transferred to the Russian front.

He enjoyed this work. To take on a mission, to do it well — this was a matter of pride, of honor. Among the Germans, there were still a few men who understood such matters. Or at least so he had thought, at the beginning.

He was aware that he might have made a mistake in allying himself with the SS. But at the time, they had held a place he wanted badly — the home of his ancestors, the castle where he had once ruled.

Times had changed. It was always necessary to adapt, in one way or another.

Free now from the pangs of his hunger, still tireless, Wolff evaded both US and German patrols as he crossed the lines back into the brooding Eifel hills. But even for him, it was a long way in a single night, and by the time he approached the rendezvous point he was growing uneasy. His contact had better be there, better be waiting.

The place had been a forester's hut once, before the last war, as Wolff remembered. The yellow light of a lantern flickered through the curtained windows, in disregard of blackout regulations. Wolff approached cautiously, passing the American jeep parked at a short distance from the hut — Scholz's latest acquisition. Scholz's driver couldn't get his long ostentatious staff car into the densely wooded hills. The driver himself sat at the wheel, shifting restlessly on the seat. Something moved too on the floor in the back of the car, and Wolff briefly caught the scent of pain and despair. He ignored it and moved on around the back of the hut, approaching the door from the other side.

Suddenly Wolff paused, went rigid. He could sense the presence of more than one man inside. Scholz was supposed to come alone — always, alone.

They were seated at a table in front of the cold ashes of the fireplace. Wolff caught the scents of expensive tobacco and cognac as he flung open the door, taking satisfaction in seeing the two men flinch. They were both wearing the black-and-silver dress uniform of the SS, an ostentation never seen these days among the troops in the field.

Wolff pulled out the folder of papers and sent it sliding across the table into Scholz's bulging lap, pages spilling out and falling onto the floor. "American secret documents," he said curtly, ignoring the second officer.

Scholz's thick-lipped grin seemed forced as he gathered the documents. "Very good. Very good. I take it the operation went well?"

"Well enough." It was a principle with Wolff to volunteer nothing to Scholz.

"Good, good. I knew I could depend on you." Scholz smirked. "Your usual payment is outside in the car."

Wolff was particularly glad now that he'd already fed. "You can keep your carrion, Scholz."

Scholz grinned nervously as he stuffed the folder into his own briefcase. The Sturmbannführer thought he had Wolff at a disadvantage, knowing his secret, but still he'd never been able to look him directly in the eye. At the moment, though, Wolff suspected it was the presence of the senior officer that had him fumbling with the briefcase lock.

Scholz glanced at his watch, a seemingly careless gesture, but Wolff knew better. Dawn was not far off. "But I see we haven't much time. There is another matter, a very important operation. As you can see, Oberführer Kessler—"

The second officer interrupted with a sharp movement of one black-gloved hand. "I think that will be enough, Scholz. You can wait outside."

Scholz's face darkened momentarily as he seemed to choke on his indignation, but he rose quickly enough to his feet to click his heels and give the Hitler salute before leaving the hut. Wolff turned to Kessler with an expression of dark amusement, but the Oberführer met his eyes steadily with a slight nod of his head.

"Herr . . . Wolff."

Wolff appreciated Kessler's cool manner. The SS senior colonel had a lean, almost ascetic face, with grey hair clipped short. Cold eyes. They had looked on enough death, was their expression, that they could meet Wolff's without blinking. Wolff had seen such eyes, uncounted years ago, in a mirror, except that his own were blue.

He acknowledged the greeting with a bow of his own. "Oberführer Kessler."

"Please sit down. I'll try to be brief. I believe you're aware that the Reich has recently suffered some setbacks in the Carpathian region."

Wolff raised his eyebrows. He had reasons—personal reasons—for concern with that region. But how did Kessler know? "I think perhaps the situation is more serious than you suggest," he said, probing for a reaction.

Kessler frowned. "This information is highly confidential, but I can tell you that steps will be taken—soon—to assert direct German control. The present Hungarian government is no longer reliable. When matters stabilize, there is, I believe, a certain castle in the northern Carpathians . . ."

Wolff stiffened. *He knows. They know.* His identity, so long kept secret. Angrily, he said, "At the moment, I believe that region is in Rumanian hands. And the Russians follow the Rumanians."

"At the moment, this may be so. But as I've said, we expect that situation to be temporary. They say—our enemies—that the Reich is finished. Those enemies underestimate the German will. They don't know what weapons we will have—soon—to turn the tide back again."

"Miracle weapons, yes, I've heard of them," Wolff said impatiently.

"I've *seen* them," Kessler answered in a clipped, intense voice, leaning slightly forward in Wolff's direction, as if he had quite forgotten what manner of being he faced. "In a matter of months, the Luftwaffe will be able to reestablish air superiority over Europe. We will have the means to reduce the cities of England to ashes. We can push their armies back into the sea again. But we need time. We need to hold them back long enough to rebuild our strength.

"The Führer is already making his plans. But there is one crucial factor." He paused. "You, Herr Wolff, can play a vital role, a role that may prove essential to our success."

Wolff shook his head. He could feel the nearness of dawn deep in his bones. "Oberführer, I'm not a soldier. It's true that I've carried out some operations for your organization, but there are particular limits to the type of mission I can undertake."

Kessler's direct gaze wavered for a moment. "I am aware—to some extent—of the nature of your limitations. And your . . . unique abilities. In fact, this is precisely the reason why you were chosen."

Now we come to it, Wolff thought to himself.

"Herr Wolff, have you ever been above the Arctic Circle? Are you aware that in the highest latitudes there are months when the sun never rises above the horizon?"

Wolff was taken by surprise. For a moment, he even ignored the approaching sunrise as Kessler went on, "It's absolutely essential to our forthcoming operations that we have accurate weather forecasts. And Europe's weather is born in the Arctic. The only way to obtain the necessary data is from reporting stations established as far north as possible, preferably on Greenland. The enemy, of course, is well aware of this factor. Less than a month ago one of our weather expeditions was intercepted at sea on the way to set up a base on Greenland. We already have sent another party to replace them, a party that was originally supposed to be sent elsewhere."

Wolff frowned, warned by the ache in his bones. "I fail to see how all this would involve me."

"Security. In the winter, the east coast of Greenland is entirely isolated by the ice packs. When this happens navigation in those waters will be impossible. The darkness will prevent effective air surveillance. Then the only danger can come from land-based patrols, dogsled patrols. For much of the year, this is the only way to travel in those regions. We have reason to believe that this winter the Americans have reinforced the local Danish patrol with trained ski troops and dogsleds."

"In winter," said Wolff thoughtfully. "In the dark."

Kessler nodded. "Exactly. In the dark. Think of it, Herr Wolff—a night that lasts for almost four months. When the need for increased security for our weather parties was being discussed—at the very highest levels—your name was brought up. Your . . . unique abilities were considered almost providential by the Führer."

"The Führer." Wolff's voice was flat. "And has the German

21

Führer any misgivings about the nature of these 'unique abilities' of mine?"

Kessler shook his head. "On the contrary, the Führer has a certain interest in . . . such persons as yourself. This is part of the greatness of his mind. In fact, he expressed a desire to meet you, personally, one day when your mission is complete."

"I see. And you, Oberführer?"

Kessler hesitated only for an instant. "I follow orders. And when the fatherland is at risk, there are no means I wouldn't employ to save it." He met Wolff's eyes again with a frigid gray stare. "No means."

Wolff stood up. His glance went involuntarily to the eastern window of the hut, where the visible sky was turning a lighter gray. "But when these four months of night are over, when the sun does come back, what happens then?"

"You'll be taken out before that becomes a problem. We've successfully evacuated a number of our remote bases in an emergency. There will be no difficulty. You'll be in contact with us by radio."

A minute passed while Wolff stood and stared at the window, at the almost imperceptible coloring of the sky. He could feel it beginning now, the slow, aching weakness starting to claim him, as it had every morning since he had put the knife into Istvan's heart and claimed his blood.

Four months without the sun. Four months of freedom. It had been so long . . .

"Yes," he almost whispered, "yes, I do think I might be interested. If you can guarantee that I'll be taken out in time."

Kessler stood. "Then it's settled."

"Not quite." There was an expression on Wolff's face that made Kessler flinch. "Do you consider yourself a man of honor, Herr Kessler? Would you pledge your sworn word?"

Kessler's straight figure went ramrod stiff. "You have it," he said. "My word."

"Then I accept it," said Wolff. "But for now, it's late."

"I'll meet you here tomorrow night, then. We have very little time—"

"No," Wolff said shortly. "The night after. Tomorrow, I have other business to finish." Without another word, he left the hut and disappeared into the fading night.

From the dark shadows of the trees, he could see Scholz pacing impatiently beside his precious jeep. Scholz. For a moment Wolff's hand crept toward his sheathed dagger, but a warning pang of weakness stopped him. No time. He had left it too long.

There was a shelter here beneath the hut, a small dugout cellar, but he didn't dare use it, not with Scholz nearby.

Instead he went deeper into the woods, through a tangle of roots concealing an overgrown gully, following it down. The Eifel was carved by countless small streams, and here a shallow cave had been hollowed out under the bank. Wolff stumbled more and more often as the spasms of weakness hit him, muscle and bone, but at last he managed to crawl into the cave and fling his body down on its damp floor.

Here, beneath the ground, with the earth as his bed, the pain was bearable. His respiration slowed, growing more and more shallow as his other functions ceased. Only his senses were alert. He could hear the groundwater seeping through the earth, the minute scrabbling of insects on the floor of the cave. He was completely helpless now, vulnerable to his enemies.

As Istvan had been two hundred years ago, lying in the deepest dungeon of the castle. And as he had been himself one evening a month ago, just as dusk was fading, when he had caught the sound of an automobile engine, the scent of combustion byproducts. Then a door slamming and footsteps, coming closer and closer—Scholz, arriving before his appointed time.

Fifteen minutes earlier, and Wolff wouldn't have been able to move. But the sun had already passed below the horizon, only the afterglow remaining in the sky. Fighting against the pain, he had forced himself to his feet and climbed, inch by torturous inch, up from the cellar. He'd barely closed the hatch on the floor when Scholz cautiously pushed open the door, feigning surprise to find Wolff already there. But the look on his fat face, the knowing smirk, had betrayed him. He *knew*.

Tomorrow night. Waiting now, with the sun rising into the eastern sky, Wolff lay on the floor of the cave and dreamed of a dungeon where he lay bound with heavy iron chains and stared into the face of his enemy, a face he hadn't seen in two hundred years. But as he waited for the spike to pierce his heart, the roof fell away above him, and he was staring into the star-filled darkness of an endless winter night.

Chapter Two

No one ever brought up the fate of Sturmbannführer Scholz, whose flabby drained corpse had been left lying on the seat of his stolen American jeep next to the larger body of his driver. Although Wolff had noticed teams of SS rounding up a number of local suspects for the usual *pro forma* reprisals, it appeared that Scholz, in the current emergency, was considered expendable by the higher authorities.

Kessler had only fixed him with a look like gray ice, saying, "I trust now that your affairs are in order and you can devote yourself to the task at hand. We haven't much time."

His reprisal was of a more subtle variety. Wolff had never, for obvious reasons, flown on an aircraft. But Kessler had him shipped secretly, by day, in a sealed, windowless compartment in back of the plane, from Bonn to Wilhelmshaven and then to Tromsø in upper Norway. It was torture, no matter that the rays of the sun never touched him directly. He lay in agony for hours, far from the soothing contact of the earth, unable to move until the sunset finally faded.

And from Kessler's expression as he stepped down from the aircraft into the northern night, Wolff could see that he had known.

"We haven't much time." Wolff heard it again and again as Kessler's urgency drove him through the endless grueling briefings necessary to transform him into a passable model of an officer in the SS. They drilled him in shifts, allowing no time for rest except in the shorter and shorter intervals between sunrise and sunset.

They knew what he was.

Kessler, of course, had known from the beginning. The Führer himself knew. As for the others, he could see it in their eyes—in the eyes of the guards, with their hands never far from the triggers of their machine pistols, escorting him from briefing room to pistol range to the shelter of his basement retreat. He wondered sometimes, almost amused, what they thought would happen if they opened fire on him, whether the bullets would pass through his flesh, whether he would disappear in a puff of black smoke. There were many misconceptions about the powers and invulnerability of his kind. But Wolff was reluctant to risk the effects of automatic weapons fire at close range. He knew how he could be killed, and a bullet smashing his heart would be more than sufficient.

At first he didn't think of himself as a prisoner, despite the guards constantly and silently at his back. It wasn't the threat of their guns that kept him from escape. He had undertaken this of his own will, had given his word to complete the mission.

Kessler disappeared for a few days early in October, once Wolff's training was underway. When he returned, his mood was even more grim than before. "The enemy has intercepted another one of our weather groups—the one you were to join."

Wolff looked down at himself in the black dress uniform of an SS Hauptsturmführer and laughed shortly. "Then . . . all this has been useless?" Would there be no Arctic, then? No long months without a sunrise?

Kessler glared stiffly at him. "Not at all. I can't deny that this has been a serious setback. But there is another weather group already established for contingencies like this one."

"And this group is your last chance?"

Kessler frowned again. "There's a weather ship in the area, as well. But a ship runs the risk of detection by enemy planes and submarines. They have to operate too close to the convoy routes to Murmansk. Your mission, essentially, is unchanged. You *must* see to it that this station keeps broadcasting its information for as long as possible."

"At least until what date?"

Kessler looked uncomfortable. "The end of December. I suppose I don't have to remind you again that this information must remain confidential."

"Of course."

They were in the windowless basement briefing room where Wolff had spent many long hours since coming to Tromsø. The guards had been left outside the door, this information being too sensitive for their ears. Wolff had never before made a deliberate attempt to intimidate Kessler. Now he sat forward in his chair and stared at him steadily until the Oberführer was forced to drop his eyes and there was a slight scent of nervous fear in the air of the room. "And you've already made the arrangement we discussed? About the property?"

Kessler pulled a large stiff envelope out of his briefcase. "The new government of Hungary is fully cooperative, as I promised. Here are the deeds. Just as we agreed."

Wolff took the envelope, permitting himself a slight bleak smile. So the castle was his, again. If the Germans ever recaptured the territory. "Well, then," he said finally, "I suppose that now I have a material interest in the success of this new offensive."

Kessler scowled coldly. "Things are moving quickly now. I think it would be best for you to leave for the Arctic as soon as possible. Transportation is being arranged."

At the mention of transportation, Wolff felt a spasm of incipient panic. "I assume you mean a ship, or a submarine."

Kessler shook his head. "Out of the question. Every day is crucial now. The pack ice in East Greenland is almost solid already. Our previous transport was caught in the ice. The risk is too much even for a submarine in those waters, at this time of year. We'll have to fly you in."

Kessler's voice was just slightly too knowing, slightly too smug. The scent of fear had dissipated. Wolff had to force himself not to react as a hot dark rage swept over him, boiling toward bloodlust. *You dare — you dare to taunt me! I could kill you. Now. While your guards are outside. Put the knife against your throat. Watch you squirm. Watch you beg. And then . . .*

"If it's necessary, of course," he replied at last, stiffly. Another flight. Dreading it. *Enjoy your little victory, Oberführer. Your little vengeance. For today.*

The suppressed rage stimulated his growing hunger. It had been almost two weeks since he had fed on Scholz and his oversized bodyguard, far too long for his comfort. Now, if they were shipping him out, he needed blood. He wanted, needed to kill.

Tromsø's night, at seventy degrees north latitude, was already more than twenty hours long, the sun's brief course low over the horizon. Wolff waited impatiently the next day for it to set, anticipating the hunt along the Norwegian waterfront, the deep shadows in the side of a tied-up ship, the drunken, careless sailors and tired whores — his prey.

As soon as he felt the day pass away, he went to the door of his solitary room, lifted the steel bar. He pushed on the handle — and the door held. Closed. Locked.

Trapped!

Terror and panic reddened his vision. It was a heavy steel door with the locking bar on the inside, provided for his own security, or so Kessler had claimed. Wolff pressed his palms against the unyielding steel surface. Could he break through? Did the Germans have any real idea of his strength? But there would almost certainly be guards stationed outside, inches away. SS with their lethal Schmeissers — at this point-blank range. They would have heard him try the latch, would be ready for him.

His hearing suddenly alerted him, he moved back a step, lowered his hands to his sides as the lock clicked open. He hesitated. To open it now? A minute passed, then another, and nothing happened. Finally he pushed down on the door handle and felt it yield smoothly to his touch. The door swung open on its oiled hinges and he faced the SS guards, the scent of their fear, the heightened pulse of their heartbeats. He fought desperately for control of his hunger. Four of them . . . the Schmeissers . . . at this range . . .

The noncom commanding them cleared his throat nervously. "Ah, Hauptsturmführer Wolff, Oberführer Kessler has . . . has requested that you remain in your room at this time."

Wolff turned on the man, who reflexively brought up his weapon between them. But Wolff ignored it. "Send Kessler to me," he snarled.

Kessler must have been waiting. He appeared within five minutes. "Perhaps you could explain your latest request?" Wolff demanded stiffly. He was in control again now, his rage and hunger held back behind the barrier of his will. "I have certain arrangements to make before the flight."

"Ah, yes. I'm afraid, for security reasons, that I can't allow you to leave the base until it's time for your transport to depart. But don't be concerned. I'm aware, of course, of your needs, and I can make whatever arrangements are necessary."

And they were duly made, that evening, when Wolff's hunger had grown to a knife-edged need that had him pacing the floor in his prison.

They brought the man to him, flinging the door open and shoving him in, then slamming it shut, closing them both inside together. The man stumbled, caught himself, staring around the room with wild, panicked eyes, breathing hard, ready to fight or defend himself or escape, if he could. The scent of his terror filled the enclosed space.

Wolff supposed he was a partisan—or what the Germans were calling a partisan these days. The SS were not extremely particular. Wolff had been in their camps, had fed there. They practiced death in those places on a scale unimaginable to anyone who hadn't witnessed it. Some, like Scholz, had supposed this made a bond between them and a being such as Wolff.

Now he got slowly to his feet, saying nothing, drawn by the inexorable demand of his hunger, damning Kessler for putting him in this position. His victim reeked of fear, heartbeat racing. The man's eyes flickered as they darted around the room, searching for anything—escape, a weapon—that might offer the slightest bit of hope. *No*, Wolff told him silently, *there is no hope here, none at all*. He'd been hungry for too long, and the nearness of the man, the warmth, the scent of sweat and gut-knotting fear all worked on his bloodlust until it clawed like a live thing inside him, demanding to be fed.

He made it sudden, then, drew the man to him in a deadly intimacy, forcing his head back, back almost to the breaking point to receive the swift thrust of the knife. It suited his mood—a quick, angry death. His victim also seemed to want it; he wouldn't let it be easy. He struggled, hard, until the very end, when his heartbeat finally gave up the fight.

It was a kill Wolff would have savored, alone in the dark with his victim on Tromsø's waterfront, on his own terms. Not here. Not this way, like a dog in Kessler's kennel.

There would be an accounting one day, when this was all over. That, he promised himself—to teach Kessler what he was dealing with, to teach him at great, painful length exactly what it was to fear and to die.

Chapter Three

Today the sun had been a dull orange glow, sullenly rising above the horizon for several minutes before subsiding again into the ocean. Now twilight was overtaking the sky once again. As Martin Dietrich watched, inhaling the smoke from a cigarette, the orange faded toward purple, toward gray. Briefly, the peaks and escarpments of offshore ice flared with reflected light, an illusion of warmth in the Arctic sea.

The long winter night was descending on Greenland, and there was no sign of the expected aircraft. Dietrich stood near the edge of the bare rocky cliff overlooking the mouth of Ursa Bay. Beyond, in the open waters of Dove Bay, icebergs clashed and ground together as the Greenland Current carried the mass of the pack ice south. The fjord was already iced over. At this season of the year, late October, stretches of open water could appear and refreeze in a matter of hours. But within a week or two the sea would be locked in ice until midsummer. There would be no escape then, for any of them.

It was said that the constant unrelieved darkness of the Arctic winter could drive men mad. Shoving his hands into his coat pockets for the warmth, Dietrich turned to look down at the bare wooden cabin where twelve men would have to live together for the next nine months. He'd volunteered for this expedition after a head injury had left him unfit to fly — most of the Luftwaffe was already grounded, as it was.

Dietrich sometimes wondered at the miracle that he was still alive. Six years ago he had fit the image of the dashing young pilot, and no one could have convinced him he wasn't going to live forever. Now his blond hair was thinning and going gray—too many missions, too many deaths. Would it ever be finished? Somewhere beyond that horizon was Germany, was Stuttgart, where he had a wife and a three- no, four-year-old daughter. Amelia and Trudi. He'd seen them last during his leave in June. It would be at least a year until he was with them again.

But as a former flier, he was acutely aware of how crucial accurate forecasts would be to the military planners this coming winter. He had impressed it on all his men: what they did here in this lonely northern outpost could be the salvation of all Germany, all their families. This was the real reason they were still fighting.

He believed—he had to believe—that they would succeed. But the situation made it hard to keep any such hopes alive. The enemy had occupied Greenland since the first days of the war, flushing out and destroying every weather base the Germans had tried to establish. Already this season had been disastrous. The trawler *Kehdingen,* carrying the Edelweiss weather group to Koldewey Island, had been attacked by a US Coast Guard icebreaker. The ship had survived the torpedoes, but the party had no choice but to scuttle the ship and surrender.

Worse had followed. A second expedition, previously intended to set up a base on Franz Josef Land, in Russian territory, had been diverted to Greenland, and had actually established its base on Koldewey, an island just over one hundred kilometers east of Ursa Bay. But again the German ship, the *Externsteine,* had been spotted by an enemy reconnaissance plane. The ship was captured, and the members of the weather group rounded up and sent to prison camps.

"It's up to us now," he told himself, standing on the lonely headland overlooking the bay. "Up to me."

He had chosen his site with care, south of the peninsula aptly named Germanialand. The steep face of the cliff protected and concealed the station from the sea. Below, the path wound up behind the headland from the rocky beach. No one would spot this place unless they were headed west up the fjord, and then only with luck, if they caught sight of the path.

It wasn't hard to believe, standing here, that this desolate place was uninhabitable. Even the Eskimos hadn't been able to survive on the east Greenland coast. Dietrich suddenly remembered a slogan he had once seen chalked on a wall in a bombed-out village in eastern Poland: *Sieg oder Siberien*. Victory or Siberia. But between Greenland and Siberia there didn't seem to be much to choose.

He turned for one last look at the bay before going back to the base, and at that moment, when all the colors had faded to different shades of gray, his ears registered the approaching drone of aircraft engines, even before he saw the shape against the dimming light.

He rushed down to the weather station, praying that this was not somehow an enemy reconnaissance flight, but the pilot had already made contact by radio, and Dietrich's men were running down the rocky trail to the beach to meet the flight. He hurried after them, concerned that the pilot might not be able to locate the base in the dark, even with the radio signal to guide him in.

Dietrich had been told to anticipate the plane's arrival, but not exactly what or whom to expect, only that it involved the security of his base. Now he paced impatiently along the ice at the shoreline while his men lit flares and the aircraft circled uncertainly overhead. He recognized it as a Blohm und Voss flying boat, the Luftwaffe's most reliable amphibian, but how safely could it land on the frozen water of Ursa Bay? There were chunks of icebergs out there that could tear the belly right off the plane. And would the ice be strong enough to hold its weight? Dietrich reflexively strained with the unknown pilot as he fought to reduce speed without stalling his engines. At last, spotting a relatively clear stretch of ice, the seaplane touched down in a spray of glittering shards while the pilot fought to hold it on course and avoid colliding with any of the frozen obstacles.

The men cheered as it finally slowed. Most of them were Luftwaffe ground crew, and they knew what a magnificent exhibition of skill they had just witnessed.

But now the plane, with its engines idling, was coasting slowly to a stop, and Dietrich saw a figure climb unsteadily down onto the ice. As soon as he was clear, the pilot, doubtless trying to keep his plane from being frozen into the ice, began to turn it back into the wind. Dietrich watched with his jaw set so tight it hurt, while the pilot fought to get the aircraft up to takeoff speed on the uneven surface of the ice. The three Junkers engines screamed with the strain. Dietrich was so intent on the desperate effort to get aloft that he almost failed to notice the man coming toward him across the uneven frozen surface of the shore ice.

Suddenly, though, he registered the long black leather greatcoat and high-peaked black cap of the SS with its death's head badge. SS? What in God's name was the SS doing out here beyond the edge of nowhere?

Dietrich stiffened and dropped his cigarette. Suddenly the casual, comradely atmosphere of the weather base had disappeared, swept away by something colder than the Greenland ice. Apprehensive faces turned in his direction, questioning, but Dietrich knew as little as his men.

"You are the commanding officer?" the stranger demanded with the sort of harsh arrogance typical of the SS.

Dietrich noted with a distinct relief that their ranks were equivalent. "Hauptmann Martin Dietrich, in command of Weather Group Flieger," he replied in a flat, extremely correct tone, bringing his heels together. He gestured toward Dr. Pflieger, who was standing nearby, scowling visibly. "And this is Dr. Pflieger, our senior meteorologist."

The SS officer bowed slightly, a curiously old-fashioned

gesture, all but ignoring Pflieger. "SS Hauptsturmführer Wolff. Here are my orders."

His face was pale, unnaturally pale, especially the forehead beneath his black hair. Was he sick? Dietrich wondered. The packet he held out was sealed. Dietrich took it, instinctively returning the bow. But his attention was drawn back to the scene out on the ice where the flying boat had once again failed to reach the necessary velocity for takeoff.

His muscles were still tensed. "I don't think they're going to make it off."

"The possibility was anticipated. If necessary, they'll have to remain here. Now, I think we'd better discuss my orders."

"Yes, of course," Dietrich said, distracted, wondering how they were going to manage to accommodate the five-man crew of the flying boat in their tight quarters. And why had this SS man been sent here in the first place? "We'd better go back up to the station."

They proceeded up the trail behind the headland, leaving behind the single bag Wolff had carried. Wolff was silent, and Dietrich couldn't bring himself to speak. The SS officer's presence was forbidding.

Once back inside the weather station, Dietrich broke the seals and opened the envelope. Reading quickly, he learned that Hauptsturmführer Wolff had been sent by the highest authority to take special charge of security for the weather expedition. He was to be given all possible cooperation. Glancing down at the signature, Dietrich gasped involuntarily. The highest authority, indeed.

"I see," he said finally, handing the papers back, though in fact he didn't understand at all. The only thing that was clear was that at least Wolff hadn't been sent to take command of the weather group itself, only security, whatever that meant. Looking at Wolff, standing there in his sinister long black leather coat that reminded Dietrich against his will of the Gestapo, he found it hard to formulate a coherent question. You never knew for sure about the SS. Wolff's pale, thin-lipped mouth was compressed, his light blue eyes . . . Dietrich had to let his own gaze fall. There was something unsettling about Wolff's eyes.

"Perhaps you can explain," he asked at last, "why this need for special security—here, on the coast of nowhere? Do they . . . does the Führer expect sabotage? Is someone here under suspicion?"

Wolff shook his head. "No *particular* suspicion. The problem is primarily one of external security, not internal. I assume you were briefed before your expedition left port. Are you aware that the second Edelweiss weather group was captured by the enemy only ten days ago?"

"Yes. We heard that news."

Wolff lowered his voice slightly. "There is more. The weather ship *Wuppertal* has been caught in the pack ice. They were operating too far north, because of the British interference. Now, they're having radio trouble. Authorities in Tromsø don't hold out much hope of finding them."

Dietrich said nothing. He was too well aware of how easily the mass of the shifting pack ice could crush the fragile steel hull of a ship.

"You understand what this means," Wolff went on. "Weather Group Flieger is the only station the Reich Meteorological Service can count on for continued reports from the Arctic. And those reports are going to be essential. Before the year is out there will be certain operations, crucial to the survival of Germany. I trust that you understand."

Unconsciously, Dietrich straightened slightly again. "Yes—yes, I understand. Of course." He hesitated. "But, already it's winter here. It's dark now. Their reconnaissance flights shouldn't be able to spot us. And the ice pack is almost solid."

"This is true. But the Americans are more determined than ever to keep German weather stations from operating on Greenland. We have reason to believe that they've set up a radio monitoring station on Jan Mayen Island. You recall that the Bassgeiger group was attacked by the Danish dogsled patrol last year. Their transmissions were probably traced."

Dietrich frowned. "I see."

"There's more. This winter we believe the Danish patrols will be replaced by American ski troops. I was sent here to counter them."

"I see," Dietrich said again, feeling slightly helpless. "Of course you'll have the full cooperation of everyone. But most of these men are scientists, technicians. They haven't really been trained for combat."

"It doesn't matter. Your only job is to make sure the weather information gets out. I'll take care of everything else, myself."

"Well." Dietrich was dubious — one man against the resources of the US Army — but looking again at Wolff, he didn't want to say anything more. "Well, as you can see, our quarters here are going to be crowded." He turned to the door, wishing he could see if the flying boat had made it into the air. "I'll see if the men have brought up your equipment yet."

"I didn't bring much with me," Wolff said shortly. "Right now I'm going to take a look outside this place, to see what kind of defenses you have."

As the door opened, Dietrich could see that it was already quite dark outside, and he almost called out a warning to Wolff to be careful on the trail if he went back down to the beach. But he said nothing. It was a sudden relief to see him gone.

Dietrich started back down to the beach, but halfway there he met a group of his men, coming back to the station. "They didn't make it, Herr Hauptmann," they reported glumly.

Soon the three flyers came into sight themselves, each man carrying a duffle. The pilot in particular looked haggard with the weariness of frustration and failure. "Well, it looks like we'll be spending the winter here with you," he said bitterly, throwing down his bag.

Dietrich felt for him. Within a few hours, the seaplane would be solidly frozen into the crushing mass of the ice. He stepped forward to meet the crew, and the pilot, seeing the Luftwaffe insignia on Dietrich's uniform, looked slightly ashamed at his outburst. "Erich Klostermann," he introduced himself and the others, "and this is Arnold Busch, my copilot, and our navigator, Hans Ziegler."

Dietrich frowned. "This is all of you?" The Blohm und Voss 138 normally carried a crew of five.

Klostermann shrugged. "Orders. *Top Secret* orders. They pulled the rest of the crew off. Whatever all this is about, I sure hope it turns out to be worth it."

So, thought Dietrich to himself, do I. He forced a grin instead. "Well, it looks like we really are Weather Group Flieger, now more than ever. I hope some of you turn out to be decent radio operators."

The name, a pun on Dr. Pflieger's name and the Luftwaffe makeup of the group, got at least some response from the stranded fliers, except from the navigator, Ziegler.

"But first of all, it looks like you could use a hot meal, then some sleep. We'll figure out where to stow your gear later." He paused. "There's probably some equipment on your ship that we might be able to use in an emergency."

"Go ahead," sighed Klostermann. "Gut the old bird."

Dietrich contemplated his small command, suddenly increased by a third of its number. Supplies would be no great problem. They had enough for over a year, plenty for emergencies. It looked like his biggest difficulty, for the moment at least, would be finding room for everyone. He glanced dubiously across to the limited space of the bunkroom. They might end up sleeping in shifts.

Just then Doctor Pflieger came up to Dietrich, whispering out loud so anyone could hear, "What is this? We have the SS now, spying on us?"

A couple of the other men were muttering under their breath, sentiments which appeared to agree with Pflieger's. Mundt, a young radioman who was the station's most vocal Nazi, got to his feet with his face turning red and his fists balled up, saying, "You'd better watch your mouth."

Dietrich found himself in the unusual position of having to defend the presence of the SS. "Hauptsturmführer Wolff is here to see to the security of the base," he said firmly, "so that we can carry on our proper mission without having to worry about enemy patrols. Which I suggest we all do — now."

The mutterings and hostile glances subsided, a little. Dietrich watched everyone return to his own job. He exhaled. One crisis averted, for the moment.

Only, he didn't think it would ever be possible to actually *like* Hauptsturmführer Wolff.

Wolff escaped out into the darkness, into the quiet and solitude of the Arctic night. It was unbearable back in the weather hut, surrounded at close quarters by so much human warmth. It had taken an effort to keep himself under control.

With a sigh, he flung himself down onto the cold rocky ground.

The flight to Greenland had been like reliving hell. Takeoff had been delayed by a British air raid on the submarine base at Tromsø, so that the sun was rising by the time the seaplane came within sight of the Greenland coast. The worst part had only lasted a few minutes, the crest of the sun just skimming the horizon, but it had been agony, even as far back into the tail section of the plane as he could crawl. A few centimeters of sheet metal were almost no protection at all, up there so far from the shelter of the earth.

Wolff shuddered, not from cold but from the lingering sensation of pain deep in his joints. He had barely been able, when they landed, to stand up and climb out of the plane.

After a moment he exhaled. It was over now. He was here, far enough above the Arctic Circle that for almost four months he wouldn't have to see another sunrise come again.

He got to his feet, brushing off the absurd impractical black leather greatcoat. It had served its purpose, though. He had felt the fear of the men at the weather station as they drew back from what they thought the coat must represent—what they thought he must be, rather than what he was.

He smiled at that notion, a predator's smile.

The starlight illuminated the terrain. Wolff walked quickly away from the crude wooden buildings of the weather station, stretching long-cramped muscles. The land here was so desolate, so different from the rugged forests of the Eifel or the fierce wild Carpathians of his distant homeland. No trees could grow in this place. Rock and ice, snow and stone—that was Greenland.

He climbed to the top of the cliff and looked out for a few moments over the sea. From the name of this place—Ursa Bay—he supposed that polar bears frequented the region, but at the moment there was no sign of the huge white beasts, nothing but sea and mountains. Turning, he looked back down on the weather base, admitting to himself that Dietrich had chosen his site well.

He supposed he was pleased with his performance. Kessler's tedious briefings had paid off; Dietrich had believed in him completely. Now, for the first time since he had come to this place, Wolff thought seriously about the American dog-sled teams and ski troops, trying to envision how they would come in through the pass, across the ice. They had a base, too, somewhere hundreds of kilometers south along the coast. Dozens of men, soldiers, conveniently designated the enemy.

But his attention kept returning against his will to the cluster of wooden huts down below—the heat, the scent of life, the only life discernible in all this desolation. He was not, he reminded himself angrily, *not* hungry, only frustrated in his bloodlust.

He couldn't escape the lingering sensation of that last, sordid killing in Tromsø. If he had known, in the beginning that he would be treated that way . . .

Wolff had intended when he first associated himself with the SS to use their war for his own purposes. He still had every intention of carrying out this mission for them, for the sake of his castle, for the sake of his sworn word. What was between him and Kessler was a personal matter. Killing him would be his own private affair.

But that was the way it ought to be—each death should be unique, personal, every drop of blood to be savored. The politics of the matter should be incidental.

But for good or ill, he had joined his fortunes to Kessler's side, had risked his heritage, his future and his past. So now he stood on the headland overlooking Ursa Bay in northeastern Greenland. Somewhere in all that expanse of ice were the Americans, and for both Kessler's reasons and his own, they would have to die.

Chapter Four

Staff Sergeant Matt Ferrier stepped around to the dog pens carrying a couple of pails of half-thawed fish guts. He was a tall, rawboned redhead who somehow managed to look like he was wearing a checked lumberjack shirt even in an Army uniform, whistling an off-key rendition of "In the Mood," which fairly expressed his feelings about things these days—because when the Army sent Ferrier to Greenland, it had finally done something right.

Like Sarge Novotny had told them over and over again in Basic, there were only two ways to do a thing: the wrong way and the Army way. And the Army didn't much like people who thought they knew better. So Ferrier had seen mechanics sent to typing school, truck drivers turned into cooks, accountants working on tank engines—and everybody and his brother carrying a rifle, whether or not they'd been able to tell one end of a gun from the other before the war.

But when it came to sled dogs, even the Army had to turn to Matt Ferrier. He'd spent ten years in Alaska running traplines before the war. He knew the northland, how to set up camp in a blizzard and mush forty miles a day when it was forty below. So he'd spent the past sixteen months as an instructor in the Army's Arctic School, and now they'd posted him to Greenland to patrol the east coast for Nazis. The Army couldn't have picked a better man for the job, he thought with no small amount of satisfaction as he went to feed his team.

A pack of three of the native dogs came running, drawn by the scent of food, but Ferrier kicked them away. "Get outta here, you damn lousy mutts!" The animals belonged to one of the guides. The Greenlanders didn't feed their sled dogs in the summer, and they ran wild, a general menace in the native villages. Not a year went by when they didn't kill some kid or a drunk sleeping it off in the streets.

"Hey, Lars," he yelled again, knowing it would do no good, "come get your flea-bitten dogs!"

Cursing under his breath, he went on to the run where his own huskies were penned, Alaskan dogs, good sled dogs, sixty pounds apiece of fur and muscle. Spotting his approach, they surged against the wire of the run, setting up a howling that had all the other teams joining in. At a distance, the native dogs skulked, ears and tails lowered. The Alaskan and Greenlander dogs had hated each other on sight, and it was war to the death if they weren't forcibly kept apart.

Sometimes dogs could be a pain in the ass, but Ferrier knew that once winter set in, a dogsled would offer the only means of crossing the Greenland ice. The Army'd tried motorized sleds a few times, trying to rescue fliers downed on the icecap, but they broke down too damn often to be any real use. In the clutch, dog teams were what you needed.

He turned his face to the west, thinking he could catch the scent of new snow in the air, then bent down to scratch the neck of Robber, his lead dog, feeling the solid strength of muscle in the neck. It would be good to get them hitched up, get out on the trail again.

Some of the other teams were being fed now, and the noise level got worse. Huskies didn't bark like most other kinds of dogs, they howled like the wolves they were related to. A driver fed his own dogs. Even officers. Even, he noticed now, Captain McCluskey. Ferrier grinned. You don't go around saluting when you've both got your hands full of seal blubber and half-rotten fish.

If there was one flaw in his paradise, it was McCluskey. He didn't think much of officers to begin with, and McCluskey was one of those blood-and-guts types who'd make a soldier's life hell just on general principles. Thought he was General Patton on a dogsled, for shit's sake. Saluting. Inspections. A couple weeks ago, when the Coast Guard picked up those krauts, McCluskey looked like he was going to crap on the spot, just because he wasn't in on the action. If you could call it action. Hell, the krauts just stuck up their hands and surrendered.

But it wouldn't be long before he could get away from the captain, the base, the whole damn Army, out on the snow with the dogs. Yeah, that was the life.

A few flakes started to fall, and he licked one from his lips. Fresh. Cold. Not too long now.

Captain Daniel McCluskey was in command of the US Army's Dogsled Reconnaissance Patrol at Eskimoness on Clavering Island, a cluster of Quonset huts put up as quickly as possible over the few months of the past summer. Eskimoness had originally been the northern headquarters of the Danish dogsled patrol, about two dozen hunters who had constituted Greenland's only local military force since the beginning of the war. But late in the spring of '43, the patrol had run into a Nazi weather expedition on Sabine Island, and before it was over the damn krauts had killed one man, captured two others, and burned down the Eskimoness base. And neither the Army nor the Coast Guard had been able to do a damn thing about it.

That was changed now. It was clear to McCluskey that the Nazis were determined to establish weather stations in Greenland, come hell or high water, and finally the Army had figured out what they needed were US soldiers patrolling the region with sled teams. Not to say that the local Danes hadn't done OK. But after all, they were really civilians, mainly hunters, when you came right down to it. Tracking polar bears meant more to them than tracking Nazis, even when they were on patrol. Even last spring, when the radio monitoring station picked up those signals coming from near Shannon Island and the Danes had tried to shoot it out with the krauts, in the end, they had to pull back while the damn Nazis went right on with their transmissions.

The fact was that despite all the efforts of the Danes, Coast Guard and US Air Force, Nazi bases had been sending vital weather information back to Germany for the last two years — letting the Luftwaffe know when airfields in England would be socked in, helping Nazi wolfpacks find unprotected convoys. It was about damn time they did something about it.

McCluskey made no effort to hide his impatience. If he'd been able to have his patrols running up the coast a month ago, he'd have been the one to take out that kraut base on Koldewey Island, not the damn Coast Guard. That's why he was over here — to fight the Nazis, dammit!

The sight of fresh snow in the air made up his mind. "Sergeant!"

Just about to leave the dog pens, Ferrier groaned inaudibly. Shit! What did he want now?

"Yeah, Captain?"

McCluskey reminded himself again that he was lucky to have a man like Ferrier, with his Arctic experience. If he'd just — once — pretend to act like a soldier. "Go find one of the guides and get your dogs in harness. I want to check out the ice conditions around the island — up as far as the north shore, at least, if it's sound."

Ferrier grunted. Just last week, both the native guides had said the ice wasn't ready, that October ice wasn't reliable. But, hell, October was just about over, wasn't it? And a short trip around the island would be a good idea. Finally to get out there with the dogs.

"Sure thing, Captain," he replied cheerfully, demonstrating his approval of the order with a slight movement of his hand that might have been taken for a salute. McCluskey, at least, decided to take it as such.

Ferrier went off, whistling, to the camp kitchen where, as he'd expected, he found the guide Lars with his feet up next to the hot coffee pot. "Let's harness up," he said, taking the opportunity to pour himself a cup, too. "The captain wants to check out the ice around the island. Thinks it's about high time to get out there hunting Nazis."

"Ice is thin," Lars said dubiously.

Ferrier shrugged. "You think it's too thin, you go tell the captain."

Lars took a long swallow of coffee, thought about it a moment. "Maybe ice is okay. Now."

Lars was a Greenlander, what Ferrier would have called a half-breed back in Alaska. Native women were real, real friendly to strangers, and as a result there weren't many full-blooded Eskimo left, in this part of Greenland, anyway. Despite his last name of Thorkilson, he had round, flat features and oriental-looking eyes like a typical Eskimo, but he spoke fluent Danish and, what was most important, halfway decent English. There'd been Americans on Greenland for three years now, plenty of time for some of the natives to learn the language.

"All right, then," Ferrier said, putting down his cup, "let's get ready."

They packed the sleds — lightly, since this was going to be not much more than a two-day trip at most. But you always prepared for the worst, just in case, so they loaded tents, Primus stoves, sleeping bags and provisions for men and dogs. It was just as well to have the sleds light if they weren't sure about the condition of the ice.

Getting the dogs hitched was more trouble. Lars's dogs had been running loose, as Ferrier knew, and not all of them were eager to get caught and put into harness. But the Greenlander decided that six animals would be enough for such a short trip, with the sleds so light. Of course, as soon as the fugitives saw the others being hitched to the sled, they came running, as usual starting a fight with the American dogs, while Ferrier and Lars waded in with their whips to restore order.

Ferrier's huskies boiled out of their pen in an overwhelming furry mass, yelping and yipping with uncontrollable excitement. While he struggled to hitch them up, Ferrier couldn't help glancing over to where Captain McCluskey was engaged in the same task. The captain's face was more than normally red as he fought with the dogs and their tangled lines, but one by one he was getting them into position. It was the fondest wish of Matt Ferrier's heart one day to see the captain's dogs running off with his sled, with the captain himself running after them, cursing helplessly. But it hadn't happened, not yet. McCluskey did everything by the book, and by the book his sled was well-anchored before he started to put the dogs into harness.

Lars, his half dozen dogs already to go, watched the American soldiers with a dubious expression. The Greenlander had his dogs hitched to a fan trace, while the Americans had theirs lined up in tandem by pairs.

Ferrier had already noticed how the Greenlanders harnessed their dogs and wondered whether it might be more efficient that way, out on the open ice. But he was used to working his dogs in pairs, and more important, they were trained to run hitched to a center trace. Old Robber made his feelings known if he were harnessed in any position but lead. Ferrier glanced back and saw that McCluskey was finally ready. "All right, let's move out," the captain ordered, and the dogs were away, muscular hindquarters bunching as they hauled the sleds into motion.

Ferrier, with his hold on the sled, was borne away in the rush. Stopping them now would have been impossible. Keeping them going in the right direction was possible — barely. Snapping his long whip, he yelled *gee, gee,* while up ahead, Lars called to his own dogs in Eskimo, making high-pitched, yipping sounds.

The dogs carried them away into the Greenland night. The ride was rough at first, with the snow cover sparse on the ground. The sleds jolted and bucked over the shore ice until the sound abruptly changed to a low, hollow rumble that meant they were running now over the open sea. The dogs picked up speed then as the surface improved, and Ferrier yelled out loud in sheer joy with the wind in his face and the sharp sting of the snow and the warm fog of his breath swept away into the dark.

The base was soon a dim yellow glow behind them. The whole land stretching ahead was in darkness. But as his eyes became accustomed to it, the dark resolved into various shades of gray, like a snapshot, often obscured by the blowing, swirling flurries of snow. But his dogs seemed to know where they were going, following the team ahead. Eventually the headlong pace slowed, and they settled into a strong, steady trot, except when rough places on the ice slowed them down.

Ferrier had been coming to realize, since winter began up here, that the high Arctic of Greenland was a far different place than what he'd known in his years in Alaska, below the Arctic Circle. Here they were at seventy-four degrees north, nearly ten degrees of latitude above the circle, and heading further north toward the absolute polar night.

In Alaska, his sled travel had been mostly on land, occasionally along the frozen surface of a river, and the worst problems had usually come from the depths and drifts of snow. But on the Greenland coast, with its mountains and outcrops of rock, the normal sled routes were across the sea ice. And the sea was never entirely still, even when its surface was frozen. There were the tides, and the cold Greenland current that carried the icebergs south. An iceberg could crop up in a sled's path at any minute. And there were the ridges of pressure ice to contend with, as impassable for a sled as a mountain, and sudden cracks or leads of open water in the ice. Ferrier had known all this, in theory. But now, mushing at full speed in the dark, across the frozen surface, he felt a jolt of uneasiness at realizing just how much he didn't really know about this new environment. All his life he'd relied on his experience and common sense. But here his experience counted for a less than he'd figured it would, and at every ridge or rough place in the surface his gut quailed just a little at the thought of the unstable new ice beneath the runners of his sled. But experience also had taught him to trust his dogs, and even more he trusted Lars ahead of him, who knew this country, whose dogs were veterans of this kind of travel.

The base was on the south shore of Clavering Island, which was about thirty-five miles across at its widest point. After a few miles, Lars called a halt to examine the pads of the dogs. "New ice," he explained. "Cuts feet. Salt ice."

Ferrier nodded in understanding and McCluskey was already conscientiously checking the feet of his animals. The dogs stood panting in a cloud of their breath. The Greenland dogs were milling together in their traces, biting at the snow that had accumulated in the lee of an upcropping of ice. Fresh water, Lars explained, untangling his team. You could get fresh water from an iceberg, too. Icebergs came off the glaciers, off the land, not the sea.

Soon they were moving out again. McCluskey's square face looked grim and eager. It looked like the patrol season was about to start for sure, Ferrier thought.

They stopped several times more along the southeast coast of the island, rounding the point and turning north across the mouth of a narrow sound to the peninsula named Wollaston Foreland. At a place named Sandodden there was a cabin where they planned to stop for the night. Over the summer, they'd gone up the coast by boat, caching provisions in most of the accessible shelters and hunting stations. Sandodden was a fairly comfortable cabin that had been a hunting station before the war. Now, after they were done with picketing and feeding the dogs, it offered shelter and the welcome warmth of a stove after the long day out on the ice.

The captain still seemed charged with enthusiasm, but Ferrier thought he was a lot easier to take, out here on the ice. On the trail there was none of that chickenshit about saluting.

Sandodden had already played a part in the war. This was where the Germans had come after the raid when they burned down Eskimoness in the spring of '43. Their base on Sabine Island had been only forty miles away. But it was at Sandodden that the krauts had killed the first casualty in this most obscure theater of the war, a member of the Danish dogsled patrol.

The fire was just getting started, but McCluskey stepped out the door again and around to the back of the house. The body was still there, lying in a small sod hut that had become a tomb. It was marked by a cross. Ferrier followed, saw the captain stand there for several minutes, staring at the grave, muttering, "Nazis. Damn Nazis."

Ferrier shook his head slightly. He knew that the cross had been put there by the Germans themselves. McCluskey had to know it, too. *Crazy war,* he thought. *Crazy.*

The captain came back inside and threw a little more coal into the stove. Then he turned to Lars. "What about Sabine Island? We could get there in another day, right? Check it out."

But the guide insisted, "No. Not Sabine Island. Bad ice, there. Thin ice, broken ice, open water. Even in spring, ice is very bad. Now — no."

Thwarted, McCluskey stared at his feet for a while, thinking. "The regular route north, then, across the foreland through Keppel Pass? That would be clear going?" he finally asked.

After a moment Lars nodded. "Yes, maybe. Maybe enough snow."

"All right then, I think I've seen what the conditions are like. We'll turn back to the base in the morning. Sergeant, when we get there, I want you to get ready to take a patrol north."

Ferrier scratched his head. "Just how far north did you have in mind, Captain?"

"Let's find out how far you can go. See if you can find me some Nazis, Ferrier."

Chapter Five

Wolff had almost immediately discarded the Gestapo greatcoat and other emblems of the SS after his arrival on Greenland. Now he wore the white, hooded camouflage uniform of the ski troops and moved almost invisibly against the ice and snow, just as he had operated in the darkness of the forest shadows at night in Europe.

"Patrolling the area," was his answer whenever Dietrich or one of the other Germans would ask him where he'd gone, what he'd been doing out there alone for so long.

In fact, his concern almost from the first had been to set up a shelter, a bolt-hole, a place of refuge in case things went wrong, even in a place without a sunrise. It had been too many years for him to able to feel secure, otherwise.

He would have settled if necessary for a cave in the rocks, but after a few days' exploration of the region around the weather station he discovered a deserted hunter's hut near the head of the fjord, close to the tongue of the glacier. It was a crude, low structure built mostly out of stone and driftwood with sod, moss and lichen for insulation. There was a rude stove, a bed-shelf and a few tattered hides, and much of the lichen had long since fallen out of the cracks, but Wolff had no great need of amenities. It was low, close to the earth, and once the drifts buried it, the place would be invisible.

Because the Germans were always watching him, he was

forced to pack supplies along in a rucksack whenever he went out on his skis. He generally left them in the hut, building up a small stock of food. When he traveled, he preferred to go alone and unencumbered, and he took pains not to leave tracks in the snow that could lead anyone in the direction of his hiding place.

He avoided the weather station as much as possible, and when he was there he refused meals and rarely even pretended to sleep. The strain was growing on him, of hunger and proximity to so many lives. He began to hope the Americans would attack.

But credibility required him to spend at least some time at the base. It was snowing, the wind working up to near-blizzard velocity when he stepped inside after one of his patrols. A few reflexive shouts rang out, "Shut the door, will you?" until they turned and saw who it was, then silence.

He brushed snow off his jacket, stamped his feet as if he were trying to warm them — these were actions he had studied, trying to act as human as he could, as susceptible to the cold. In fact, the sudden warmth of the hut was like a blow in the face. Body warmth, blood warmth. It had been too long since he'd last fed in Tromsø, and his need was starting to be acute. Outside, in the solitude of the Arctic night or his own dark shelter, he could force himself to ignore the hunger pangs. Not in here.

The hut was full, with the crew of the flying boat added to the weather party. Wolff focused on them avidly, straining his control. His needs would be provided for, Kessler had promised, although the Americans were obviously his intended prey. But it had also been tacitly understood that the crew of the flying boat was expendable. There should have been five of them, but the gunners were yanked at the last minute at the insistence of some other authority. The German command was fragmented.

Now he glanced around the main room of the cabin. In the back, a few men were asleep, but out here four of them were

53

sitting at the table playing cards, with the remains of a recent meal pushed to one side. Wolff caught the scents of sausage, coffee and plum preserves. The Germans supplied their remote weather stations generously, no matter what the shortages were at home.

Dietrich turned from the radio, came across the room to Wolff and took him aside. There were lines of concern on his face. "We've just heard from Tromsø. About the *Wuppertal*. It's been two weeks now with no word since their last transmission. Officially, the ship is considered missing, but . . . they don't really hold out any hope."

Wolff nodded gravely, pretending sympathy. Dietrich had followed the fate of the doomed weather ship with almost obsessive interest. "That leaves us," he said almost desperately. "The only team left."

"They should be able to do something—send a plane for them," one of the men protested.

No one else said anything, most particularly Klostermann and the rest of his crew, although the pilot did dart a quick, resentful glare in Wolff's direction. They had all gone through this argument before. Weber, one of the radiomen, had claimed to have caught a faint distress signal four days ago, which could have come from the *Wuppertal*.

The ship's fate concerned them all, Wolff noticed. He could feel every heartbeat, every intake and exhalation of breath of the dozen men in the room. Clearly, they could see in the *Wuppertal* some mirror into their own situation.

Wolff had no idea if it might realistically be possible to mount an attempt to rescue the men on the icebound ship. Apparently their location wasn't really known for sure. And the surrounding waters were enemy-controlled. He supposed it was more likely that the Germans had already written them off as lost.

It was Weber who tentatively suggested, "Maybe if someone would contact the Amis or the English . . ."

"Enough of that kind of talk," Dietrich snapped. "We'd do

better to remember exactly why we're here."

The reprimand made Weber's face flush; his heartbeat was rapid. Wolff's attention was immediately drawn to him. Weber was too much the good soldier to argue with his commanding officer, but Dr. Pflieger, the civilian meteorologist, knew no such constraints. He muttered quite audibly, "And who knows exactly why we're here? While the Amis are at the Westwall."

The radioman, Mundt, always ready to defend the Führer, started to protest. But Weber was quicker. "It's true! What are we doing here? The war is already over—"

"That's enough." Wolff spoke before Dietrich could step in with his own authority. He used his SS voice, and the Walther automatic was in his hand. Everyone in the room turned to stare at him, and the scent of their fear had an acid edge. Pflieger turned pale. Weber stammered, "I didn't . . . I didn't mean . . ."

Wolff made a slight gesture toward the door with the hand holding the gun. "Outside."

"Herr Hauptmann?" Weber's voice broke as he pleaded with Dietrich, who hesitated, looking from his radioman to Wolff. But Wolff gave him no chance to intervene, grabbing Weber by the elbow with his free hand and shoving him toward the door. No one even protested aloud.

The wind had intensified in the short time Wolff had been inside. He could feel the heat of Weber's body through his thick sweater, could hear the frantic, panicked throbbing of his heart as he begged, "Herr . . . Hauptsturmführer . . . please . . ."

Wolff made no reply, pushing Weber in front of him, by means of a painful grip on the elbow, past the radio tower, past the supply sheds, down toward the path to the beach. Weber didn't struggle, though he was young and strong—it would have done him no good, not against Wolff, but he only begged, stumbling in the dark on the rough uneven path: he hadn't meant it, wouldn't say anything against the Führer again, his mother was a widow and his only other brother had been killed at Stalingrad. Terror radiated from him like heat.

Wolff had already put away the gun. Now the thin-bladed knife was in his hand. He stopped next to a large rock, pressing the tip against the soft pulsing flesh of Weber's throat. He whispered, very soft and chill. "Turn around."

Weber whimpered. He couldn't make himself do it. Wolff spun him around, slamming him back up against the rock. He bent over him, letting him see his face as clearly as possible in the dark, letting him see death.

It was too much for Weber. With the knife at his throat, he started to sob, uttering inarticulate choking sounds. The harsh acrid scent of his urine flooded the air.

Wolff plunged the blade in, then drank long and deep, filling himself with the warmth of lifeblood. It was interesting how Weber kept whimpering while he died, much longer than usual. At the very peak of sensation, Wolff shuddered and let the body fall into the snow at the foot of the rock. The Arctic wind blew snow into his face, and he felt as if he could sweep the storm away, or fly with it, far out onto the sea.

Then his head cleared. He had the body to deal with now. There'd been polar bear tracks the other day, down at the foot of the headland. The animal had probably been attracted by the scent of the Germans' garbage. Something would have to be done about that. But at the moment it was a convenient complication. He lifted the body — drained of blood, the inert weight always seemed heavier than when they were alive — and carried it down the path.

The tracks and scent of the bear had been obliterated by the storm. Out in the bay, a mound of snow marked the resting place of the gutted seaplane. Wolff carried his burden further out toward the open bay, leaving it for the bear, knowing even the faint scent of blood would draw the beast.

By the time the corpse was disposed of he was less than satisfied with what he'd done. Operating under the strain of hunger had its risks. His whole ostensible purpose for being here was the protection of the weather station—to keep it transmitting, as Kessler had put it. Now he'd just eliminated one of the radiomen. Hardly what the SS had in mind.

Wolff was aware that Weber might well have been right, that Germany had already lost the war. If it was true, he'd linked his own fortunes to the wrong side. Wryly, he thought of the deed at the bottom of his bag—he might as well sell it to Dietrich for cigarette paper.

But the castle hadn't been his for the greater part of a century; he supposed he could continue to exist without it. The fact was, though, that his agreement with the Germans had never been entirely material. He had given his word, and taken Kessler's.

And what had he done? Waiting here for the Americans to attack was accomplishing nothing. Worse than nothing. The Amis were his proper victims, not the German weather party.

He picked up a shard of ice and sent it flying, disappearing into the driven snow. It was time, past time, to begin. While there were Germans still alive.

It had all happened so fast, before Dietrich could react.

Of course, talk like Weber's couldn't be tolerated, even if he had only said out loud what was on everyone's mind. Certainly Dr. Pflieger should have known better than to speak out that way, especially with the SS in the room.

But mostly he blamed himself, for letting the talk go on, get out of hand. He should have intervened. But suddenly Wolff was holding that gun, shoving Weber out the door. And Weber had called out to him, to his commanding officer, for help: *Herr Hauptmann* . . .

And I did nothing.

Bitterly, he came back to it over and over again. He'd done nothing. He let Wolff take Weber out through that door—without a word, without a protest.

But, God damn it, there were regulations against defeatist talk! And for good reason. Weber knew, should have known, what he was saying. He was old enough . . . he was only twenty . . .

I was in command. I should have said something, done something to stop it.

But it had happened so fast, the frigid gust of wind had blown in through the open door and they were gone, Wolff pushing Weber in front of him. And it was too late.

Weber was gone, with the rest of them standing stunned, Pflieger opening and shutting his mouth, Mundt and his Nazi friends looking embarrassed, as if a bad practical joke had gone too far. All of them staring at *him*. The commanding officer.

He had to say something now. But what? What could he say?

"I hope there won't be any more defeatist talk around here," he managed finally. "Germany isn't beaten. The Führer is already planning a counteroffensive that will drive the enemy back off German soil, back to the sea. The details are secret, of course. But our mission here is a vital part of his plans." He took a breath. "So vital that Hauptsturmführer Wolff has been sent here expressly *by the Führer himself* to ensure the security of our operation. Neither he nor I will let anything, anyone obstruct our operations. I hope this is clear to every man here."

Mundt, Dienst and Manstein all got to their feet and gave the Hitler salute. A few others, including Doctor Pflieger, stared at the floor. Then Köbler, the cook, began to clear away the rest of the dishes from the table, although no one seemed in a hurry to take up the card game again. A few men mumbled that they had business at the latrine. Then there were readings to be made, checks of the instruments, technical difficulties at the balloon shack.

But no one left the room. Dietrich lit a cigarette, stood staring at the eddy of the smoke. The men had all been too long in the German armed forces to doubt what must have happened to Weber, but when the door opened again and Wolff came in, alone, they all looked away.

Dietrich got slowly to his feet, meaning to say something, he wasn't sure what. The set, determined expression on Wolff's face stopped him. "I'll be leaving in hour or so—as soon as I have my gear put together. I may be gone for some time—weeks, possibly, or even longer."

In his surprise, Dietrich was hard put to conceal his relief. Still, he couldn't let the other matter go. He owed something to Weber. "Listen. About Weber—he was one of my best radioman. Was it absolutely necessary—"

"The man was a defeatist," Wolff said shortly, cutting him off. "He was a security risk, and we can't afford that. Remember, he spoke of contacting the enemy."

Dietrich nodded. Wolff was right. But . . .

"Busch—the copilot—is a good enough radio operator, isn't he?"

"Good enough," Dietrich agreed.

"Then the traitor was expendable. The matter has already been disposed of."

And Dietrich didn't dare to ask how. He knew.

Chapter Six

There would be three of them in this first patrol: Ferrier in command, Archie Blackburn, and Lars as their guide. Ferrier had come to appreciate Lars's profound knowledge of the land and the ice, and he was now willing to admit that there might even be some sense in the way the Greenlanders handled their dogs.

This time the sleds were heavily loaded with nearly a half ton of provisions and gear. They were going to be out on the trails for weeks, maybe longer, and whatever they left behind they were going to have to do without. The dogs had to strain to get the loads into motion, and the men sweated behind the sleds, shoving and manhandling them over the ridges of shore ice. Once they were out on the broad stretch of the sea ice, the going was slightly easier. The snowfall of a few days ago had settled on the surface, smoothing the way across a lot of the rougher spots and protecting the dogs' feet from the salt.

The sky was clear now, though, and the stars and moon brighter than Ferrier had ever known them, even in Alaska. The snow and the ice seemed to reflect and re-reflect all the light, and he could see the dark shape of the mountains miles away. He could imagine somebody passing overhead in a plane and seeing the three of them down below, tiny dark specks moving slowly across the vast, vast surface of the ice. It made him feel — almost religious, somehow, just thinking about it.

He had Blackburn ahead of him so he could watch how he handled his dogs out here on the ice. Blackburn was a short, sharp-faced guy with an accent right off the New York streets, and he was slightly clumsy on his skis, but Ferrier was more used to snowshoes than skis, anyway. Still, after a while they all settled into a steady pace, around the eastern shore of Clavering Island and up across the sound to Sandodden. Ferrier and Blackburn grinned at each other as the cabin came into view across the width of the sound, seeing the wool of their balaclavas, even their eyebrows covered in the ice from their breath. It had been a long, hard day's traveling, but the three of them were shaking out well together as a team.

They fed and staked out the dogs, then cooked their meal from the stores in the hut — saving the provisions packed on the sleds — and settled around the stove with mugs of coffee. The dogs, securely picketed for the night, were curled up outside in relative peace. Ferrier didn't figure he could want much more than this. There was only the silent, snow-covered grave behind the hut standing as a reminder that there was anything like a war going on.

But after a while he turned to Lars. "You say it was the krauts put up that cross, right? The Germans?"

"Danish patrol find it there, like that, when they come back next summer. Not me, I stay in Scoresbysund. See German prisoner there."

"That so?" asked Blackburn, who hadn't heard that part of the story before. "They got a Nazi prisoner, huh?"

"Patrol take him, keep him all winter, until the boat come, Army come."

"Whaddya know!"

"Tall man. Quiet. They take him away. To Iceland."

Ferrier said nothing, only stared at the stove. Hard to believe there were German soldiers out there. How the hell was he supposed to find them? With all the fjords, bays, and islands along the coastline, they had maybe a thousand miles or more to cover. In the dark. He'd never seen a German before, never shot at another human being to kill him. Or been shot at himself. And yet the Nazis had been here, in this very house. Had waited in ambush for the unsuspecting Danish patrol to come through the pass and opened fire, killing one man, taking the other two prisoner.

"Hey, look," he asked Lars, "how did those guys spot the Germans out on Sabine Island, anyway? How'd they manage to find them in all this?" He waved his arm to mean the entire coast of east Greenland.

It was no mystery to the guide. "Patrol hunts up and down coast so many years. They know all hunting stations. And dogs know, when they smell bear, smell man." He grinned. "And, that one time, they get lucky. Germans are out hunting, too."

"Great," Ferrier muttered. The more he thought about his luck, the more he worried. Hell, for all he knew, the Nazis were right outside, surrounding the place. But then he remembered the dogs, who could scent the approach of a stranger for miles, and he felt better. Well enough to get a good night's sleep, anyway.

The next morning—or moonrise, anyway—the patrol set off through the pass across Wollaston Foreland. This was one of the few overland routes that the hunters traditionally used, avoiding the treacherous ice south of Sabine Island. It was the sort of terrain Ferrier was more used to, with the newly fallen snow piled up in drifts. On the soft surface the dogs made much slower time than on the ice, and after an hour or so he exchanged his skis for American snowshoes, Blackburn doing the same. Lars eyed them with interest and agreed that such things might be useful later on in the year, when the passes were *really* choked with snow.

Once across the peninsula, they checked out Sabine Island—the north side of it, at least, then started toward Shannon Island, where the krauts had set up another base just last year. Krauts never seemed to know when to quit. Ferrier knew just how much territory he was missing, all the sounds and fjords and islands to the west of Shannon. On the return trip, maybe they'd be able to check out some of the more likely spots. He sighed. The captain was going to want it all in his report when he got back, every chickenshit little island they'd passed and what about all the ones he'd missed.

Their progress was slowed by Lars. The guide insisted on stopping to hunt. Ferrier had a good idea of what Captain McCluskey would've had to say about that, but to Lars it was simple—the dogs needed fresh meat, more meat than they were carrying on their sleds. And so he and Blackburn were forced to wait with the dogs off the ice, restraining them while the hunter, ever so slowly, ever so stealthily crept up on the blowhole of a seal and then stood motionless over it, waiting.

"Shit," Blackburn complained over and over, "shit, Sarge, it's cold! Don't think I'm ever gonna get the ice outta my feet!"

They felt the cold a lot more, just standing there. Both of them shifted from foot to foot. It was the moving that kept you warm in the north, running with the dogs. Ferrier's feet were getting dangerously numb. How could the Greenlander stand it?

But then came the sharp *crack* of the rifle across the ice, and they whipped up the dogs, who smelled the blood and ran eagerly to the hole where Lars was hauling the seal out of the water. Soon the animals were gorging themselves on the meat and guts. Grinning, Lars offered the soldiers a share, and Ferrier reluctantly chewed on the raw liver and managed to get it down, but he drew the line at the eyeball. Blackburn gave his opinion that they were both crazy, eating that kind of shit.

Ferrier figured, if the captain complained about their slow progress, that he could tell him they'd run into quite a bit of bad ice.

After a little more than two weeks, they'd checked out the larger islands and moved on north to the mainland, a barren piece of ground named Hochstetter Foreland, almost a hundred miles north of the base, although they'd traveled about three times that distance altogether. They were well above seventy-five degrees of latitude, and the night was almost absolute. There was hardly even a glow in the sky at noon, and day and night didn't seem to have much meaning any more. But Ferrier found himself getting used to the dark, even when the moon was down. One night there was an aurora, a rippling arch of light across the southern margin of the sky. "Looks kinda like an air raid, doesn't it?" Blackburn remarked.

"Yeah, with no sirens, no bombs," Ferrier answered. It seemed strange suddenly to have to think about the war, to remember why they were supposed to be out here.

For the sake of appearances, Wolff set off down the trail loaded with a full pack of unnecessary survival gear, including a Schmeisser machine pistol strapped to his back. Most of the gear he left in his shelter. In the end, he took little more than a single blanket. The Schmeisser, of course, was useless for his purpose, but after a moment's thought he slung a rifle onto his back, in addition to the Walther he always carried.

The sky was utterly still and clear, like hard crystal. The moon and the stars overhead blazed with a fierce white light, so that every outcrop of ice or rock cast a sharp black shadow onto the snow. The only sound was the crunch and snap of Wolff's footsteps. If he paused there was nothing, not even a whisper of wind, only the silence of a vast and empty land.

When he came to the foot of the headland at the mouth of the fjord, onto the broad expanse of Dove Bay, the air was so clear that he could see the dark length of Koldewey Island a hundred kilometers across the bay, where the last two German weather expeditions had so recently come to grief. Well, he was bringing the war to the Americans now. Let them see how they liked it.

Before setting out across the bay, he paused near the foot of the cliff where he'd left the body of the dead radio operator. To his satisfaction, there was little of it left, not even a stain on the snow, only a few fluttering scraps of uniform snagged on the rocks near the shore, which the winter gales would doubtless soon tear away.

He came closer, knelt, and finally saw the clear imprint of a bear's track pressed into the snow. The bear scent still lingered faintly. He stood again, looking across the ice as far as he could, but the bear, wherever it was, couldn't be seen. Suddenly there was a familiar harsh cry. He jerked his head up and saw circling overhead the black form of a raven come to scavenge the remains. Slowly Wolff's pale, grim face showed a smile, and he lifted an arm to wave at the bird. "There'll be more," he promised the bird, "later."

Pleased with such an auspicious meeting, he started south. No one traveling by dogsled would try to go overland across the mountains. Wolff, on foot, would have had only slightly easier going. Instead, he began to cross the broad, open stretch of Dove Bay. Alone, unburdened, he moved at a steady lope, across pressure ridges of ice uplifted and folded by the relentlessly moving current, passing icebergs frozen into the pack ice, dazzling bright in the moonlight. On his right, the broad iceways of fjords cut into the mountains, where the ridges of bare rock contrasted darkly with the snow. Beyond the farthest peaks was the vastness of the icecap, its white at this distance merging with the gray western horizon.

A number of islands studded the bay, some ten miles or more in length. Coming close to one, Wolff caught a familiar scent and followed it to the den of a sleeping bear, dug out of the snow drift piled against a rock. He glanced up, but for the moment the raven was nowhere in sight.

Hours had passed, one kilometer after another, and still he kept moving. After a while, the pace came to be almost hypnotic. In the clear northern air, mountains a hundred kilometers away seemed as close as the nearest island, but constantly retreating in front of him, like a mirage in the desert.

He still hadn't crossed Dove Bay when he felt a warning

twinge down the length of his spine. Instantly, he glanced toward the southeast. Almost imperceptibly, the sky in that direction was taking on the stain of red that meant dawn. Wolff cursed aloud, his voice echoing off the ice. Out here, he felt exposed, vulnerable. It was only pain and weakness, and in an emergency he might have gone on, but it had already been a long, wearying way, and there were nights and nights of it yet in front of him.

There was an island not too far in the distance, and he made for its western side. Once he was there, with the earth between him and the sun, he unrolled his blanket and curled up inside it like a bear in its den. He still wasn't quite used to going entirely without rest. Like a bear, he slowed his heartbeat, all his metabolism. His body temperature dropped even lower, but there was no possibility of his freezing. He barely felt even the most biting cold.

For an hour he rested, until the angry tinge was gone completely from the sky, and then he brought himself back and got to his feet. The mainland still seemed as distant as when he had started across the bay. Rolling up the blanket, he went on.

Hours later, the land finally seemed to be coming nearer, and by the second noon sunrise Wolff had made the crossing. According to his map, he was now on the northern margin of a coastal peninsula named Hochstetter Foreland. The enemy, according to the best estimates of German intelligence, was two hundred kilometers further south on Clavering Island, where the Holzauge weather group had burned out the headquarters of the Danish militia. It was a fairly well-known spot on the east coast of Greenland, where there had been a weather station before the war. It might take him, traveling without rest, as long as two weeks before he reached it, and by then his hunger would be acute. It was a temptation to try to cut the distance by going overland, but a glimpse of ice-capped peaks in the distance was enough to rule out that alternative. There might well be an easy pass through the interior, but nothing of the sort was marked on his map.

With a sigh, he waited through another false dawn and then moved on, continuing to skirt the coast. After a while he began to regret his decision. The current had broken up the pack ice, and there were long stretches of open water. A few of the cracks he was able to jump, but one time he had to backtrack for several hours until he found ice sound enough to cross safely. While he was retracing his steps, the sound of the raven made him look up, and in the very far distance, he could make out a movement in the water, a bear, most likely after a seal that had come to the open water for air.

But Wolff was intent on his own prey. Once on Hochstetter Foreland, he had started to discover an occasional hunter's hut along the coast. They were all deserted; from the absence of tracks, no one had been near them since the beginning of the winter. But they were an unmistakable sign of a human presence in this empty land, and the sight of them gave him the will to go on. He was increasingly conscious by now of the need that would soon be starting to make its demands on him, and misgivings were coming into his mind. What if he couldn't find the American base? What if it wasn't on Clavering Island? What if German intelligence had been wrong and there was no base at all? He hated to think of the condition he would be in then. The next nearest humans were the natives living almost a thousand kilometers down the coast at Scoresbyound—or the American airfield at Thule, about the same distance across the entire width of the icecap.

No—the nearest humans were back at the German weather station. The fact was reassuring in more than one way. The Germans were depending on those weather reports. They never would have sent a being like himself to this place if they hadn't been certain the enemy was here. They never would have risked their own men—while they still needed them.

The dogs were picketed outside the cabin, half buried in the snow with their tails curled around over their muzzles. They were gorged and content after bolting down—bone and hide and all—the second half of the musk ox Lars had shot yesterday. It was always amazing how much the animals could eat, just like starving wolves.

The men had saved a few steaks from the ox and cooked them over the stove, enjoying the welcome taste of fresh meat, even if it hadn't come, as Blackburn said, from Kansas City. Just as welcome was the comfort of the hunter's station. This far north, they were almost as far up the coast as men usually went, and now they'd had to spend a few nights in their tent, warmed only by the flame of a Primus stove and their own body heat. It was tolerable enough, but cramped, and it was a lot more work putting up the tent than settling into one of the hunter's stations. Though they'd only gone half a day, Ferrier had called a halt when they came to this hut. It was snowing already, with a wind that cut through his parka and was slowly turning the exposed flesh of his face numb and hard. It might turn into a blizzard, and then they'd need all the shelter they could get.

Now there was coffee, and Ferrier was sitting with his boots off, next to the stove, when the dogs suddenly started howling outside. The three men looked at each other in some alarm. "What the hell set them off?" Ferrier demanded irritably.

"Bear, maybe," Lars offered.

Ferrier reached for his boots. This far north, this time of year, there were really only two things that could set off the dogs the way they were howling, and a bear was one. The other was men, and men meant—almost certainly—Nazis. But how could it be Nazis? Unless their base was somewhere right over the next hill and someone there had noticed the smoke from their stove.

"I'll go check," Blackburn offered, putting his arm through the sleeve of his coat. He still had on his boots. "Probably just a bear. Hey, after tonight we could use the meat!" Taking his rifle, he went out into the night, swearing at the dogs to shut the hell up.

"Probably a bear," Ferrier said, but he quickly put on his

own boots again. The howling was growing more frantic outside. He and Lars looked at each other, really worried.

"Better go see what it is."

Outside, the wind had picked up, blowing snow. Cloud cover had done a blackout of the sky. Coming out of the lighted hut, Ferrier strained to see beyond the leaping, lunging forms of the tethered dogs. No sight of Blackburn. He didn't like this, didn't like it at all. "Hey, Blackburn! Archie! What's going on?

"Goddammit, Lars, can't you shut them *up*? Blackburn! Where are you?"

He could hear nothing but the howling dogs—like being surrounded by a pack of wolves trying to tear out his throat. He pulled a mitten off his hand to keep it on the trigger of his Thompson submachine gun, aiming blind out into the darkness. He was almost afraid to shoot if something moved, in case he hit Blackburn. Almost afraid not to.

Then his foot kicked something, and he knelt down, very carefully, to pick it up. Blackburn's weapon. He dropped it, whirling around, trying to *see*, but there was only darkness and the sound of the wind. *"Blackburn!"* he screamed, his voice breaking.

He and Lars searched around the cabin in wider and wider circles, all the way down to the shore, but there was no sign of the missing Blackburn. Nothing, nothing at all. In the dim red glow that passed for noon, when the wind had died down a little, they searched again, with their flashlights, this time for a body, or a trail of blood—anything. But if there had been any tracks, the snow had covered them.

Ferrier finally let loose one of Blackburn's dogs, hoping the animal could catch the scent and put them on the trail of the missing man. But the dog, after running forward a few yards, cringed with its tail lowered and refused to go on.

Throughout the day, Lars had grown more silent—sullen, even. But if there was something bothering him, the guide wouldn't say.

Ferrier finally had to make the decision. "I guess in the morning we'd better go on. Whatever happened to Blackburn . . . If it could have been krauts, we'd better check it out, at least."

He knew, even as he said it, that this was all wrong. A Nazi patrol wouldn't do like that, take out one man and leave the rest, when they had a clear shot at all of them. But he was thinking of the captain and what he was going to say when they got back to base.

"We'll get some sleep. Maybe the wind will die off some, make it easier to see some tracks."

The Greenlander didn't answer, just sat there hacking at a piece of leather with his knife, staring at the floor. Ferrier pulled off his boots, crawled into one of the bunks. Lars, slowly, silently, did the same.

For all his exhaustion, Ferrier found it hard to sleep. The sound of the wind outside, the hiss of the snow as it hit the walls. There was no one out there. No one. Blackburn . . . was gone. Swallowed up without a trace.

He woke suddenly, to silence. The cabin was dark. What time was it? How long had they slept? "Lars!" he called out, striking a light.

But the other bunk was empty.

Seized by panic, he ran to the door, flung it open. His dogs broke out of the snow, shaking themselves, when they heard him yelling, but the other team, the other sled was missing.

Tracks, almost filled with snow, led south into the darkness. His guide had deserted him, left him there, alone.

Chapter Seven

He had caught the scent of them first, warm and compelling, from across the lifeless cold foreshore. Wolff stopped abruptly, ignoring the snow lashing his face. The scent of life — dogs and men — in all this desert of ice. His buried, dormant hunger came awake like a polar bear roused from its winter sleep.

The scent was upwind of him. Cautiously, he moved toward its source, his senses eager and acute. The wind carried the sounds of dogs to him, the howls and snarling of a pack of hunting wolves as they fell on their prey. But wolves were extinct on Greenland, as the caribou were extinct, and the presence of dogs meant men.

And light meant men, the warm yellow glow faintly visible up in the hills ahead, despite the blowing snow. In all of the surrounding night, it was like a signal flare. But more than the light it was the scent that drew him on, the scent and the warmth of blood.

The dogs had gradually quieted, and Wolff supposed they'd been fed and were settling for the night. He could see the hut now, glowing almost like a lantern with heat and light. Nearby, the long forms of sleds and the smaller mounds which were the dogs, denned up under the snow. He was careful to keep downwind of them, well aware that their senses were almost as acute as his own. But for all his caution, the animals caught his scent. Suddenly, the sleeping hummocks of snow burst into life and the silence exploded with the frenzy of three dozen howling beasts, lunging against the lines that tied them down.

Wolff halted with a low curse. He'd known wolves before, as he'd known dogs, but these beasts were neither and both, all at once. Like wolves, they loved the hot lust of the kill, the savage pleasure of tearing at living flesh. But as dogs, they knew the hand of a human master. He came closer to them now, letting them have his scent, letting them know him, that his scent was not human, not human at all.

The howling grew louder. Suddenly the scene was illuminated by the door of the hut swinging open as a man stepped out into the night, carrying a weapon. He cursed the dogs, shoving the frantic animals back with the butt of his gun. Wolff grinned with elation, baring his teeth. An American! Yes! He'd found them at last!

He moved quickly, ignoring the dogs, only taking enough care to keep clear of their teeth. He had minimal concern for the gun under these conditions. In the dark, in the driving snow, there was no chance of his being seen by human eyes.

The cries of the dogs reached an unearthly pitch as he seized their master from behind. Wolff pulled the gun out of his hands. The man kicked out, screaming, as Wolff wrenched his arms back, but with all the noise from the dogs it didn't matter how loud he screamed. Wolff's main concern now was getting his victim away before the rest of them came out of the hut.

With a dull crack the man's shoulders dislocated. The peasants had trussed their livestock this way to carry them to market; it cut down on the struggling. Wolff lifted his victim bodily and ran. As he disappeared into the blowing snow, he could hear the others from the hut running out, trying to quiet the dogs, calling for their missing companion, Blackburn.

Blackburn was still conscious enough to try to call back to them. Wolff scowled. There wasn't much cover in this place, except for the curtain of driven snow. He wanted to feed in relative peace, not have to deal with the rest of the soldiers. He held Blackburn up in one hand, hit him once to break his jaws, then flung him down. The man thrashed, trying ineffectively to get to his feet, still fighting even as he gasped and spit blood from his broken mouth. Wolff appreciated that, and a warning thrill of bloodlust ran through him. He ripped open the front of the man's coat, where the pulse was rapid with pain and rage and fear.

He wanted badly to prolong the kill, to savor the pain, but in the near distance he could still hear the other Americans, searching for this one, crying out his name. This was not the time or place to give in to the extremes of his bloodlust.

The bright blade of the dagger plunged in.

When the body was drained, Wolff turned around. The other Americans were coming closer, sounding more and more desperate — two of them. He knew he could take them. It would be simple to finish the matter here tonight. But he wanted more than that.

He lifted the inert body and carried it farther away, out onto the ice where the bear had been hunting near the lead of open water. He left it there, a gift of sorts for the massive white beast.

Behind him, the driving snow soon obliterated his tracks.

Let the Americans wonder what had happened to their comrade. Let them wait. He had time.

Once he made himself believe that Lars had driven off and deserted him, Ferrier wasted no more time. He loaded up his own sled, got his team into harness. It was a struggle. Something had the dogs spooked, bad. Blackburn's team gave him a few moment's hesitation. He didn't want them running loose, but the alternative was to shoot them all.

Finally he cut them free, then cracked his whip and drove out into the night, following the rapidly disappearing tracks of the Greenlander's sled. There was no more question of trying to go on, not in this unknown country, without a guide. Mushing across the broken ice, fighting the sled, the snow and the dogs, his curses were all for Lars, and his rage gave him the strength to shove the load ahead of him over the roughest pressure ridges.

The driven snow flayed his face. There were times when he couldn't see his own lead dog, fifty feet ahead of him. Driving in a blizzard like this, with almost no visibility, there was no way of knowing if he was following the guide, except for the dogs instinctively following the trail of the other team.

He flogged the dogs on, pressing for speed, but they were only capable of so much. Not knowing what was ahead of him, he didn't dare lighten his load. From time to time he could make out the gray form of one of Blackburn's dogs, running free alongside his sled at a distance.

He drove himself almost past the point of exhaustion. It was the condition of the dogs that finally made him stop, and when he stopped moving, the wind cut through his sweat-damp parka, chilling him instantly. His hands were too numb to let him unharness and feed the dogs, and it was almost impossible to get the tent up. At last he got the Primus lit, but then, with his fingers frozen, he still had to force himself to go back out into the blizzard to tend to his ravenous team. After a run like that, they needed meat. He was too good a driver to abuse animals the way he'd done, no matter how much he wanted to catch up with the guide who'd deserted him.

The animals were restless, like there was something they could sense out there in the dark. They bolted their food stiffly, growling, and afterward they didn't settle down to sleep, even after the long hard day on the trail. Ferrier could see a few of Blackburn's dogs skulking around the edge of the camp. He had no intention of feeding them, not when they hadn't pulled, but with them hanging around he had to unload the sled completely and drag all his stores inside the tent to keep them from getting into it. Every musher he knew would swear a hungry sled dog could eat three times its own weight in harness leather.

Back inside the tent he huddled, shivering convulsively, over the stove's tiny hot flame, almost at the end of his strength. But he knew what he had to do, and he made himself strip off his damp clothes, hanging them to dry as much as they could while he pulled dry things from his pack. He was cursing himself by now, because it was his own fault. He should have known better than to let himself get into this condition, especially out here alone. It wasn't the cold that killed you in the Arctic, it was always your own stupid mistakes.

But then, whose fault was it that he was out here alone? The damn guide, that's who.

Getting dry made the difference. And being inside out of the wind. The cold wasn't all that bad — he didn't think it was more than twenty below. After a while he began to melt some snow and started to fix himself some rations. It had been close. His fingers were starting to thaw and the pain made his eyes water, but he told himself it was going to be all right.

He thought it was. But when he crawled into his sleeping bag, but he couldn't close his eyes. Outside, the dogs were still restless. He could hear them, whimpering, growling. It was almost . . . and he didn't want to think about it, but again it was like they knew something was out there. Like they were being followed.

There'd been a wolverine once, back in Alaska, that had followed his trapline one winter. Mean, evil-minded beast. Left a trail of sprung traps all the way up and down the river. He'd tried everything — poison, even the nasty Eskimo whalebone wolf traps. Nothing could stop it. At night, in camp, he knew the thing was out there, could hear it snuffling sometimes no more than a few yards away. But all that winter he never laid eyes on it. A whole season of trapping, ruined.

Now, nervously, he checked his gun. Procedure in the Arctic was to stow the weapons inside the tent, but under the groundsheet, where the moisture wouldn't collect on moving parts and freeze them shut, make them useless. He wished he could sleep holding the Thompson.

The next day, by his watch, the wind still wasn't letting up. Ferrier knew he ought to wait out the weather here in his tent. He had plenty of supplies — enough food and gas for the stove.

But he knew somehow that Lars, up on the trail ahead of him, was going to keep going, no matter what. And he still couldn't shake the feeling that there was *something* out there somewhere, following him.

The dogs whined as he got them into harness. Setting out food, he managed to capture a couple of Blackburn's team. Fresh dogs might help him catch up with the guide. Though it hardly seemed worth the trouble when Robber led the team in turning on them. Ferrier kicked them apart, cursing and using his whip. He didn't have time for this crap.

The blowing snow had obliterated any tracks that might have been left by Lars's sled. It hardly seemed possible that even the dogs would be able to pick up the Greenlander's trail. All Ferrier really knew for sure was that keeping the vague dark mass of the mainland on his right, he had to be heading more or less south, in the direction of the base. But there were hundreds of inlets and sounds and islands between him and there, and it was hard to make them out in the dark, when he wasn't really sure of the way.

He drove for hours through the worst of the weather, keeping up a good pace but careful now not to overtire either the dogs or himself. After a while it seemed to him that the wind was dying down. He could see the line of dogs pulling ahead of him, the fog-cloud of their breath. It was getting colder.

He was starting to think of looking for a good spot to set up camp when the dogs suddenly surged forward, making an excited racket. Ferrier's first impulse was to grab his gun and look behind him, but there was nothing he could see — there never was. Just this feeling in the back of his neck. Then he looked forward again, and there ahead was something moving.

He whipped the eager dogs into a run — it would have been harder to try to hold them back — and they quickly started to close the distance. Over the noise of his own team, Ferrier could soon hear the growls and snarls of a vicious fight. Then slowly he made out the form of a sled. As he drove up, he saw the dogs snarled in a tangle at each other's throats.

The last thing he needed now was his own team crippled. Swearing, he hauled back on the sled, ordering the dogs to stop, but they wanted into the fight, and he took a couple of bites, hauling on the ganglines, before he had the sled stopped and anchored so the frantic bloodthirsty beasts couldn't drag it off.

Lars must have seen him coming, but the Greenlander was too busy trying to separate the frenzied fighting dogs. Ferrier could see that some of the animals were the huskies from Blackburn's team that had run free ahead of him on the guide's trail. He should have shot them all back there, he knew now. With the instincts of years of dog handling, he waded into the fight with whip and boots, dragging the Alaskan dogs off the Greenland team. Some of the animals whimpered in pain. The snow was dark with blood and dog shit.

As soon as he had them secured, he turned on Lars, who was kneeling next to an injured dog. He dragged him to his feet.

"You *bastard!* Filthy, yellow bastard! Running out on me!"

He backhanded the Greenlander hard across the face, making him stagger. He advanced to hit him again, but Lars held up his hands to protect himself. Blood streamed blackly from his nose. "I knew you will follow me. I wait for you."

They were both breathing hard, white clouds of it in the frigid air. Ferrier suddenly felt the bite of the cold. "The hell you were," he snarled, but it was getting to be a lot harder to remember how mad he was. The fingers he'd frozen last night were throbbing.

"What the hell did you run off for? Leaving me there like that? Not saying a word?"

Lars shook his head, looking down at his boots. "Not Nazis," he mumbled. "Not Nazis out there."

Ferrier said nothing. He remembered his own feeling in the tent last night, alone, with the dogs whimpering outside, the feeling he couldn't shake that there was somebody out there, somebody following. And not Nazis. He couldn't say why, but that's how it was.

He stuck his tingling hand inside the crook of his elbow to warm it. "Maybe we'd better make camp," he said finally.

Wordlessly, Lars agreed.

Two of the dogs were plainly dying, one Greenlander and one Alaskan. Dispassionately, the guide slit the throat of his own animal and skinned it with efficient strokes of his knife. While Ferrier watched, fascinated and slightly disgusted, he disjointed the steaming carcass and tossed the meat to his team, which bolted it down. It was the way they did things around here, that was all.

By the time both teams were fed and staked, the tent was up and the stoves going. It would be warmer, at least, with two of them sharing the space in the three-man tent.

Three men — for the first time since that night back in the hut, Ferrier thought of Archie Blackburn. Gone. Not just dead, but . . . gone. He hadn't known the guy very well before they went out on the patrol, and now he could hardly remember him, what he'd looked like, the sound of his voice.

"So," he said finally, confronting Lars, "running out on me that way, leaving me up there alone . . ."

The guide stared at the floor of the tent. "I'm afraid."

"Afraid? Afraid of what? Look, you knew we might run into Nazis when you took this job!"

Shaking his head, "Not Nazis."

"Oh yeah? And what happened to Blackburn that night, he just decided to take a walk in the storm and got lost? C'mon, I heard the dogs, there was somebody out there!"

"Somebody, yes. Not Nazis. Not men. Dogs . . . know men. This is not men."

Ferrier remembered the wolverine. But there were no gluttons on Greenland. "You mean some kind of animal? A bear?"

"Maybe bear. Maybe . . . not."

Ferrier felt his anger starting to build up again. "I don't know what the hell you're talking about, but I want to be there when you tell it to the captain back at the base."

Lars's hands twisted in his lap. "The old ones — they say, the inland-dwellers live on the ice, the high ice. Not men. They have great shamans. They fly — where they want. They take shape of walrus, of seal . . . of bear. Long ago, men live here, villages of men. Inland-dwellers come in the dark, kill them all. Leave only their bones. All the men gone. All. No more. Only at Scoresbysund."

Ferrier snorted skeptically, but the Greenlander went on, "They get dogs, then. Dogs know inland-dwellers, know their scent. Dogs always know."

Ferrier wanted to tell him he was crazy, but outside the tent one of the dogs whimpered restlessly.

Lars went on, "That night, I hear the dogs. I think, maybe bear outside. We go out, but Blackburn is gone. In the dark."

And Ferrier, despite himself, felt a kind of crawling sensation down the back of his neck, remembering how the dogs had acted on the trail, remembering his feeling that something was out there . . .

He was going as crazy as the guide, that's what it was. Polar madness or something. He suddenly wanted a drink, wanted to be back at the base in a warm bed — anywhere but here.

"We'd better get some sleep," he said finally. "Maybe . . . one of us should stand watch." He shifted the position of his Thompson, safely stowed under the groundsheet, so it was near the door flap of the tent, close at hand. "I'll take the first go." He knew he wasn't going to be able to sleep anyway, not right now.

He stared at the entrance of the tent, waiting, listening for the dogs. *The dogs know.*

They come in the dark.

Chapter Eight

The chase: it had been a tradition for centuries at the castle, in Wolff's time, in Istvan's before him. They would take a serf guilty of some petty crime—or not, but there was hardly a serf who wasn't guilty of some crime or other—and set him loose in the castle courtyard at sunset. If he managed to reach the boundary of the estate by sunrise, he would go free.

Those were the stated conditions, but in fact no serf had ever gone free, not in Wolff's time or in Istvan's. The point of the game had been the chase, to prolong it as long as possible—let the quarry get to within a few yards of the boundary, let him stare in growing hope at the sky starting to grow lighter in the east.

But here in the Arctic there was no sunrise to end the game. The night went on and on without end, with no escape on the broad empty stretch of the ice, nowhere to hide. All they could do was run, and keep running.

Wolff had been easily keeping up with the pace of the dogs. The blizzard had been like a cloak of invisibility at the beginning of the chase. Now, with the clouds blown away from the stars, the Arctic landscape was starkly illuminated and he had to take more precautions, but this only sharpened the thrill of the hunt.

For much of his existence, he had tried to control the feral side of his nature. He had been brought up to appreciate civilization, the social order—the old order, with all its privilege and, yes, its responsibility. The castle had prospered while he was lord there. But so much of what he valued had been lost. He'd agreed to this mission as a way of trying to regain what he had lost, his castle and lands, if not his title. With the Germans losing the war, it was probably a futile hope. But here on the ice, existence reverted to its essential elements: kill or be killed, survive or die.

It would be good to have Kessler out here on the ice. Alone, without his SS guards behind him. To see how well he would run, how far, how long.

But thinking of Kessler made Wolff recall his purpose in coming to the Arctic. The Americans were not just his personal prey. He had to track them all the way to their base, to leave one of them, at least, alive for that purpose.

It was easy, trailing them. Even when a storm cut down on the visibility, he could follow them by scent. They were afraid. The scent of it was as clear to him as their tracks through the snow. Even the dogs smelled of fear.

The animals could sense what he was, the difference in his scent—not human, not human any more. He was one of them, a predator. But there was only one kind of prey that could satisfy his need. Only one kind of blood.

How many men at the American base? Ten? Twenty? There would be enough—certainly more than enough.

His ears caught the sound of raised voices. The American was quarreling with his guide, accusing him of wasting time trying to catch a seal. Their tempers were very short. It had been a long time since either man had been able to get any real sleep.

The dogs sensed Wolff's presence, hidden behind the rocks at the shore's edge. They whined and pulled at their anchor lines, making the men turn on them with whips, cursing. They were breaking, on the edge of breaking. Wolff licked his lips, exposing white teeth.

The guide finally seemed to prevail, taking his gun and

walking further out onto the ice where a fissure hinted that there might be a seal's breathing hole. Wolff watched the hunter until he was a dark indistinct shape standing motionless over the hole, waiting for the seal to emerge for air.

Wolff's attention turned to the American, left behind to set up camp. The hungry dogs were fractious, and the man's efforts were hampered by the two quarrelsome teams lunging and snapping at each other. Every minute or so he had to stop and try to warm his hands. As Wolff drew closer, taking advantage of the uneven ridges of shore ice as cover, the animals grew more and more difficult for the soldier to handle. They had Wolff's scent, they knew him, were afraid.

The man was distracted. As he moved down the line of dogs, Wolff caught the eye of the nearest animal, held it—yes. Slowly, the dog lowered its head, whining in submission and fear.

Wolff looked past it to the American, as he kept struggling with the other animals. Wolff's bloodlust had been aroused by the long chase, and now the closeness of his victim was sharpening his need. Political considerations were irrelevant. Enemy or ally, nothing now could stop him from taking this man's blood.

But the soldier was wary. He never took more than a few steps away from the submachine gun slung on one of the uprights of the sled. It was too close, the atmosphere was too clear. He could take him when his back was turned, but not with the dogs to give the alarm. If he could only quiet all the animals, now, while the other man was out on the ice, concentrating on the seal.

Suddenly the crack of the rifle broke Wolff's concentration. The American's head jerked up, he ran a few steps out toward the figure on the ice.

Wolff withdrew a short distance, frustrated for the moment. But there would be another opportunity. Like the hunter on the ice, he could wait.

* * *

It must be thirty below. At least. Not as much wind, maybe, as the storm a week ago, but the cold was like a knife.

Goddamn dogs!

Ferrier kicked two of them apart, checked the harness on one that had been chewing the leather — the Greenlander dogs were the worst, they'd eat their own harness in a minute if you didn't watch them. But none of the animals wanted to be tied up, not with . . . whatever it was, following them. He didn't blame them. He'd been in bad places before — times when he wasn't sure he was going to make it. But never like this. God, never like this.

He stuck his hands into the relative warmth of his armpits, trying to get them thawed enough that he could tackle the job of putting up the tent. He didn't know how Lars could stand it, out on the ice like that — no shelter, not moving. You couldn't move, he said, not even stamp your feet to keep warm. The seal could hear it. When the sun was up, the seal could see your shadow through the ice.

But it was weeks since they'd seen the sun. It was dark — so dark you couldn't even tell night from day. The inland-dwellers came in the dark.

Lars was a dark shape against the ice, waiting for the seal. Ferrier thought of a seal's open, steaming belly, of plunging his frozen hands into the heat of the guts. The warm, chewy liver. His empty stomach spasmed. He pulled the tent off his sled.

At the sound of the rifle shot, his head jerked up, he stared out to the shadow that was Lars on the ice. The dogs went crazy, howling and pulling on their tethers. They were capable of bolting down the whole seal — bones, hide and all. Fill their bellies with fresh meat, and they'd pull a lot faster next morning. So maybe Lars was right, it hadn't been a waste of time, after all.

Once the animals were finally fed and the men were inside

their sleeping bags, Ferrier closed his eyes, listening for the sound of footsteps outside, someone coming closer to the tent. The dogs, gorged on seal meat, had dug into the snow to sleep, quieter than they'd been in days. If only it was over, if only they were back at the base.

Ferrier opened his eyes and stared at Lars's motionless shape in the fur sleeping bag. *Do you think it's over,* he wanted to ask. *Do you think it's finally gone, whatever's been following us?*

Lars never stirred, but Ferrier could tell from the pattern of his breathing that he was still awake, listening, both of them, listening. *No, it's still out there, somewhere. In the dark. The inland-dweller.* Shape-changer. Prowling outside in some terrible form. Blood on its mouth.

Ferrier had seen wolves in Alaska kill a moose — running the animal to exhaustion, crippling it, then tearing at the belly while the animal was still standing and trembling, tearing it open, snapping at the entrails, pulling them out, eating the animal while it was still alive, still alive . . .

He sobbed wordlessly, a sharp intake of breath. The wolverine had followed his trapline for two months. All that time, the only thing he'd seen had been its tracks and the other signs it had left — the severed paw of a fox or martin in his traps, the shredded remains of a cache of furs. It had been out there, yes, out there behind him, waiting, silent, unseen, always waiting.

It was the vision he saw now whenever he closed his eyes, because his exhausted imagination insisted on giving the fears a shape — evil black-masked face, a snarl of vicious teeth, wolverine grown huge, as big as a bear, padding silently after him, in his footsteps. Blood on its mouth — black blood shining in the starlight. A light in its eyes . . .

Ferrier reached for the Thompson, drawing it to him, clutching it against his chest. He could feel Lars, lying next to him in the tent, stiffen inside his sleeping bag. Neither of them had been able to sleep in days, in nights. God, they were going to start hallucinating soon, seeing things, hearing things.

He wondered what Lars was seeing, what crazy vision.

The wind hissed, shards of snow striking the edge of the tent, and he flinched, holding the gun tighter. It could rip open the canvas with its claws, dig them out . . .

He couldn't tell, anymore, whether he was hearing anything or not. The brain plays tricks — you listen hard enough for something and you start to hear . . . things.

It was only when he felt Lars move next to him that he knew the guide had heard it, too. The crushing of ice crystals underfoot. Coming closer. He tried not to breathe. His heartbeat, painfully rapid, was too loud, drowning out the sound. No — there it was again. Yes, it was out there — out there for sure now.

One of the dogs whined, then another. The dogs knew, the dogs were afraid . . .

It was out there . . . coming closer . . .

The explosion of fire ripped through the tent, so loud, so sudden that at first Ferrier didn't realize what he'd done, not until he could hear himself breathing again. And, outside the tent, the sound of dogs howling, whining, yelping in pain.

Lars, sitting bolt upright in panic and shock, stared at him a second, then cursed in his own language and crawled quickly out of the tent to see how much damage Ferrier had done, to tend to the wounded dogs.

Ferrier looked numbly down at the gun in his hand, at the shredded fabric of the tent. *What did I do? How could I shoot* . . .

He was going crazy, that's what it was. A Section-Eight case. Firing through the tent — at what? At nothing! Shooting his own dogs.

The noise from outside had turned to snarls and cries. What was going on? The dogs, especially the Greenland dogs, were capable of turning on each other. What was Lars doing out there? *I ought to do something* . . .

Ferrier stumbled out into the night and stood still. The moon had risen, almost full, and the white light cast stark black shadows against the snow. Some of the dogs were growling and snapping over a bloody patch in the snow, others were straining on their tethers, wild to get in at the kill. Lars . . . was nowhere. Ferrier tried to call out the guide's name, but his voice was frozen. Suddenly he thought—*the dogs, did the dogs get him?*

Frantic, he tore into the pack of snarling, bloody-muzzled beasts, kicking and using his gun to beat them away, but the carcass they were savaging was one of their own kind.

"Lars!" he screamed, then made an choking cry of despair. First Blackburn, now the guide. Disappeared. Swallowed up by the dark. Now he was the only one left.

But the sky was clear this time and the moon lit up the terrain. A little past the margin of the camp he found tracks in the snow, leading inland. The tracks of one man—only one. They were deep, irregular and scuffed, suggesting someone carrying a burden, suggesting a struggle. But no blood. And—they were *human* tracks, the soles of thick soft boots. Ferrier took a breath, a fresh grip on his weapon. Better to face it this way. Whoever—whatever—it was. Better than lying awake in the dark, night after night. Better than waiting.

He started out to follow the trail. The enemy (he was starting to think in terms of an enemy again—a human enemy) was moving fast, almost too fast for someone carrying something the weight of a man. But the depth of the tracks argued otherwise.

He could face another man, a German, a Nazi. Who else could it be? Who else but the Germans were on Greenland?

The inland-dwellers, who lived on the icecap? The shapechangers, taking human form?

No, that was crazy. Lars might believe in that native superstition crap, but a white man could not.

The trail led down the shoreline, toward a tumble of boulders that could easily hide a man—even two men. Ferrier paused and shivered. His breath hung in front of his face, white in the frigid air.

The horizon was open, empty. No way to flank this position. No real use in trying to take cover.

Because there was no other choice, he finally took another

step forward, then another, until a sound made him pause again—a faint, muffled moan. Ferrier clutched the Thompson, flexing his fingers again and again so they wouldn't go numb on him. Closer yet, close enough . . .

Then he saw, though it took his mind another split second to register the sight: a figure in white bending over another, mouth pressed to his victim's throat. Bending over Lars. The guide's eyes, staring. Staring open, dead. Then they blinked once. His mouth opened, he tried to say—

Just at that instant the killer looked up. Blood ran from his mouth—blood, black in the moonlight. And his eyes, a lurid glowing red . . . *glowing* . . . *eyes* . . .

Reflexively, Ferrier's hand closed down around the trigger of the submachine gun, and the night erupted with fire. He was still screaming when the gun went silent, empty.

Now there was only Lars, sprawled on the bloody snow. Still. Motionless. Dead.

And no killer. No sign of the killer, anywhere. He was gone, as if he'd evaporated into the air, into the mist.

Chapter Nine

Wolff cursed under his breath, gritting his teeth against the pain. *Stupid! Careless!*

If the American's magazine hadn't been half-empty . . .

He'd come close, too close to dying this time.

A few hundred meters away, the American gibbered in shock, spun around and fled, stumbling, slipping once to his knees and crawling a few meters before he could get back on his feet. Panic — sheer mindless panic. Wolff was used to it in his victims.

Now he fell back in relief against the ridge of ice that had hidden him near the edge of the shore. His leg throbbed excruciatingly. He was sure the kneecap was shattered. He swore again, with bitter self-accusation. Pure carelessness, nothing else. He'd let himself be carried away again by his lust for the kill, and this time it had almost been fatal.

It had been the fear. The long chase, with the two men fleeing ahead of him, and at night inside the tent, lying awake, feeding their private nightmares. He'd been aware of every breath they took, every beat and stroke of their hearts, feeling the American's rising terror when the dogs started to whine. The bloodlust fed on their fear.

And then in the confusion, with the maddened frenzy of the dogs tearing at each other, the blood spraying the snow — the native guide rushing out of the tent, almost into his arms. It had been, simply, too much of a temptation, too much for him to resist.

The guide had been a strong man, almost insane with panic when he looked into Wolff's eyes, hard to subdue easily. He'd known it was going to have to be a quick kill, and there were some rocks upshore that offered concealment. Quick kill and leave the body there, retreat.

But the guide had fought to the end, resisting even as Wolff pulled his head back to expose the throat to the knife, blood pulsing hard under the smooth brown skin. Strong blood, rich, rich blood, pumping out with each heartbeat. The sound of that heart was all he could hear, and the deep, pagan scent of fear overwhelmed all other sensations.

He fell into it, savoring it, anticipating the end. Until the moment, too late, when he finally looked up to see the American, eyes wide in shock, bringing up his weapon to fire . . .

Careless.

Setting his teeth, he tore away the stained knee of his pants to face the damage. Dark pulp and white bone shards. As bad as he'd feared.

The knee would heal. At least he'd just fed. But it was going to drain his resources, and it would be days before he was ready to match the pace of a dogsled again. Even now the American was probably whipping his dogs up to speed, heading south, back to his base. It was suddenly frightening to be alone in the middle of this harsh, empty land. The only human within a hundred kilometers was escaping, getting farther and farther away while he sat here, helpless.

Wolff frowned, remembering something. The end, the instant of death — he hadn't felt it. Could the guide still possibly be alive?

He licked his lips and swallowed at the thought of more blood. Shock was setting in, and need. Cautiously, he tried to stand. A few minutes ago his instincts for self-preservation had shut down his nerves long enough to let him run on the shattered knee, but now it buckled when it put his weight on it. So instead he crawled, dragging the broken leg, back across the ice to the shoreline boulders where he'd left the guide, perhaps still living.

But dead, now. Very dead, in fact, and the reason easy to see — the bullets had torn his chest apart. The panicked American had fired without thinking, killing his own guide. Wolff suddenly realized — without the body as a shield more of those bullets would almost certainly have hit him. He'd come closer than he'd realized to dying.

Now he looked down at the corpse, the bloodstained snow, and considered the empty distance between him and the American base, the soldier getting closer and closer to escape. Like it or not, he was going to need as much blood as he could get.

With a certain feeling akin to nausea, he pulled out his knife and punctured the dead flesh. A dark trickle welled out, and he put his mouth to the wound, sucking hard. It was a long, distasteful process, and a few times the revulsion threatened to overwhelm him. Sucking blood from a corpse, feeding on the dead, like a ghoul. There was a foul taint of death already in the fluid, chemical processes at work, the first steps of decay. Grimly, Wolff extracted what he could, then turned to scooping up the stained snow into his mouth.

When he'd finished, he limped away from the remains, retrieving his rifle and using it as a crutch. A bank of snow had drifted up against the cliff face, and he dug himself into it, curling up like a bear in its den, with only his broken leg extended its full length.

Then he let himself go, sinking into rest. Around him, the silence expanded to the horizons. Each snapping crystal of snow sounded in his ears like a gunshot, and in the distance the massive, restless blocks of sea ice shifted at the fracture zones.

It was a solitude as close to infinite as he had ever known, both comforting and disquieting at once. It seemed somehow that he had been destined to come some time in his existence to this lifeless, sunless place.

Destiny—he rejected the notion. It had been his own will that had brought him to the Arctic, his own free choice, to live, to die or be damned.

And if it had been a mistake? To die for the sake of the Germans? Was that what it all had come to?

It was the SS that had attracted him first, the Order of the Death's Head, as they liked to call themselves. One of their researchers into the primal Germanic myth had discovered an old woodcut of his castle that he hadn't known existed. There was a brief correspondence that came to nothing when he realized how absurd their racial theories were. But the connection was made, and later, more practical arrangements. The SS had deaths to offer, and he had his unique abilities.

The missions had come to mean something to him eventually. A sense of purpose, a matter of pride. It became a point of honor with him that he'd never failed. Never yet. Not until now.

Failure. The American had escaped. The knowledge rankled, but it couldn't be denied. The soldier was going to make it back to his command, report how his patrol had been attacked, two men killed. And the longer Wolff waited to heal, the harder it would be to follow.

Wolff flexed his leg experimentally, stiffly, and the slight movement was without pain. Slowly, he began to dig himself from the snow.

He could hear the stiff flutter of wings, and the sound of ravens disputing over some piece of carrion. Limping, careful not to put too much weight on the newly mended knee, he walked the few meters back down the shoreline to the place where he'd left the drained body of the guide. One bird retreated a few beats from the carcass at his approach, the other stood its ground defiantly. Wolff had no interest in disputing the rights to that particular piece of flesh. He went on down the coast and across the shore ice to the site of the American camp.

Here were more ravens, and the tracks of foxes. Wolff stood and considered the ruins. The soldier in his flight had abandoned a great deal. The bullet-riddled tent, one sled, along with some of its supplies, a pair of skis . . . Wolff searched among the scattered leavings of the camp. No weapons left behind. The American had at least had the presence of mind to take what was essential to survival, discarding the rest as excess weight. He would be armed, he would be moving fast, as fast as he could drive the dogs. When well fed, the animals could cover over sixty kilometers a day on a good trail.

Wolff frowned, pulling out his map from the inside pocket of his coat and tracing the shortest possible route to Clavering Island. He'd been almost two days under the snow, healing. By now, the American might be almost halfway back to his base.

White teeth bit down on almost colorless lips. The tracks of the dogsled led south, down the coast. He had recently fed, his knee was almost sound. Almost. There was a chance he could catch up with the fleeing soldier before he could report back. A remote chance.

Again he checked the map. No. It was too far. He couldn't make it, not in his present condition, not if he couldn't catch up with the American. The healing had taken too much of his strength, and he was going to need blood again soon. Too soon.

He turned his back on the American base and headed north, limping back toward Ursa Bay and Weather Group Flieger.

Chapter Ten

The work of the weather station had settled into a regular routine. Most days, despite the cold, it was simple enough to take the readings of temperature, humidity, air pressure, wind direction and speed, to send the radiosonde balloons aloft into the upper atmosphere. To perform the same tasks in the teeth of an Arctic gale was more of a challenge, but that, after all, was why they were in this place.

With nothing but the clock to mark the intervals between night and day, time often seemed to stand still. It was an effort sometimes to keep all the men busy, to battle the constant threat of depression. Some of them were more susceptible than others. The Luftwaffe navigator Ziegler was one of the worst cases, and Dietrich even noticed the tendency in himself, the dragging reluctance to climb out of his bunk in the morning—what they still arbitrarily called morning, even though none of them had seen the sun for over a month.

But work was the best cure, and the routine of the weather station imposed it on everyone. Every day, the readings had to be made, at precisely the same times. Twice, again on schedule, they had to radio the data back to Tromsø.

Dietrich carefully checked over the coded message, then laid it down on top of the radio, nodding to Mundt, who was adjusting something in the back of the set. "Very good." He lit a cigarette and glanced at his watch. Everything was in order.

The radio was their link to the real world, their homeland, their families. At certain times Dietrich allowed them to tune into the official German broadcasts for news of the war, but the only way they could get personal news was through the Tromsø link. There was no mail call for them on Greenland.

As 0900 hours approached, the hut was full of men pretending to have something else to do, just as Dietrich himself was, going through the motions of being in command. Waiting, all of them. Dietrich looked down again involuntarily at his watch, saw that ninety seconds had passed. His fingers rotated a loose button on his uniform. Have to take care of that, later.

He always made sure his uniform was in good order, as an example to the others. They should never forget they were in the service of the German Reich. And such tasks kept the men occupied, with laundry, mending, heating water for shaving — all the necessary tasks of daily life that took so much more effort in this place but helped them remember who they were and why they were here. That it also kept the commanding officer occupied with the necessary inspections was no small consideration, either.

At exactly 0900 hours, Mundt began to key in the transmission. There was a pause when he finished, all the men waiting openly now, no more pretense of having other business.

But there was no news for anyone at the station.

Several men grumbled their disappointment out loud, but most of them stayed around the set to listen to the broadcast, impatient with Mundt when he was slow to tune it in. But this news was the same as usual. German troops had repelled yet another Allied assault and the war was going well — except that every time the assaults came from closer and closer to the German heartland. Everyone knew that the Amis had already crossed the Rhine.

There were a few mutterings about the official optimism before the men turned away to their various tasks, but nothing outspoken. Privately, they clung to their own beliefs — that the war was already lost, that the Führer would produce a miracle — but no one anymore spoke of those things openly. They all remembered what had happened to Ernst Weber.

Erich Klostermann, the stranded pilot of the flying boat, came up to Dietrich with a worried expression. "It's been almost four days, and they're not back yet."

Dietrich looked again at his watch. "Yes. I know. But the weather's been good, and they had a tent, sleeping bags . . ."

A week ago, a polar bear had been spotted prowling around at the foot of the headland. Dietrich had immediately authorized stricter procedures for garbage disposal, but after a number of requests he'd authorized a hunting expedition. It would be good for the men; it would get them out of the confines of the hut for a while, let them have some exercise, some freedom. Three men had left four days ago — Klostermann's copilot Busch was one of them. They should have been back by this time.

But Dietrich didn't feel there was too much need for concern. The men had been trained for survival in the Arctic and were already accustomed to the subfreezing temperatures. The weather was holding. Still, it was one more worry. Should he send men out to search for them?

He supposed if he ought to worry about anyone, it was the SS officer, Wolff, gone now for all of three weeks. Whether he'd run into the enemy or fallen through a crack in the ice or simply frozen to death in a storm, Dietrich supposed he'd never know. But Wolff had been a law unto himself. And Dietrich had profited from the example. It was a rule now that no one could go off base alone.

Maybe allowing the hunting expeditions had been a mistake. He glanced at his watch again. Almost four days. Where *were* they? Busch, Schaus and Rohde. What could have happened to them?

"Maybe someone should go out after them," Klostermann prodded him.

Dietrich was about to agree when Feldwebel Dienst, one of the weather technicians, came into the hut. "Herr Hauptmann, I was just up on the tower and I think I spotted someone coming across the bay. Three men."

Dietrich grinned at Klostermann. "Well, it looks like they're back! I wonder if they got a bear? Some fresh meat would be good for a change."

"Bear schnitzel," muttered the pilot, but his grin showed his relief.

They were all joking about how to cook the bear and what to do with the pelt when the door was flung open. Into the hut came Busch, Rohde and — not Schaus. Following the others instead was the SS officer, Wolff.

The hut went suddenly silent. Dietrich felt dread rush over him. Everyone stared.

The three men were haggard. Busch and Rohde had white patches of frostbite on their faces and red, exhausted eyes. Wolff's shoulders slumped, and he was limping slightly. He had no pack, only a rifle. The other two dropped theirs heavily onto the floor.

"What happened?" Dietrich finally demanded.

"We lost Schaus," Busch said, wearily. "We thought we spotted a bear. We separated, to try to pick up the trail. But he never . . . we never . . .

"We searched. We went up and down the fjord, up into the hills — we . . ."

Köbler came up with three mugs of steaming coffee, handed them to Busch and Rohde, who flung off their mittens and took the hot mugs with infinite gratitude into their hands. Wolff waved him away.

Despite his apparent weariness, Wolff's voice was clipped and unemotional. "I found a body out on the ice. There was enough left of the remains that I could tell it had been a German soldier. There were bear tracks in the vicinity. Unfortunately, it wasn't possible to identify the body, but from what I understand, it must have been your signalman, Schaus."

Dietrich was stunned, almost as much by this sudden, impossible reappearance as by Schaus's death. How had Wolff managed to survive, alone out there, for so long—for weeks? What *was* the man?

"I'll need to send a report," Wolff said abruptly.

"Of course. Just give it to the radioman on duty."

"There's more to this situation. Questions of security."

"Yes. Of course," Dietrich said again. They retreated to the corner next to the radio, waving the operator away from the set.

Dietrich lowered his voice. He was suddenly and uneasily aware how relieved he'd been when the SS officer had never come back. But he found his voice to ask, "You don't really think Schaus was killed by a bear?"

Wolff shook his head. "It's possible, but I doubt it. I think the animal found his body."

"Just south of Dove Bay I came on an American reconnaissance patrol. Two soldiers and a native guide, traveling by dogsled."

"Americans? Here? No, I—"

"Do you doubt my word?" Wolff demanded.

"No! No, of course not. It's just that no one saw anything, no one heard—no shots."

"No. There might not have been shots," Wolff said shortly. "These were dangerous men. You were fortunate they didn't have a chance to report your location back to their headquarters."

Dietrich didn't have to ask to know the dogsled men were dead.

"What I want to know," Wolff demanded, "is what those men were doing so far away from this station."

"Hunting. It gives them a break from the routine here—"

"No, it can't be allowed. There's too much risk. From now on, no one leaves the base—not for any reason."

It was an order, and Dietrich accepted it as such, pulling out a cigarette. Hearing of the Americans had shaken him, realizing what could have happened. If it hadn't been for Wolff.

"I thought you'd been lost. You were gone for such a long time."

Wolff shook his head, a grim smile on his face. "Never write me off too quickly, Hauptmann. I'm not that easy to kill."

Landfried, the medic, had treated the frostbite on Busch and Rohde and declared it not too serious. The two surviving hunters had been filled with hot soup and pushed into their bunks. Wolff had declined treatment or food and taken only a mug of coffee after encoding a message for transmission.

Now, incredibly, after only a few hours of sleep, he was gone again, back out into the cold to "check something."

"It's like he can't rest," Dietrich said, half to himself.

Klostermann frowned. "How much do you know about him?"

"Only what was in his orders. And whose signature was on them. I'm ordered to give him full cooperation."

"Because of the Americans?"

"I suppose so."

"But . . ." Klostermann lowered his voice. "Do we know there really were Americans? Did anyone else see them? Besides Wolff?"

"They killed Schaus!"

Klostermann shook his head. "All we really know is that he's missing."

"Do you have some reason to doubt Wolff?"

The pilot shook his head. "It's just—the way he was, on the flight. We get orders to stand by for a 'special' mission: top secret, special orders from Berlin—you know. We're real happy about *that*, I can tell you. Especially when our CO comes around with the news that the gunners won't be going along on this one. Then we get our flight plan. No deviations, they tell me.

"So, we're waiting to take off, and a car pulls up, full of SS. This one gets out—Wolff—and he looks like he's spent his whole life down in the Gestapo cellars poking people in the eye with lighted cigarettes. But the way they're escorting him, it's like he's a prisoner. Pale as death. I think, he's afraid to fly. Then he won't take a seat up front. He crawls as far back as he can into the tail. Stays there the whole time.

"We land — well, you know how that was. All the time, I kept hearing something from the back of the plane — sounds. Then he staggers like a drunk when he tries to climb down. I tried to give him a hand, and it was like ice, touching him. I swear, I thought he was going to kill me.

"I don't know, I guess it doesn't sound like anything. There's just something not quite *right* about him. Even for the SS."

"I know what you mean," Dietrich thought.

"But I had my orders," Klostermann went on. "What else could I do?"

And Dietrich knew the answer to that one, too.

A few hours later, Helmut Rohde woke up and stumbled stiffly over to the coffee pot. Dietrich sat down next to the civilian weatherman at the table, giving the card players a look that made them fold up their hands and leave. "Herr Rohde, I'd like you to tell me in your own words — what happened out there?"

Rohde rubbed the stubble of his beard, stopped, held the hands out to stare at their discolored condition. He spoke slowly. "It was the way Leutnant Busch said. We'd gone as far as the big bay when we spotted something moving down along the shoreline — a bear, we thought. We followed it, lost it. Then we spread out to see if one of us could pick up its trail. We'd agreed to fire one shot as a signal to the others if we found anything.

"Well, after a while I met up again with Busch. Neither of us had seen any tracks. We started back to see if we could find Feldwebel Schaus. We went all the way around the other side of the headland. Busch fired his gun, the way we'd agreed." He looked up at Dietrich with reddened, weary eyes. "Maybe you heard the shots?"

Dietrich shook his head.

"No. Well, we tried to signal him, tried to pick up his trail from where we'd separated. There was just nothing. We kept on searching . . ."

"Until *he* found us."

"You mean Hauptsturmführer Wolff."

Rohde nodded. "It was like . . . he'd walked out of the ice. All white. Not a sound. He was just . . . there. Like a ghost. Of course we asked if he'd seen Schaus. And he said, if one of our party was missing, he was afraid he had. But there wasn't any use in our going to look, because the bear . . . there wasn't enough left to be able to tell who it was. So he brought us back—"

"You didn't try to recover the body?"

Rohde looked down. "Wolff ordered us not to. He told us to get back to the station right away."

"I see."

Rohde was still staring down at his hands. "I don't know what could have happened to him. If there were Americans, we never heard any shots."

"Well, from now on there'll be no more hunting parties. I've already given the order to the rest. We can't afford the risk, not if the enemy's in the area."

Rohde looked worried. "Shouldn't we post sentries—do something to protect the station?"

"That's up to Wolff. He's in charge of security matters. Right now he says that no one should leave the base."

Dietrich spoke firmly. But a few moments later he sat down and started to draft a message back to Tromsø, a request to confirm the authenticity of Wolff's orders. It couldn't do any harm, after all, just to check.

When it was encoded, he handed the paper to Manstein, the radioman on duty. "Send this out with the next transmission."

Just to make sure.

Chapter Eleven

Matt Ferrier drove south, whipping the dogs into a run, pursued by monstrous terrors rising up out of the darkness at his back.

The thing he'd seen — *eyes glowing red in the night, blood running black down its face, fangs* . . .

He hadn't given in entirely to his panic. There had been enough sanity remaining that he remembered the cold and the miles that lay between him and the safety of the base. There was more than one way to die on the ice.

He threw only the most essential supplies onto the sled, leaving a lot behind but not the tent or the stove. Most of all, not the Thompson and its ammunition.

He'd fired at the thing killing Lars. Had hit it, he knew he had. At that range, only a few yards, he couldn't have missed.

Yet he *knew* it wasn't dead, was still behind him, out there in the dark, behind him in the dark . . .

The dogs seemed to know it, too, the way they ran, heaving against their harness, none of them holding back, not now, not when they had its scent. *The dogs know,* Lars had told him.

Ferrier sobbed, tears freezing on his lashes. Lars. He'd *seen* it bending down over him, blood running down its face. And Oh God that last, worst moment when Lars's eyes had moved, begging for help . . .

He'd been alive.

Oh, God, still alive. *And I fired. What have I done, what have I done?*

Tears froze, sealing his eyelids shut, and he was blind, running blind across the ice through the endless night, and God help him if there was an open lead ahead, or a bad pressure ridge.

Eventually he managed to rub away the ice, painfully, and restore his vision. But all he saw was darkness.

How long had he been seeing the world in shades of black? The endless dark surface of the ice stretching ahead, faintly reflecting the starlight, the darker mass of mountains looming against the horizon in the distance, the surging dark shapes of the dogs just in front of him — all gray and darker gray and black. It was hard to make himself believe there had ever been daylight or color in the world. That in the spring, only a few months from now, it would all be white, a fierce, bright glare of sunlight off the packed, frozen snow.

He sobbed, thinking he'd never live to see the sun again, the blue of the sky, or to feel the warmth of spring on his face. Then ice crystals stung, forming on his lashes, and he remembered, wiped them away with the back of a stiff gloved hand.

The world seemed to blur and change shape around him. His eyes felt raw. It had been so long, so long since he'd been able to close them and sleep. Couldn't sleep, not when it was there in the dark, out there, watching, waiting, following . . .

He stumbled on a rough patch of ice, and he jerked himself awake. *Can't sleep . . . can't close my eyes.*

But at the far distance of his vision there were dark shapes moving, loping. *Wolves,* he thought in confusion, not remembering that he was in Greenland and not Alaska.

He drove on, afraid to stop, whipping the dogs to a trot whenever they faltered. He couldn't stop, couldn't, it was out there behind him, following . . .

But at last his sleep-deprived brain realized that the animals simply couldn't go on any longer, that he was killing them, keeping up this pace with no rest, no food. He'd die if he ran the dogs to death. Die anyway if he didn't take care of himself, get food, rest.

He'd left it too late. By the time he called a halt, he was too exhausted to unharness the dogs. The beasts were ravenous, lunging and snapping, attacking the sled. Too much for him to handle. Kicking them back, he dug through the supplies, dismayed to see how little dog food he'd packed. Finally, desperate, he threw it all to them while they were still in harness, letting them fight over it while he made the ultimate effort, shivering in spasms, to light the stove with hands that felt like formless lumps of ice.

He was remembering the Jack London story he'd read when he was a boy, about the man who died because he couldn't do what it takes to light a fire in the woods. But finally the Primus caught with a whoosh of blue flame, and Ferrier huddled over its tiny point of warmth there on the sled, a blanket forming a makeshift tent around him while the dogs snarled and fought over their food.

The meager heat of the stove couldn't compensate for the growing chill in his body now that he wasn't moving anymore. The shivering was getting worse. He was experienced enough to recognize the signs of hypothermia, knew he had to do something to get warm. But it just was so hard, right now, to move — so much more easy to lie down, to sleep. The way the dogs could sleep, curling up under the warm snow. It was easy for the dogs.

Just one more minute . . . a little rest . . . so tired . . .

Somewhere in the night, a dog's howl broke through the fog of his brain, and terror jolted him awake. *It was out there! It had followed him!*

In an unthinking panic, he fumbled for the Thompson with numb hands and fired blindly into the night. Around him the dogs leaped and surged in a savage frenzy of howling and snarls. Ferrier's sleepless, tormented mind no longer knew where he was, or when. *Lars is out there! I've shot my own dogs! Lars! No, Lars was dead. It was the thing with the red eyes* . . .

A sudden jerk of the sled knocked him off-balance, and he remembered, too late, that he'd left the dogs in harness. At the limit of his vision, dark shapes fled, the wolves bounding away into the night. Then he recognized them at last as dogs — Lars's dogs, maybe even some of Blackburn's, that had been following his team for so many miles. And his own team, frantic to attack the Greenlander dogs, tangled in their traces, snapping now at each other, still dragging the sled.

Ferrier waded into them, kicking and beating them with the stock of his gun until they subsided. At the bottom of the heap an animal raised its head and shoulders, fighting to get to its feet, then fell back again.

Ferrier knelt with his knife and cut the wounded beast's throat. It went still, and he could almost feel the warmth of the body seeping away into the chill Arctic air. He shivered. But the rest of the dogs, his team, only subdued for seconds, had caught the scent of the blood, were surging back toward him, Robber as always in the lead.

He cursed, then backed away, letting them have their meat. He didn't dare approach the pack while it fed. The Primus stove had been knocked off the sled onto the ice and some of the fuel spilled. Ferrier picked it up, then anchored the sled. While he still could think, still move, he got the tent up and the stove lit inside, got a pan of snow melting. It was all automatic, tasks he did without even thinking.

By that time the dogs had finished with the carcass, even to bolting down the bloodstained snow. Now he could untangle their harness and stake them down away from the sled. With full bellies, worn down after the long forced run, the animals wanted nothing but sleep.

Ferrier was at least as exhausted as they were, and every movement was an effort, but he forced himself to stay awake. At last the water was boiling, and he stirred in oatmeal, watched it thicken, and finally spooned it down in huge, burning mouthfuls. The welcome warmth of the food spread through his body. Before it could fade, he crawled into his sleeping bag and gave himself up.

* * *

It was much later, after he'd been driving south again for another day, maybe longer, when he realized at last — the *thing* he'd seen bent over Lars, that had killed Blackburn, that had been trailing him for so many days — it was gone.

He could finally sleep, finally shut his eyes without hearing the whimper of the dogs, without the vision of red gleaming eyes in the darkness. He'd gone too close to the edge, had almost gone over. Now he was very very careful not to make any mistakes, convinced that he'd already survived more than his share.

He was south of Hochstetter Foreland now, or so he thought, onto the open ice of the bay. The dark mass of the land had fallen away on his right and dimly visible ahead was Wollaston Foreland — or else he was lost. Lars would have known. Lars would have been able to find the hunters' shacks where the three of them had stayed on the way north.

Ferrier couldn't remember anymore what it had felt like to be warm, to sleep on a bed near the heat of a stove. Night after night in the open, waking up to find his sleeping bag crusted with ice. The fuel for the Primus was almost gone, his provisions almost gone. He'd been able to shoot a couple more of the Greenlander dogs to feed his team, but the half-wild animals stayed out of range now, and the previous night he'd had to kill one of his own. He had seven dogs left, enough to pull the empty sled back to Clavering Island, back to the base. If he could find the pass across the mainland. If he was anywhere near where he thought he was.

Lars would have known. Lars would have gotten them home. Ferrier remembered how the guide could read their direction from the ridges the wind left in the drifted snow. How he'd set out following their own trail back. Skills learned in a lifetime on the ice, but they hadn't been enough to save him. Not from that. Not from that thing.

It was the dogs that caught the scent first. They'd been running silently, day after day, night after night, a slow steady trot across the endless ice with no sound but the hiss and crunch of the runners over the surface and the panting breath of the dogs. Suddenly Robber let out a howl and the rest of them lifted their heads. Weary as they were, they picked up their pace, making Ferrier have to grab onto the stanchion to keep up.

Then, out of the darkness ahead of them came a faint answering cry, the call of another team, another sled, and it was what Ferrier hadn't dared to hope for — they were coming for him!

It seemed like hours before he saw them, dark forms moving out of the darkness, the shapes of dogsleds heading toward him. He whipped the dogs into a run, and by that time there was no holding them. The sleds converged in a tangle of animals, and then there were men surrounding Ferrier, men seizing him by the arms.

"Sarge, what the . . ."

"What happened?"

"We thought you were . . ."

"Where are they, Blackburn and the guide?"

"You meet up with the krauts?"

It was too much. He couldn't say anything, could only shake his head. Finally the lieutenant, Lieutenant Wexler, took him by the shoulders and shook him, hard. "Come on, Sergeant! The rest of your patrol, Corporal Blackburn and the guide — are they lost? Are they behind you? What happened out there?"

He shook his head, groping for words. It was hard. Finally, "Gone. Both of them."

"Gone? What do you mean? Snap out of it, Sergeant!"

"Dead. Blackburn. Lars. Both dead."

"Was it the Germans? Did you find the kraut base?"

"No. No Germans. No . . ." His voice trailed away, with the image in his mind — the red glow of eyes, inhuman eyes.

His head shook again, and someone was saying, "We have to get him to the shelter."

He was bundled into a sled, wrapped in blankets and sleeping bags, and someone whipped the dogs into a run.

In minutes his eyes were frozen shut again.

It was over. They'd found him. They were taking him back.

Chapter Twelve

Exhaustion, dehydration, hypothermia, frostbite on his face, his fingers and toes—lucky he hadn't lost any of them, Doc Martino had muttered. And shock, too, from whatever had happened out there.

They told Ferrier that he'd been delirious back at the hunter's shack, raving about monsters in the dark. In his condition, it was no wonder. He was lucky to be alive, to have made it back over such a distance, all alone. They thawed him and warmed him and fed him and brought him back to the base, where Doc Martino, the medic, had put him to bed and talked about having him shipped back to the States. Back at the base, warm, fed and bandaged, it was a temptation to tell himself it had all been a nightmare, a hallucination. A bad case of polar madness.

It was still in his dreams: Lars with his bloody throat, trying to warn him against the inland-dwellers. Archie Blackburn calling out from the darkness that he was lost. And the eyes, glowing red like the coals of hell, rising up slowly to meet his own . . .

Shock, Doc said when he woke up screaming. *Poor bastard, after what he went through.*

But Captain McCluskey was having none of that crap—shock, polar madness. Captain McCluskey was going to have the facts and he was going to have them now, dammit, standing over the bed where Ferrier sat up with bandaged hands and feet.

He swallowed and chose his words, one by one. "We drove north. Eight, maybe ten days—I can't quite remember now."

"You can't *remember?*" Scorn and more than just a hint of a threat in the captain's voice.

But Ferrier shook his head firmly. "No, sir. Out there . . . no day and night—"

"Okay, okay, so then what happened?"

"We were on Hochstetter Foreland, just south of that big fjord—I can't remember the name. We stopped for the night at the hunter's shack there and picketed the dogs. There was no sign of . . . anything—"

"No Germans?"

"No, sir. The guide was positive. No sign of Germans in the area. Then . . . the dogs started up something. Corporal Blackburn had the first watch. He went out to see what it was . . ."

"So *you* didn't see anything. You don't know it couldn't have been krauts, right?"

"We thought . . . maybe it was. You know how the dogs are when they scent a stranger. Or maybe there was a bear out there or the teams were getting into a fight. So Blackburn went to check it out, and . . . the dogs, they started howling. I followed him to see what it was setting them off. I called Blackburn. He was . . . gone. Just . . . gone."

"You're telling me he just disappeared?"

"It was like that, yes, sir. We searched, both of us did. It was a bad night, a lot of blowing snow. We never even found any tracks."

"This is a goddamn incredible story, Sergeant."

"Yes, sir. We searched for hours, there was just . . . I mean, it was a bad night, but not so bad he would have gotten lost in the blizzard. There weren't any tracks. Maybe, Lars said, it could have been a polar bear or some kind of animal."

Ferrier took a breath. He was heading onto dangerous

ground. "We finally gave up and went back to the cabin. Lars—the guide—he was acting kind of strange. I kept asking him, did he really think it might have been a bear. He said, maybe. Or else—he didn't really want to talk about it—but maybe it could have been . . . what he called the inland-dwellers. Some kind of . . . I don't know what. Native stuff."

"And you believe that kind of crap?"

They come in the night. In the dark.

"No, sir! But the guide—he was afraid of *something* out there. And he didn't think it was krauts. I could tell he didn't want to go on. But I said we had to check it out, make sure."

He was avoiding McCluskey's eyes. "I told him we'd move out as soon as we got some sleep. But when I woke up—he was gone. I saw his sled tracks, heading south. I went after him."

"So your guide didn't just disappear, like Blackburn."

Ferrier shook his head. "I went after him. The dogs followed his trail. It took—I don't know—two, three days of hard driving before I caught up. I . . . we had things out, but by then I figured we'd better both go back to base, report what had happened. We drove out together.

"It was . . . we were camped for the night, and there was . . . outside the tent . . . a noise . . . the dogs . . ."

This was the hardest part now. He swallowed. So much he couldn't explain, couldn't say. They wouldn't understand. McCluskey, especially, wouldn't understand. He'd never seen it, felt it.

"The dogs—for a couple days they'd been acting . . . I donno, like there was something out there, following. Lars, he always said, the dogs would know when there was something out there. The way they did when Blackburn . . . the same way.

"I thought I heard something. I fired. It was night . . . I couldn't see. The dogs, they were like wolves, fighting over a kill. It was . . . I must have hit one of them, they were fighting over it. There was blood. And I saw . . . the tracks, followed them—"

"What kind of tracks?"

He shook his head. Here was where his memory went all wrong. There were human tracks, soft boots. *No. Not with those eyes. Not, not human eyes.*

"Lars. Must have been . . . Lars's tracks. Gone after it, the animal, whatever it was. I followed. Behind the rocks. I saw . . . saw . . ." *Eyes. Red. Glowing red. Blood.*

"Snap out of it, Sergeant!"

Ferrier shuddered. "The thing had Lars. I fired, hit it. It ran."

"What *thing?*"

"I don't know. Don't know. Couldn't see. I think . . . maybe it was a bear. Some kind of animal. It ran away. I hit it, I know I hit it."

"You didn't go after it?"

"No. Lars was . . . I had to get Lars."

"The guide was alive then?"

"I don't . . . I thought I saw . . . not by the time I got back. He was torn up. His throat. It was too late."

"So this *thing,* as you call it, got away."

"It was too late. By the time—"

The captain cut him off. "All right, Sergeant, I don't know what the hell kind of Section Eight you're bucking for here. But you've got two men dead you can't account for. And let me tell you this: Our radio direction finding station says there *are* Nazi transmissions coming from that area, not too far north of the cabin where you claim Blackburn turned up missing. *Nazis,* not polar bears, not any native monsters."

He was standing over Ferrier now, punctuating his words with stabs of his forefinger. "They've got a station up there, Sergeant, transmitting weather back to their fatherland. Attacking *your* patrol. Well, we're going back out there. We're going to wipe out that nest of Nazis once and for all. And there's going to be none of my men disappearing, and no *things* out there in the dark. Is that clear, Sergeant?"

Ferrier closed his eyes. "Yes, sir. It's clear."

* * *

Day followed day without a sunrise. The same routine, the four walls, the same faces. No way to escape, especially now that Wolff had forbidden the hunting parties.

Richard Mundt had started a fitness group. Every morning before breakfast a half dozen men stripped to shorts and undershirts and lined up outside on the packed snow next to the east wall of the hut, working up a sweat with vigorous calisthenics. Dietrich imagined their Hitler Youth leaders looking on with approval. By some miracle, none of them had frozen to death yet. A couple of men had wanted to build a sauna as well, but he'd vetoed that plan on the grounds of fuel conservation. So far, at least, no one had suggested cold dips in the frozen bay.

For himself, Dietrich had his own ritual: once a day, no more often, he let himself pull the picture out of his wallet and remember his family, what he had to go back to, what he was fighting to save, why they were here in this place. He dreaded becoming one of those men who had nothing to live for, no reason to want the war to end. He'd seen too many of those the last few years.

Against his will, his eyes went to the figure of Wolff, standing over the radio transmitter. What did a man like Wolff do when there was no more killing?

He turned his face away, so Wolff might not catch him staring. Every time Wolff entered the room, he seemed to bring the deadly chill of the Arctic in with him. Conversations came to a stop, men stared at each other, trying to remember if they'd just said something incriminating. At least he'd put away the terrible black leather greatcoat. But even in his white camouflage uniform there was still something deadly about him, something almost unhuman. He hardly ever spoke, except to give an order. Dietrich couldn't imagine asking Wolff about his own family. Did he carry a picture of them in his wallet — a stern-faced Frau Wolff and scowling little boy in a Hitler Youth uniform? Did he ever smile at home? Did he have a home?

At the stove, Köbler sliced onions into a stewpot. Two men off duty played a game of cards, no joy on their faces when either of them won a hand. In the darkened bunkroom, a few men slept, or seemed to sleep. The door opened and Feldwebel Wederling came inside from the balloon shack, stomping his feet to restore the warmth, rubbing his hands as he took off his gloves. Doctor Pflieger recorded the data in the log. Day after day it was the same, except that now Wolff was watching them.

When 0900 hours came, the whole group gathered around the radio, but once again there was no news from Tromsø. Wolff frowned, and his lips moved in an unvoiced curse. Dietrich could hear the whole cabin hold its breath, then exhale with relief as the SS officer finally shrugged on his white parka and opened the door to leave, all without saying a word aloud.

"Where does he go, I wonder." Without turning around, Dietrich knew it was Erich Klostermann. The pilot was staring at the door. "He won't be back for hours. Out there all by himself — what does he do?"

Dietrich took a drag at his cigarette and shook his head. "He has to check to see that no more Ami patrols are infiltrating the area. It's a lot of distance for one man to cover, alone."

"If he is alone."

"What in the devil's name do you mean?"

"I don't know. Nothing." Klostermann looked pointedly around the room, where no one seemed to be paying particular attention to the two of them speaking together. Dietrich nodded, they both put on their outdoor things and went outside into the cold.

The faint rippling colors of an aurora were visible in the southern sky, making it more than usually bright. Klostermann looked nervously over his shoulder, as if Wolff might be somewhere behind him. Dietrich couldn't help it — he did the same. "So, what's this all about?" he demanded.

A gust of wind made Klostermann shiver, and he pulled up the collar of his coat. "I know — you've confirmed his orders by radio. But, think, orders can be forged."

"But *why?* What would be the purpose? If the Amis knew where we were, they'd have bombed us out this fall."

"Maybe . . . I don't know. Maybe he's sending out false information. You saw the way he was watching the radio, just now? How do you know what's in those messages he sends?"

Dietrich threw down his cigarette into the snow. "Now you're carrying this too far, Erich! What possible reason do you have to believe anything like that? Besides, think about it—how often is he even here?"

"Well, that's another thing. Where does he go? All alone? He's *got* to have someplace he goes. He could have a transmitter there! Just think what kind of information he could be sending out."

"Where would he get a radio? He didn't bring one with him."

"I don't know. Maybe he meets with someone out there. Maybe the Amis brought it to him. But, damn it, Martin, think—how long was he gone the time Schaus was killed? Almost three weeks. He comes back, he's got no pack with him, no supplies, no tent, no sleeping bag—nothing. No man could survive by himself like that out here, not for so long!

"Schaus is missing from the hunting party, and then, suddenly, Wolff shows up—out of nowhere. He says he's seen the body eaten by a bear, but *no one else* has and he won't take them to it. How do we know Schaus was killed by the Amis? How do we know he didn't stumble onto something out there that he wasn't meant to see? Don't tell me you can't imagine Wolff killing in cold blood?"

Dietrich stared out at the dimming colors of the aurora, remembering Ernst Weber. And other things. The way Wolff had ordered the hunting parties to stop. And thinking, yes, if Schaus had happened to see something . . .

Absently, he lit another cigarette and said slowly, "It could be. But think—he's SS. They sent him here. Maybe this station is a cover for . . . some secret weapon project. Something no one is supposed to see. We wouldn't be told."

"That's as implausible as some of my ideas," Klostermann admitted.

Implausible, but Dietrich couldn't quite put the doubts out of his mind once he was back inside.

Mundt was at the radio now, but Mundt was a young Nazi hothead.

He waited till Manstein was on duty.

"Yes, Herr Hauptmann?"

"Manstein, I have some concern about our radio security here. Would it be possible for you to discover if some other transmitter is operating in this area?"

"Well, yes, Herr Hauptmann, I could try. But, I thought the Hauptsturmführer was taking care of that kind of thing."

"No, not exactly. Radio isn't his field."

"No, I suppose it isn't. Do you have any idea how strong a signal it might be? How near by?"

"No, this is just a notion I'd like to check out. But, Manstein. No matter what you find out, this is to be mentioned to *no one* else. Do you understand me? No one."

Manstein nodded. "I understand, Herr Hauptmann."

"Very good." Dietrich looked at his watch. How long had Wolff been gone now? And where had he gone? Just what was he doing out there?

Chapter Thirteen

Wolff had been badly in need of rest after the long, relentless chase, the bloodloss, the slow journey limping back to the weather station. He was starting to realize, here in this place without days, that his need for blood would be more acute if he went without rest altogether. Finding the German, Schaus, out hunting, separated from his party—he hadn't been able to resist. It might have been a good thing, after all, that he hadn't gone after the American base in his condition.

But he couldn't rest in the weather station, lying on a narrow bunk in the wooden hut, surrounded by so many living men. Their breath, their heartbeats, their vital scents filled the confined space, agitating his senses. The instinct for survival was too strong in him. To make himself so vulnerable required solitude, a safe refuge deep in the earth.

As often as he could, he retreated to the darkness and quiet of the primitive hunter's shack at the head of the fjord, where he could slow his breathing and shut his eyes, secure with no human eyes watching him. It was December now, the solstice nearing, with the sun so far below that horizon that he no longer felt even a moment of the old weakness and pain, even at noon.

It had been so long . . .

A sigh relaxed the harsh austerity of his features. This, he admitted to himself, was why he had really come to the Arctic, to escape the sun, if only for a few months. He thought he had known, two hundred years ago, the price he would have to pay—to live an eternity in darkness, never again to see the sunlight. *I can endure that,* he had told himself, young and craving power. And in fact he had come to love the night, the cold silent light of the stars, the blaze of the moon. No, he had no regrets for the day. But he hadn't realized there would be so much pain.

If I had known . . .

Two hundred years ago he had seen the sunlight for the last time, standing with a pounding heart at the head of a staircase leading down, down into the darkness beneath the castle of his ancestors. The air was cold, with a faint, dusty stench of old graves. Behind him the door stood open, his key still in the lock. He pulled it out with a hand that was far from steady.

There was a legendary curse, well known to all of his blood, that whoever turned the key in that door, whoever went down those stairs, was damned. But the key was his by right.

He took the first step, expecting to feel his soul shrivel and die within his chest. Terror had made him sweat, and he shivered in the chill draft from below. The torch he was carrying flickered. He turned to close the door, shutting out the sun. Then he locked it behind him and went down into the dark.

The stairs were stone. The walls, stone—stone and cold. This was a tomb. The stairs went down, deep, deep into the earth, leading to a place the sun had never reached, never touched. Not to see it again. To be a thing of darkness, a power of the night. To be feared. And the castle would be his, Imre's rightful heritage. His body tingled with fear and the sense of the enormity of what he meant to do, to become.

Damned.

At last at the bottom of the stairs, the corridor bent to the right. Knowing this place as if he had walked these stones a hundred times before, he followed it. His steps rang on the floor, echoed off the walls. He paused, holding his breath, waiting, listening for a response, but there was only silence.

He paused at a door, partly opened. He stepped inside. It was a dungeon: old, long unused. Rusty chains hung from brackets on the walls. At the bottom of a pit in the center of the room was a black substance, partly ash. He knelt and unearthed a few splintered, charred fragments of bone.

His ancestors had chained their enemies down here, at least as far back as the time of the Turks. He crossed to the far wall, curiously picked up a chain and tried to open the corroded hinge of the shackle attached to it. In moments, this would all be *his*. He could bring his victims here and chain them to this wall; they would beg him for mercy, sob and plead. In vain. He tried to imagine the taste of their blood.

Soon, he would know.

Resolute, he left the room. Other doors opened off the corridor, other dungeons, where skulls stared up at him from the floor. He wondered if they recognized him.

But he had come to the end of the passage now, to another door of thick oak planks banded with iron. He stood before it, heart pounding. He knew this place. Here was the innermost chamber, the dark heart of the castle, where the deathless lord slept away the hours of sunlight.

If he were wrong, if he failed . . .

With sweating hands he took the key from his pocket, the key that had opened the upper door — Imre's key. It had been put into his hand by his father at his death, and by his father before him, the one thing he had taken when he fled the castle so long ago, leaving it in Istvan's bloody hands.

But now Imre was back.

He inserted the key into the lock, and the door opened onto absolute darkness.

He had a momentary impulse to cross himself, but suppressed it. From the time he set foot on the staircase, he had been damned. So be it, then. He stepped across the threshold into hell.

And the devil's eyes were red. His heart almost stopped to see them from across the room, the lurid, malevolent glare. He felt an impulse to run and at the same time his limbs refused to move, until he realized that the being was as motionless as he was.

There was no bracket for the torch. He held it high above his head. Lying on the stone floor was Istvan, the Lord Istvan Bathory, staring at him with recognition and impotent hate. With an effort, the pale lips moved, the voice exhaled his name: *Imre!*

"Yes!" They had been brothers, once. But Imre had died, leaving a son, and a son's son. While Istvan . . .

Closing his eyes, the being who now called himself Wolff remembered how he had taken his grandfather's knife in his hand, the knife with his crest on the hilt: the three wolves, rampant. How he had knelt, trembling with dread and anticipation of what he was going to do. He could feel Istvan's body tense, straining to move, but the sun was high over them, even though it was dark here in this tomb beneath the castle. The undead lord's skin was white as veined marble, cold as the stone he lay on, cold as death.

And I looked into his eyes while I drove the blade into his heart. While I pulled it out again. And the blood was black, welling out, and I put my lips against the wound, and it flowed into my mouth, cold and black, and I swallowed it, and it tasted like knives, slicing open my throat as it went down.

And at the first swallow, my heart turned to ice inside my chest. And I kept my mouth sealed to the wound, and the blood flowed, and I swallowed it and swallowed it, and my chest went cold, and my belly, and my manhood froze, and it spread to my limbs, and the blood was still flowing, and I was ice. Then the blood ran more slowly, but I sucked it out, all of it. And when he was empty I looked at his face again, and it was like stone, with the lips drawn back from his teeth. But the eyes — the eyes were still alive, staring at me. Staring.

I took the knife, and I drove it back into his heart, and I watched the eyes die, watched them turn to stone like the rest of him.

Then, while I still knelt there, I felt the first pains, and I knew what it meant to be damned.

Two hundred years. So long. And there had been times, in those years, when Wolff had wondered whether it had been more than complacency or carelessness that had made Lord Istvan Bathory trust his safety to that ancient lock.

And now the castle was his again, he had title to it, at least — if by some miracle the Germans managed to win the war. He thought of the men in the weather station, crowded around the radio, waiting anxiously for news, any news. And when it did come it was always the same — the enemy advancing on all fronts, held back only by the most suicidally desperate measures. Whatever Hitler's plan, whatever this great counterstrike they were preparing, it had better come soon, or all Germany would be lost, and his own heritage with it.

He stood, rubbing his knee where the bullet had smashed it, the lingering ache a bitter reminder of his failure. He'd made excuses for himself — that he couldn't realistically have gone on in his condition — that he'd kept the enemy from discovering the weather station. The last American had still escaped, to report to his superiors. It was still failure.

The American, he supposed, would probably have made it back to his base by this time — or died on the trail, but Wolff knew better than to count on luck like that. The question was what the soldier could actually report: Weather Station Flieger was still almost two hundred kilometers from the hunter's shack where he'd first encountered the American patrol. The survivor had seen him, but he hadn't actually seen a German soldier — Wolff's white coveralls bore no insignia, nothing to mark him as a member of the German armed forces.

In fact — Wolff grinned slightly at the thought — from the American's reaction, he *knew* what the man had seen. And that was a sight he could hardly explain to his superiors. They would discount his entire report.

Still, Wolff knew he had failed. Once again he'd been unable to control that part of his nature that lusted for blood, that lost itself in the ecstasy of the kill. No matter what harm it had or hadn't done, the fact remained — he'd been too careless in his lust to kill the native guide, he'd let the other soldier get too close.

And now, while the enemy might be sending a new patrol to search out and destroy the weather station—where was he? What was he doing to stop them?

Setting out to return to the weather station, Wolff could feel the alteration in the pressure as the air masses clashed overhead and the temperature plummeted. A storm, birthed on the ice sheet, was moving down the eastern coast.

In his renewed state of resolve, he ignored the gathering clouds. A storm might be on its way, but the cold and the wind didn't concern him. His nature made it impossible for him to freeze, and his senses were far more acute than an ordinary man's. Even with the clouds blotting out the moon and stars, he knew his way. In fact, the worse the weather, the greater his advantage. It was common knowledge that no one ventured out into an Arctic blizzard. Even the polar bears retreated to their dens to wait out the storm. Any American patrol out on the trail would be immobilized.

But when he'd gone no more than halfway back to the German base, the full fury of the blizzard struck. The wind screamed. It tore the breath from him. It exploded in gusts that drove him to his knees. And the snow, driven on the wind, flayed his exposed skin with the force of exploding glass.

If Wolff had been a warm-blooded living man, who could freeze, who could die, his life would have been over in minutes. Another blast of wind sent him staggering. Snow filled the air. The shards lashed his eyes when he tried to open them. It was an effort just to move through it, even with the gale at his back.

In that short time, he lost all sense of direction. There was only the wind and the driven snow, and it had blinded him. Wolff crouched low with his arms over his head and tried to think. The prevailing direction of the wind was from the west. He knew how far he had come from the hut, his location relative to the fjord, to the weather station. The distance was about equal in either direction, but to reach the hut again he'd have to struggle against the wind, and he was beginning to suspect he might well lose.

In the lee of his body a drift had already formed. It would be possible to dig into the snow, to bury himself the way the bears did, and the dogs. With an effort, he stood upright and shook himself, feeling the snow that had gotten inside his coat. He knew he might have to resort to that expediency in the end, if he failed to make it to the weather station. If he failed again.

He bent his head down and started to push his way across the wind. It was hard, hard going. In the middle of the blizzard, his senses meant nothing. He was blind, deafened by the screaming of the storm. The weather station was downwind, and the gale snatched up any human scent and flung it away from him, out onto the empty, barren ice of the bay.

He staggered on for a few meters, maybe as much as a kilometer before another brutal gust spun him around and threw him to the ground. Again, he was totally disoriented, lost. With the shifts of the wind, he couldn't always tell which way he was headed, whether he was backtracking or going around in circles. The driving snow scoured away his footprints. He could barely see his own hand held up in front of his face.

Dying wasn't a possibility, not for him. The storm could bury him for centuries and he would still survive, although the hunger would be a constant torment. But that was no risk in this situation. Yielding to it, he stretched himself out on the snow-covered ground, hugging it to make himself as low as possible a target for the wind. It battered him, howling, enraged, as if it were trying to rip him away from the clutches of the earth.

In all the fury of the storm, he was a center, a silence. As he was pressing himself into the ground, his extremities tingled slightly, the sensation crept down his spine. Even with a thousand miles of earth between them, he could somehow sense the faint shadow of its power, far off to the south. He shifted his position until he was aligned with it — the sun.

He stilled himself further. His body was a lodestone, exquisitely sensitive to that force. Though he carried a watch, it was impossible to see it in the white-out. He had no idea of the time, or for that matter of how to calculate his exact position if he had known it. But that the sun was in the south he knew deep in his nerves, in the marrow of his bones.

Slowly, hunched against the force of the wind, he got to his feet again. Again, he knew where he was going.

After a long struggle, the difference in the ice beneath his feet told him he had finally come onto the frozen surface of the fjord. He grinned in triumph, though the ice-edged winds had flayed his face so any movement pained him. But now he could turn to follow the shore with the confidence that it would lead him eventually to the German weather hut.

In fact, it led him past it, out into the open bay, until he was downwind of the station. And then, at last, he caught the human scent, the warm musk of men and the smoke from the stove. He forced his way back against the force of the gale, up the bluff, following the warm familiar scents, toward the isolated glow of heat he could feel but still not see.

His hands finally contacted the rough boards of the hut, he groped his way around the corners, encountering ropes strung from the main cabin to the outbuildings. Taking hold of one, he followed it to the door and flung it open to stumble into the stove-heated interior, more grateful for the warmth than he could remember in two hundred years.

Chapter Fourteen

The door slammed open, so hard it rattled the hinges, and startled Dietrich out of sleep in the back room as the blizzard rushed into the hut, filling it with a cloud of driven snow. In the midst of it he saw an apparition — a ghost, or one of the abominable snowmen of the Himalayas. While men cursed and ran for the door, the figure forced it shut, then took another step forward into the room. It seemed to sag at the knees, and braced itself against the table, and with growing disbelief Dietrich recognized it as Wolff, emerging alive out of the storm.

He shook his head, denying it to himself even as he sat upright in his bunk. It couldn't be. It was fifty degrees below freezing out there, with winds gusting up to over sixty knots. No one could have survived in that.

A couple of the men swore softly under their breath in disbelieving awe. Köbler crossed himself. Even Dietrich, a good Lutheran, felt the impulse to do the same. No one moved.

One hand still steadying himself against the table, Wolff reached up and pulled down the hood of his white parka. Crusts of snow fell from it, like a broken carapace, as he slowly pulled the coat off over his head.

His face was raw from windburn, and he blinked his eyes as if it were hard to open them. With slow, painful movements, he pulled off his gloves and boots, one by one.

And still no one moved, until he lifted his head with a wan,

123

almost apologetic look on his face. "Sorry about the disturbance. I was lost for a while in the storm."

Then, with the spell broken, Dietrich crossed the room toward him. "You're all right?" he asked, unable to keep the incredulity from his voice.

Manstein came up with a steaming mug, coffee laced with brandy. Köbler the cook was backed into the corner by the stove, useless.

Wolff took it with a very slight bow, as if nothing at all were wrong. "Thank you. It's a little . . . raw out there."

Dietrich was too stunned to reply. It was the first time he'd ever seen Wolff this way, almost human — even shaken.

But he should be dead! Out there in a storm like that — he should be frozen to death!

Klostermann came to stand next to Dietrich with an anxious frown, as if he urgently wanted to say something.

Wolff finished his coffee and put the cup down on the table. "I think I'll rest for a while."

At that, the medic, Landfried, approached him nervously. "You could have frostbite. Perhaps I should take a look . . ."

Immediately, Wolff straightened, and the familiar forbidding stiffness returned to his face. "No," he snapped. "I'll request your attentions if I think it necessary."

"Yes, . . . ah, Hauptsturmführer," Landfried mumbled, retreating.

The entire weather party tried not to stare as Wolff went into the bunk room and stretched himself out on his mattress. One by one, most of the men who'd been asleep wandered back out into the main room of the hut.

There was something wrong, Dietrich thought, about the way Wolff was lying there — on his back with a hand flung over his eyes. Lying *on top* of the blanket. Wouldn't a man caught out in a blizzard like this — wouldn't he wrap himself up in as many blankets as possible? He turned away, rubbing his face. There was no way now he was going to get back to sleep. He lit a cigarette and headed for the stove and the coffee pot, with Klostermann behind him, saying nothing. A look in Köbler's direction brought the cook out of his corner. "As long as we're all up, you can make some more coffee."

He sat down at the table and sipped the hot black brew, thinking about Wolff. As little time as the SS officer spent at the weather station, despite the fact that he almost never used the bunk allocated to him, no one ever intruded on that space. As crowded as they were, no one ever sat on Wolff's empty bed or tossed his coat on it. No one would dare. *Because we never know when he'll show up*.

Klostermann sat down next to Dietrich with his own mug of coffee. He glanced meaningfully in the direction of the bunk where Wolff lay motionless, not even seeming to breathe. A moment later someone in the room shut the door.

"Think he's asleep?" Klostermann whispered so low Dietrich almost couldn't hear. "Did you *see* him?"

Dietrich nodded wearily. He was too tired to play detective games.

But Klostermann went on relentlessly, "No frostbite! Think about it! And another thing — no beard."

"What the hell difference . . ." Dietrich paused, rubbing his own chin.

Klostermann went on, his point taken, "Think how long ago he left here, and he comes back without needing a shave. Every time he's gone, has he ever needed a shave when he comes back? Wherever he goes, it must be someplace with hot water. And no more than a few hours away. Just think about it!" he insisted again.

Dietrich shook his head. Erich was prone to extravagant suspicions and improbable theories — Wolff conspiring with enemy agents, Wolff meeting with a clandestine submarine out on the frozen bay. But it was true that he'd given orders to keep them from exploring the area near the station. That no one else had ever seen the American patrol he claimed to have eliminated — the Americans who were supposed to have killed Schaus.

It all kept coming back to the same question: where did Wolff go?

"Did you check into the business of the radio?" Klostermann persisted.

"Yes, I looked into it. There was nothing."

Klostermann looked disappointed. Dietrich had also submitted another, cautiously worded inquiry through Tromsø explaining his concerns, but so far there was no response. He still assumed there was some reasonable explanation. Even the war hadn't entirely shaken his belief that the universe was basically orderly, that there were proper and natural causes for all phenomena. That it would somehow all come right in the end.

So he waited, with his cigarette and his empty coffee mug, trying not to look up at the door of the room where Wolff lay on his bunk, as still and pale as death.

Up till that time the men had been talking about Christmas, planning a small celebration. For most of them, with family at home, the season brought more worry than cheer, especially for the men with children. On his last leave, Dietrich had bought a music box as a gift for Trudi. There was a ballerina that twirled on tiptoes as the box played the theme from *Swan Lake*. Lately he'd found himself playing the tune over and over again in his head, and the music seemed inexpressibly sad.

But with Wolff back at the station the heart had gone out of everyone's plans. His presence inhibited all conversation, and men thought twice about opening their mouths, even to talk about Christmas. Maybe wishing someone peace on earth could be taken as defeatism.

The storm had made prisoners of them all. It went on without letup, day after day, and with Wolff's cold, forbidding presence constantly among them, no one dared try to tune in an illicit radio broadcast for news of the war or even lighten their mood with some American jazz. It was only a matter of time, Dietrich worried, before the polar madness got to them and someone cracked.

Rohde and Dienst had quarreled over a hand of cards and refused to speak to each other. The Luftwaffe navigator Ziegler could hardly be gotten out of bed. Baumgartner, their carpenter, had started muttering to himself in a gibberish no one could quite understand. Mundt said it sounded like Yiddish, which almost started a fight until Wolff intervened with a look. Dietrich braced himself to see Baumgartner taken out and shot — or to stand up to Wolff, he wasn't sure which. But Wolff ignored the matter after that, while Mundt and Baumgartner confined themselves to murderous looks.

To add to their problems, the Weather Service had been screaming for their data, demanding to know why it was incomplete. Doctor Pflieger's explanation that there was a blizzard raging was rejected out of hand. The Führer wanted weather reports, not excuses!

"Matters must be at a critical stage," said Dietrich, with a wary glance over at Wolff, who sat and stared like a basilisk, turning everyone to stone.

Only Doctor Pflieger fumed recklessly, "Critical stage! They don't think it's critical when the wind breaks the anemometer! Critical to send up balloons in a hurricane-force gale! It's a miracle the antenna mast hasn't blown down."

They did their best, Pflieger and his weather crew, venturing out into the dark maw of the blizzard to take their readings and send up the radiosonde balloons, groping their way holding onto the safety ropes because no one could see through the storm-driven snow.

"It's as bad as Russia," a few men muttered.

"Worse," pronounced Wederling, who had been there.

You had to be in awe of such a force, Dietrich thought to himself. And he stole another furtive look at Wolff, who had survived it alone — for how long?

The anemometer broke again, the cups torn away by the gale, and this time it was Dienst suiting up, pulling the wool knitted mask down over his face, adding a scarf, exposing as little skin to the cold as possible. He stamped his feet in the thick felt boots that had probably once been worn by a Russian soldier, then hunched up his shoulders in anticipation of the cold. It was no good for a man to wait inside once he was dressed that way. It would only make him sweat, and for that he would pay, once the wind got to him out there.

The door was flung open, and for an instant the storm was at large inside the cabin, swirling loose papers around the room and covering everything with snow. Bent over against the force of the wind, Dienst battled his way into the storm, his flashlight glowing faintly, and then the men behind him had forced the door closed.

Several minutes passed. Pflieger paced up and down in front of the door. Dietrich glanced down at his watch. Mundt and Manstein stopped prodding the entrails of the radio. Baumgartner, mumbling to himself, sat on his bunk reducing a stick of wood to shavings, littering the floor at his feet.

Another minute, and Pflieger stopped in front of the door, looked anxiously at his watch. Dietrich did the same. Wolff got to his feet.

Pflieger said it first. "He should be finished. He should be back by now."

"He's an experienced man, he knows what he's doing," Dietrich said, thinking that if Dienst didn't come back through the door in another minute, or maybe two minutes, he was going to have to send someone else out after him. Time was critical if you were going to save a man out in this weather. But who to send? Who was most expendable? Or should he go himself? Dr. Pflieger, of all of them, couldn't be spared. Or either of the other experienced weather men—Wederling and Rohde.

He looked at his watch one more time, lighting another cigarette. He couldn't let it go any longer. But Wolff forestalled him. "I'll go out after him."

His tone left no room for argument. Quickly, he pulled the white jacket on over his head and then picked up his gloves. With no more protection from the storm than that, he disappeared into the dark and the snow.

Dietrich felt a strange relief—*If he can't find Dienst out there, no one can.* None of the men said anything, either hopeful or otherwise. Dietrich supposed some of them might be thinking: *At least it wasn't me who had to go.*

More minutes passed. Dietrich stared openly at his watch now, most of the rest of them did. With each sweep of the second hand the odds on Dienst's survival diminished. About Wolff—who could say about Wolff?

Then the door was flung open, and the figure that came in out of the storm was white, snow-covered white, brushing it off to reveal the white jacket underneath. Wolff pushed back the hood. "He's not out there."

"You didn't find him? Not out by the tower?" Pflieger demanded.

Wolff shook his head. "He must have let go of the safety rope and got disoriented. I know how easily it can happen."

"We'll go out in pairs," Dietrich started to order, but Wolff gave him no chance.

"No. No one's going to find him out there. Not until this dies down. I'm not going to chance the loss of any more men." Dietrich felt a brief flare of anger and opened his mouth to object. This was *his* command!

But a glance at Wolff's face sent a chill up his spine and stopped him. He suddenly remembered Ernst Weber, and the look in his eyes as he was dragged away to his death. Somehow Dietrich knew that Berthold Dienst was already beyond saving.

Chapter Fifteen

Well, thought Matt Ferrier, the storm had really thrown a monkey wrench into the captain's plans.

McCluskey was maybe a fire-eater, but he was a by-the-book fire-eater. From the way he talked, you might have figured that he was going to jump right on his sled and whip up his dogs, go out there and take on those damn krauts. But no, instead he went to his office to fill out the paperwork. Yeah, that was the Army for you.

He had to radio the brass. He had to wait for a reply. He had to organize and allocate supplies and equipment, weapons and ammunition among the men who'd be going. He had to conduct an inspection to make sure it was all in order. All of that chickenshit.

But Ferrier hadn't cared, one way or the other. After almost dying out there, he was only glad that Doc Martino had put his foot down and insisted he wasn't fit to go along on the patrol, using a bunch of fifty-dollar words for frostbite like "tissue necrosis" and writing it all up in his report. So in the end McCluskey'd had to depend on the only other guide they had with the outfit, a cousin of Lars's named Piet, though everyone on the base called him Pete.

It was Pete who'd dragged his feet and muttered something about the weather, that it was a storm coming up, a big one, and they shouldn't start out. But McCluskey insisted there'd been enough delay already, and he wasn't going to let the weather hold him back.

The patrol had barely managed to make it across the sound to Sandodden before the blizzard struck in its full force. It was two weeks before it started to let up.

They'd been lucky, Ferrier thought, that they could wait out the storm inside the cabin, instead of on the ice, in tents. It was bad enough at the base, where only a skeleton crew was left under Lieutenant Wexler: McCluskey's clerk, a few radiomen, the weather techs, and Ryan the cook. None of them wanted the daily chore of going outside to feed the dogs, the more so when the weather got really bad, so Ferrier ended up with it in the end, despite his frostbite. It wasn't so bad, there weren't too many dogs left on the base. It kept him off KP.

He was out there in the pens the day after the storm finally died down, checking the feet on his own dogs, scratching Robber's torn ears, when every animal jumped to its feet and started to howl. For an minute, he almost panicked. *It's out there, it's followed me all the way to the base!* But then he realized it was only a dog team coming in.

It was two teams, McCluskey and Piet, come back to base for more supplies to replace all the stuff they'd used up while they were waiting out the storm. The captain was mad enough to shit bricks. And that was before he heard the news that'd just come in over the radio while he was on the trail back.

It was about the war. It seemed that the Germans had counterattacked, in force, through the Ardennes. At least two Panzer armies had smashed through the American lines, and nothing seemed to be able to stop them. Allied air support, which had been an overwhelming force ever since D-Day, was grounded due to weather conditions. *And how had the Germans predicted the weather?*

Orders for McCluskey had come right from the top. Get that German weather station. Take it out of operation. Or, failing that, pinpoint the location so the Air Force could send in a strike force. And do it *now*.

Ferrier wasn't surprised when he was ordered to the captain's office a couple hours later. McCluskey, with his gray, stubbled face, was seething.

"I suppose you've heard the news."

"About the Germans? Yes, sir."

"At least two dozen Nazi Panzer divisions! Busted through our lines like they were wet toilet paper! The whole army caught with its pants down! And you know why?"

Ferrier said nothing, standing at attention on the other side of the desk. He knew enough to recognize the kind of question that wasn't really looking for an answer.

"The goddamn *weather*, that's why! Cloud cover so thick the Nazis could move their whole damn army into place with nobody spotting them! And now the Air Force is socked in on the ground!

"And you know how the Nazis pulled off this move, Sergeant? Cause they've got a goddamn weather station broadcasting just a few miles up this coast! The weather station that *you* failed to locate!"

"Yes, sir." Ferrier didn't like the way this was going. The captain's color was up, and he wondered if he was going to burst one of the veins standing out on his forehead.

McCluskey slapped a hand down on a map spread out on his desk. His finger stabbed at the mark indicating the position of a hunter's shack on the northeast coast of Hochstetter Foreland. "You're sure this is where you were, the night you were first attacked?"

"Yes, sir. Lars knew that region."

"That guide of yours, you sure he knew what he was doing?"

"Absolutely, sir."

McCluskey scowled. "The radio boys think the transmissions are coming from further north. Like around Koldewey Island. I suppose you could have run into a kraut patrol . . ." He gave Ferrier a sharp look. "Of course, your guide didn't think they were krauts at all, did he?"

Treading on thin ice, here. "No, sir. He didn't."

"As for your story . . ."

"Sir, it was dark, hard to make out what was going on, but I *saw* the thing that got Lars. I *hit* it, I know I did. And it wasn't . . ." —*red eyes, glowing in the dark*— ". . . I know it wasn't anything human, sir."

"But you can't say what it *was*."

The inland-dweller, it comes in the dark. "Not . . . for sure, sir. Like I said, in the dark. Lars thought, maybe, it could have been a bear. Rogue polar bear. They roam out on the ice sometimes in the winter—the boars, not the sows."

"A bear, huh? Not a Nazi? Not a Nazi in a white camouflage uniform, like the ski troops wear? You suppose it's *bears* out there, operating a radio transmitter, sending out coded weather signals?"

Ferrier shut his eyes, "No, sir. I'm not saying there's no Germans. But what I saw . . ." *It was on all fours, crouched over the body. Red eyes, and the blood running down from the mouth, the gleam of the fangs. Feeding on him.* "I just can't say that I saw any krauts, Captain."

Abruptly, McCluskey started to refold the map. "We'll see. Get your stuff ready. We leave at 1600 hours."

"But, uh, sir. Doc Martino said—"

"Bullshit, Sergeant! If you're fit to be outside in a blizzard feeding the damn dogs, you're fit to travel, in my book."

Ferrier knew when he was cornered. Six hours later he found himself at the back of a sled, mushing across the shore ice on his way to take on the Nazis and, this time, do the job right.

So the blizzard hadn't done anybody any good. Except maybe the krauts.

McCluskey set the pace himself, calling back. "I hope, Sergeant, you can manage to keep up and not get lost—this time."

Ferrier was grudgingly impressed—not with McCluskey's dog-handling—but with the fact that the captain had driven down from Sandodden and was now heading back again after only a few hours rest and no sleep. The guide, Pete, brought up the rear, saying nothing. His native blood was more obvious than Lars's had been. He controlled his dogs with cracks of his long whip, no commands. He never even cursed, which made Ferrier shake his head.

His own team was a mix. He had Robber in the lead, as usual, and a few of the others from his old team, but half of them were strangers, including a pair of Greenland dogs that he had to keep apart from the rest, using them together as wheel dogs. He knew he was going to have his hands full keeping the animals off each other's throats.

The way to Sandodden was easy — even the captain could navigate his way around the island. But as he followed behind McCluskey's sled, Ferrier could only think of what was ahead of them, what might be out there in the dark. The half-healed frostbit places on his face tingled and burned in the bitter cold. The wind howled in his ears. A real Arctic man would have ignored it, but Matt Ferrier wasn't quite sure he was a real Arctic man anymore.

The ice was full of shadows now.

Chapter Sixteen

Wolff had held out as long as he could, forcing himself to rest despite the human presence surrounding him, watching. But his nature was that of a predator, and his victims could somehow sense it. He could perceive the effect his presence had on the men. The scent of their fear aroused his own instincts, the lust for blood.

He made himself fight it. He would *not* lose control, not this time, not again. His proper victims were elsewhere, and if the storm kept him from reaching them, he would have to wait.

If his need got truly desperate, he kept telling himself, there was the flying boat's crew, sent here as a reserve in case of necessities of this kind. Oberführer Kessler had understood his needs — understood them far too well for Wolff's peace of mind, in fact.

It was Klostermann he wanted. He was quite well aware of the pilot's suspicions, had overheard his whispered conversations with Dietrich; they had no idea how acute his hearing was. Wolff wasn't worried. Most of Klostermann's imagined conspiracies were absurd. Wolff knew his orders were genuine, "from the highest authority," in fact. And Dietrich — good, loyal soldier Dietrich — would follow orders, no matter what he thought privately about SS Hauptsturmführer Wolff.

Klostermann, though. Klostermann had piloted the seaplane. Wolff knew he could never forget that last nightmare journey by air, the sun cresting the horizon with all its force while he lay knotted in agony at the back of the plane, helpless. Klostermann's plane. He must have seen, heard — sensed — something, and that made him dangerous. For that reason alone Wolff meant to kill him. At the thought, a feral smile had twitched at his lips. That would be one kill he intended to enjoy to the utmost. Klostermann would finally learn exactly what kind of being he'd transported to Greenland.

But the pilot was wary. There was never a chance to get him alone, no excuse to arrest him and take him away. Locked up inside these walls — sometimes Wolff thought he was going to go berserk. How much longer could the storm last?

He had shifted impatiently on his bunk, waiting. Had sat pretending to enjoy a cup of coffee, waiting. Had watched Dietrich light one cigarette after another — every one of the men smoked — and he thought of taking up the habit himself, if only to have something to do.

Outside, the blizzard clawed savagely at the doors and windows of the weather shack, screaming like a wild animal to get at its prey. As soon as it died down, as soon as he could *see,* he would set off again to reach the American base. This time he meant to kill them all, to completely eliminate the threat to the German counteroffensive. If Kessler was correct, it would all be over by the time the Americans could ship in a replacement force to the desolate eastern coast.

He cursed the German high command. Why were they taking so long to start their attack? But then, the timing depended on the weather.

How much longer? The meteorologist hadn't been encouraging. A blow like this could go on for weeks, he informed Wolff. "Although, it's true that the most severe storms usually come later in the spring — by then, of course, we can hope the war will be over." His tone was heavy with sarcasm. Dr. Pflieger did less than most of the Germans to hide his dislike for Wolff, for all the SS reputation. Not a good Nazi, this weatherman. Perhaps he felt his position made him immune.

Wolff gave him a cold look. "I see you have great confidence in the Führer's latest counteroffensive, Herr Doctor."

Pflieger had gone pale, stuttering some excuse. But Wolff turned away, clenching his fists. *No.*

A while later one of the weather technicians came staggering in, his face so stiff from the cold he couldn't speak coherently. They gave him a steaming mug of coffee, and he clasped it between his near-frozen hands as he reported that the anemometer had broken—again.

Another man started to pull on his outdoor clothes, cursing the storm dully. The conditions were so severe that none of them could stand it for more than a few minutes; they had to go out in shifts.

Dienst had failed to come back. The minutes passed, they were all staring at the door, waiting for it to open, knowing how short a time a man could survive out in the storm.

"He should be finished," Pflieger said nervously. "He should be back by now."

"He's an experienced man," Dietrich said, but Wolff noticed he kept looking at his watch. Another minute, and he'd order a search party.

Wolff was on his feet. "I'll go out after him."

It was as much to escape from the cabin as for any other reason. But it was also a fact that none of them had a devil's chance of locating the missing man out in the storm.

He paused outside the door, heedless of the lashing wind and snow, ignoring the ice-crusted lifeline. If he stepped two feet away from the cabin it would disappear into the driving, blinding storm, but the human scent and heat still glowed through, almost tangible to his senses. He was searching, though, for a much fainter scent, and after a moment he found it, traced it beyond the radio tower, already buried beneath a growing drift, so deep the feeble light of the flashlight was invisible.

He pulled the man out and felt at once that his life's heat was fading, almost gone out. Dienst was unconscious, his heartbeat irregular and slow. One or two minutes and it would stop forever, and Wolff didn't hesitate. He plunged in his knife. The blood flowed into him, satisfying his long-denied need. It flowed slowly, already cooling—a strangely arousing sensation, almost like feeding on one of his own kind, like the time he had taken Istvan's blood. But Dienst never stirred. His consciousness had already crossed over the line dividing life from death, only his heart kept stubbornly beating in the innermost core of his body. Wolff had heard that freezing was a peaceful way to die, and now he supposed it might be so. In his own case it was no option.

After, he carried the corpse to the headland and flung it down onto the rocks. A bear would certainly get it before the spring thaw.

By the time he made his way back through the gale to the weather hut, his satisfaction in the kill had faded. Had he failed again? Had he been so eager for blood that he'd overlooked the chance to bring the man back alive?

In all honesty, he doubted it. Dienst's vital functions had almost ceased by the time he'd found him. It would have been a waste to leave him there, buried frozen under the snow. But no matter the reason, the fact was that the station had lost one of its most essential men, compromising the success of its mission.

Scowling, Wolff came back into the hut and curtly ordered Dietrich not to send any more men out there to search. There was Klostermann, staring at him, imagining—impossible to tell what he was imagining. *He* should have been the one. If he had to feed again . . .

But now was the time to go, when his need was sated, when he was rested and ready to take on the Americans.

One night later, as he lay wakefully on his bunk, pretending to sleep, his sensitive hearing caught a change in the sound of the wind outside. He slipped noiselessly from the bed and out of the bunk room. One of the weather technicians—Wederling, he thought the name was—had just taken the readings.

"Well?" Wolff demanded.

"The wind's been falling for an hour now. It's down to twenty-eight knots."

Wolff stepped to the door, eased it open. It was true, the wind was dying down. Through the blanket of driving snow he could now make out the vague gray form of the radio tower a few dozen meters away. It was enough. As long he could see to make his way south, he had no fear of the storm. And it would be another day, at least, before the enemy would dare stir.

Everything he needed was under his bunk. Without a word, Wolff pulled on his white coverall, picked up his boots, gloves and rifle.

"But, you can't go out there! Not like that! Those are still almost gale-force winds!"

Wolff ignored him. The Americans were out there, and he was ready for them.

The interest in Christmas had suddenly revived. They had endured the storm.

And Wolff had left them again.

"He just walked out, Herr Hauptmann!" Wederling reported. "Just opened the door and walked out. With nothing, not even a pack."

"He *can't* have gone far," Klostermann insisted. "Not into that weather. If we sent out a team to search—"

But Dietrich would have none of it. Wolff had been gone for three days now, and as far as he was concerned, it was just as well. Let him go. The storm clouds were passing away overhead, the moon was out—

"My God! Oh my God!"

Mundt had just tuned in the radio to a news broadcast and most of the men were already gathered around him. Now the rest of them pushed their way closer to the set. Dietrich had never before heard Mundt call upon the name of the Diety. But now his voice was choked with elation. "Herr Hauptmann! They've broken through the Ardennes! The Fifth and Sixth Panzer Armies! The American lines have collapsed!"

The faint scratchy voice of the newscaster confirmed it. The men exclaimed to each other. "There's no opposition! Their Air Force is still on the ground!"

Dietrich ordered quiet. Everyone needed to hear.

So it had begun. At last.

On the radio, with the men silent now and standing at attention, the newsman was reading aloud the text of von Rundstedt's message to the German forces: "The hour of destiny has struck. Mighty offensive armies face the Allies. Everything is at stake. More than mortal deeds are required as a holy duty to the fatherland."

Outside, the thin moon illuminated the frozen expanse of Dove Bay as the sound came from the weather hut—a dozen men's voices raised in a hymn of thanksgiving: *"Deutschland, Deutschland, über alles . . ."*

But Wolff had already crossed onto the mainland, too far away to hear.

Chapter Seventeen

McCluskey pushed them at a hard pace leading the patrol north, making up for the time they'd lost due to the blizzard. Matt Ferrier thought that sometimes he could see the captain looking back at him with an expression on his face. It meant: what the hell took you so long? Ferrier wanted to tell him, remind him that his patrol had gone all the way out around the islands, checking out the dozens of hidden inlets and bays. It wasn't the same thing at all.

And conditions were different for the sleds. The snow made travel out on the sea ice a lot less rough, packed down to even out the cracks and pressure ridges, and, it sure was easier on the dogs' feet. But going overland across Wollaston Foreland through the pass, the drifts bogged them down. One after the other the men went ahead on snowshoes, breaking trail, while the drivers coming behind shoved the sleds by main force through the deep loose snow, then dropped back to let the next man take over at the front. Ferrier didn't especially mind the work. It was more like what he was used to in Alaska. Working up a sweat when it was fifty below — that was the Arctic for you.

But the dark. They traveled by moonlight as much as possible, but even when the moon came up — and every night it was fuller, brighter — the shadows were still deep and black, capable of hiding . . . anything. To the west the looming high peaks rose up between the patrol and the vast inland ice sheet, but things could come crawling down from the mountains, down off the ice. And when the moon set, the shadows spread over everything, black hiding beneath black.

He couldn't help it, he constantly had to be looking around, behind his back, for the sight of something stalking them. Even knowing that he'd never been able to catch sight of it when he was out here before. Only once. Only one sight of those eyes . . .

At night, when he tried to sleep, the eyes invaded his dreams, the red glowing stare, the fangs. The eyes looked down into him, the fangs ran blood.

Even with a half dozen men sleeping next to him Ferrier was afraid to close his eyes, even in a hut, with four solid walls to keep out the night. Walls hadn't been enough to save Archie Blackburn, that night when the dogs started to howl.

Driving straight up the coast, they spent most nights in one or another hunter's shack. Dirty and cramped a lot of them were, but at least they had walls and a stove, and none of the trouble of putting up the tents. The captain didn't think much of tents, and Ferrier noticed that on a bad day he'd push them on for hours to reach the next cabin up ahead, but other days they'd halt, even when they had good ice and an hour or so of moonlight ahead of them, because the next shack was out of reach. This, even in spite of how eager he was to catch up with those Nazis.

It occurred to Ferrier, once they had crossed onto Hochstetter Bay, that if the captain was right, if there were Nazis out here or any ordinary enemy, the Americans were setting themselves up for an ambush, keeping to the huts the way they were, on the predictable route. Well, at least they had the dogs to warn them. Though what if the enemy had dogs of their own?

If they were Nazis. If they were human.

Ferrier wasn't quite sure anymore. Whatever he'd seen out there, what it was. According to Doc, he might well have been hallucinating. Exhaustion, hunger, panic—they could cause it. Make a man see . . . things. Like red eyes in the dark. Make a man have bad dreams.

Now, when he tried to remember, when he was awake, the images shifted in his mind. Sometimes he saw a bear, sometimes a man. Sometimes . . .

He couldn't tell anyone what he really saw in his dreams. Even Doc. He didn't want them to think he was crazy, bucking for a Section Eight, like the captain kept saying. He supposed Doc could be right, that it was all in his imagination, and it was really a Nazi soldier he saw bending over Lars that night. He couldn't really convince himself that it'd been a bear. But the only other explanations were just . . . hallucinations. That was all.

Except the closer they got to Hochstetter Foreland, where it had happened, the feeling at the back of his neck kept getting worse. Even the dogs could sense something. Or was that his imagination, too?

No. Ever since they'd passed Kuhn Island, the animals had been spooky, balking at commands, howling at nothing. Robber, at the head of his team, kept his ears back and his tail lowered.

Ferrier went up to Pete one night while they were making camp, staking out the dogs and getting them fed. "Do you notice the dogs?" he asked, raising his voice a little to be heard over the din. "Does it seem to you like there's something . . . wrong, maybe?"

The guide's face was like a dark wooden mask. He looked at the ground and wouldn't meet Ferrier's eyes. It reminded him suddenly of Lars's face, just before he ran, right after Blackburn disappeared.

He looked quickly around, but there was no one else who could hear. "There were some things your cousin told me—Lars." The guide inhaled sharply, and his dark brown eyes rose to meet Ferrier's for an instant. "Lars said, there were stories about *things* that lived up on the inland ice. The inland-dwellers. Do you know what I mean? I think . . . Lars was afraid there was something like that out here. He told me, 'The dogs always know.' "

The guide had lowered his eyes again. He kicked apart a couple of dogs that were snarling at each other, checked the harness on another one, notorious for chewing his traces. "Maybe," he mumbled so low Ferrier could hardly hear. "Maybe."

Ferrier stared after him. Was it just native superstition, the way the captain kept saying? He wondered if Pete would run off the way Lars had.

He went back to his where his own team was staked. Robber was bolting mouthfuls of grease-stained snow. The husky snarled at his approach, laying his ears back for a minute before he allowed him closer. Ferrier rubbed behind his neck, the thick warm ruff of fur. "You saw it before," he whispered to the dog, "you know what it is. Is it out here now?"

Robber whined, then started to circle, hollowing out a den in the snow. Ferrier stuck his mittened hands into his armpits for the warmth. God, it was cold. He might as well go back to the shack. There weren't any answers out here.

But inside there were only more questions. The captain must have been waiting for him. Before he could even get his coat off, McCluskey was on him. "Sergeant, the place where you lost your guide — how far north of here was it?"

"Uh, I wasn't . . . I'm not really sure. A few days." Ferrier shook his head. They'd gone over this, back at the base. Over and over again, looking at the map. He just couldn't remember. It was all blurred into something like a bad dream. "We made camp near kind of a bay, there were big rocks on the shore."

Half the Greenland coast fit that description. But McCluskey waved him over to a plank shelf where he had the map spread out. His finger pointed to a mark where a hut was supposed to be, way up in the north-east of Hochstetter Foreland. "This is where you were, right? The night you lost Corporal Blackburn. Then you drove south — what, three days? — after that guide." His finger traced a line down the map. "Right, Sergeant?"

"Uh, I guess so. Yes, sir."

The captain raised his voice for a general announcement. "From now on, we're going to assume we're in enemy territory. Those Nazi bastards are out here somewhere, and they've already got two of our men. So, I want every man alert. Don't take any chances. Anything that moves is the enemy."

The men nodded, they'd heard it all before. But the protests erupted when McCluskey announced that from now on he was going to post sentries outside. The men had just gotten comfortable and warm around the stove.

"Aw, c'mon, Captain! Nobody can stand watch out there! It'd freeze the balls off a brass ape!"

Ferrier, though he said nothing, agreed. It was one thing to mush for hours behind a sled. The constant activity kept you warm. But to stand on watch, even for an hour, would leach the heat from a man. It was just inviting frostbite, and then where would they be? Besides, they had the dogs. Any stranger coming near would set them off.

But the captain had made up his mind, and so guards were posted, each man condemned to spend an hour muttering curses outside in the bitter dark, stamping his feet and clutching his weapon with hands gone too numb to fire. No one got any sleep, what with waiting till it was your turn for stand watch, or being tripped over as the next victim stumbled through the crowded shack on the way to the door, letting the frigid air blast into the room as he went out. Even the dogs were restless, stirring from their snowy dens as each new man came out the door, whining at the disturbance.

From inside the shack, Ferrier lay tense and rigid in his sleeping bag, listening to the cries. *Out there. Out there in the dark.* When it was his turn to take the watch he thought desperately that he'd refuse to go. No threats of McCluskey's, no distant court-martial could possibly compare to the terror of an hour outside, out there alone. But in the end he went, and as he stood there alone in the darkness he realized bitterly that this was how they did it — armies, how they got men to climb out of trenches in the face of machinegun fire, to face tanks and men with flamethrowers. It was the thought of the sneer on the captain's face, of the other men in your patrol turning their backs on you, knowing you were afraid to go where they'd gone, to do what they'd done. Even if you died for it.

So Ferrier stood there, with his back against the wall of the hut, thinking at least this way it wouldn't come up from behind him. It was dark, he couldn't see, and he *knew* this was how it had happened before, to Blackburn, to Lars. A low growl sounded just a few feet away, and his heart jolted, he thought for a panicked moment that he was going to piss himself. But it was only a dog.

He took a couple of deep breaths, trying to steady himself. *Remember the dogs.* One of them stirred in its sleep, whimpering restlessly. What was it dreaming about? What could it hear, what could it smell? *The dogs, they know.*

The pressure in Ferrier's bladder wouldn't let up. Fumbling with his layers of clothes, he pulled out his cock, careful not to expose the bare flesh to the naked cold, and released the stream into the snowbank at the side of the hut, hearing the crinkle of shattering ice as it struck, frozen already, even before it hit the ground.

Finished, he leaned against the wall of the shack, shivering, imagining he could feel some warmth seeping through the wood. Constantly shifting his weight from one foot to the next, trying to keep his blood going. It was only for an hour. He might, maybe he might make it.

He could hear them inside through the walls, the sounds of a half dozen men trying to sleep. Someone snored, another man swore in a tired voice. And in front of him the low snowy mounds where the dogs were dug in, curled with their tails over their muzzles, stirring from time to time. Ferrier glanced up. The cloud cover was thinning. It had been hours since the moon had set, and now where the sky was clear the stars were brilliant, like diamonds on black satin in a jeweler's window. He blinked. His eyes were getting used to the dark again by now, and when he held his breath the starlight reflected off the snow made everything seem very clear and sharp-edged.

He stared out into the distance as far as he could but nothing stirred, nothing moved. His face tingled with the cold, and he pulled up his balaclava to cover it, jogging in place for a minute or so. This was the kind of clear, still weather when — as they said back in Alaska — you could hear the mercury in the thermometer freeze as it hit bottom.

He flexed his fingers inside his mittens, hoping they wouldn't freeze too stiff and numb to be able to fire a gun. He hugged the Thompson to his chest and remembered. The thing out there — whatever it was — could be hurt. He had hit it, he knew he had, that time. He could remember the cry of pain. Maybe — maybe he'd killed it. Maybe it had crawled away in the dark to die.

The silence seemed to grow deeper and deeper the longer he stood there, with all the stars unmoving above his head. It seemed like time had come to a stop. Nothing could be out there. Nothing could be moving in all that stillness. Even a single footstep would sound like a gunshot as it broke through the snow.

He stomped his feet again, he tightened his scarf. And when Ned Court came outside to relieve him, Ferrier stepped back into the shack where the heat of the stove seemed to flare red like a blast furnace, and he crawled into his sleeping bag to spend the few remaining hours until it was time to move out onto the ice again.

There was a lot of grousing when the captain tried to get the patrol out on the trail again. The men were tired, they were slow to get moving. And the dogs weren't helping any — snapping at each other, trying to bolt. McCluskey chewed the men out, ranting about the Nazis overrunning the American lines and Panzer divisions breaking through to Antwerp, but the dogs, anyway, didn't seem to give a damn about Antwerp.

The moon was well up into the sky before they finally got going. Almost a full moon. Ferrier calculated in his head and realized it must be almost Christmas. He wondered if the krauts would stop their offensive for Christmas and didn't suppose they would. War was crazy.

This part of it sure was. The men were all having trouble with their dogs, cursing and snapping their whips. Doc Martino's team bolted and ran off with his sled while he clung to the uprights, dragging him three or four miles in a huge circle before he could get them back under control. The captain was livid. "The hell—Goddammit, Martino! Get back here! Stop those . . . Goddammit, go after him! Somebody! Ferrier! Stop him, bring him back!"

Ferrier wheeled his own sled around, and the dogs, scenting a race, charged off in pursuit of Martino's renegade team. Paul Jablowsky's dogs, unordered, took off after his, while Jablowsky shouted orders for them to halt. Then, when Ferrier caught up to the runaways, the three teams erupted into a fight, a boiling mass of fur and snapping teeth and tangled harness. By the time the drivers had them all straightened out and back with the rest of the patrol, all three teams were exhausted, with at least two dogs too badly injured to pull. The captain, red-faced with rage, reamed them all out again. If there was any justice in the world, Ferrier hoped, the captain's team would bolt next, but McCluskey managed to keep his dogs—barely—under control.

Next time they took a break, Ferrier made a point to try to talk to Pete. He gestured toward the dogs. "What's the matter with them? What do you think?"

The guide had been having almost as much trouble with his team as the rest of them. He clearly didn't want to say anything, but Ferrier pressed him. "You think it's a bear out here somewhere?"

Pete made a mark in the snow with the toe of his sealskin

boot and stared at it. "Maybe," he mumbled finally. "Maybe."

"Or maybe something else? Your cousin Lars said—"

But the Greenlander shook his head and walked away. Ferrier was starting to follow him when the captain called him over, acknowledging at least that he knew something about dogs. "Take at look at that leg. What do you think?"

With the flashlight, Ferrier took a good close look at Martino's injured dog. There was no doubt. The foreleg was broken, and not a clean break, either. Back at base, the animal might recover. But out here? He met Doc's eyes, and they both shook their heads.

McCluskey said out loud what they were thinking, "We can't afford to hold back the patrol, not for a dog." He pulled out his Colt .45 from its holster under his parka. Ferrier tried to stop him, "Captain, no, wait—" but the captain shouldered him aside, put the gun to the dog's head and fired.

The gunshot was shockingly loud. The report seemed to echo and re-echo off the mountains. In the empty silence of the Arctic, the sound would carry for miles. McCluskey stared at the gun in his hand, while all around him the huskies erupted into a frenzy at the scent of fresh blood.

That did it. Ferrier knew what everyone was thinking—if there were any Germans around, they sure as hell knew the patrol was out here. The captain had just told them, loud and clear.

For a while, it was chaos. By the time they'd gotten the dogs straightened out again the moon had already crossed more than half of the sky. No matter how much time they made up, Ferrier knew it would be hours still until they reached the next hunter's shack along the coast. Shelters were scarce up here. Not too many men had ever hunted as far north as Hochstetter Foreland. When the moon set they were still on the ice, and Pete acknowledged they weren't likely to reach the shelter any time soon.

The men were grumbling to each other by now, growling mutinous curses. They were tired and hungry, they were frozen down to the bone. Their teams were tired. It was crazy to keep on going in the dark, for god knows how long, until they reached the next hut. They'd be better off pitching the tents, firing up the stoves, getting some food and some rest.

McCluskey finally gave in. He picked a site by the shore of a small bay, sheltered by the cliff at its back, and the men started in to picket the dogs and unload the tents from the sleds. Ferrier heard Ned Court yell, "Hey, dammit, Jablowsky, get over here and give me a hand!" A minute later, "Jablowsky! Hey! Where the hell are you?"

Ferrier straightened from his work of staking out the dogs. He glanced quickly around the camp, counting: seven sleds, seven men. Seven, not eight. Someone was missing. His heart turned to a cold, heavy lump. *Not again. Not again.* But it was no use. He knew what had happened. It was starting again, all over again.

Court was telling McCluskey, "Captain? Listen, I can't find Jablowsky."

"What do you mean?"

"He's . . . I think he's missing, Captain. I think maybe he got lost or something."

McCluskey swore with a passion. Ferrier almost felt sorry for him. Jablowsky had been bringing up the rear. Some of his dogs had been limping a little after the episode in the morning. He'd certainly been with them at the last halt. But then — well, it was dark, hard to see. Anyway, somehow, he wasn't with them anymore.

McCluskey swore again, then sighed in resignation. "Okay. He fell behind. Maybe he got lost out there. Pete. Ferrier. You two harness up and go back after him. See if you can pick up his trail. The rest of you, get the tents up, get the stoves fired up. Maybe he'll be able to see the light. In the meantime, I'll stand the first watch."

The captain was still thinking it was Germans. He was starting to realize all of a sudden how vulnerable they were, how exposed, out on the open ice. Shaking his head, weary to the bone, Ferrier went to his sled, started to harness the dogs again, hauling the reluctant animals by main force into the traces. He was cold, he was almost frozen stiff, but there was nothing else he could do. He kept telling himself Jablowsky might just be lost, he might just have fallen behind the rest of them. They couldn't just leave him out there. Not like Blackburn. But they'd looked for Blackburn, hours after hours. Finding nothing. Nothing.

He drove off next to Pete, back out onto the empty stretch of the ice, the tracks of their sleds clear even in the starlight. Once they were around the headland, he yelled out, "Jablowsky! Paul!" but the echo faded away with no response.

A few minutes later he signaled for the guide to pull up. It was just the two of them alone on the ice. "Listen. What do you think? What do you really think? Is it Nazis? Germans?"

Pete stared ahead into the darkness. "Maybe. Maybe Germans."

"Goddammit!" Ferrier grabbed the sleeve of his fur parka, pulled him around, made him *look* at him for once. "Maybe a bear! Maybe Germans! Look, I *know* what Lars said, what he thought was out here. I *saw* it!"

Something changed in the Greenlander's face. He finally looked straight at Ferrier. "What? What you see?"

Ferrier's throat suddenly closed up. To say it, finally. To say it out loud. He swallowed hard. Who else was going to believe him? "It . . . was white, the size of a man. Almost . . . like a man. But its eyes—they were red." He shuddered. "There was blood on its face. Blood, running down from its mouth. And it had—I think it had fangs. Teeth, you know, like a dog's, like a bear's. Tearing open Lars's throat. And the blood . . ."

Pete made a moaning sound and said something in his own language.

Ferrier went on desperately, "I couldn't tell them. Not the captain, McCluskey. He thinks it's Germans. He wouldn't believe, none of them would believe . . .

"I knew it wasn't a German. I said I thought it must have

been a bear. Lars said, maybe it could have been a bear. But I know he didn't believe that. He told me—before he died—he said there were something he called the inland-dwellers. He was afraid it might be them—what's out here."

Pete shook his head, pulled away. "I don' know. Don' *know*. Never see . . . what you say." He said something again, what he'd said before. His English wasn't as good as Lars's had been.

After a few more minutes, with nothing more to say, the cold started to cut them, and they moved on. A mile or so past the headland, Pete stopped his dogs and moved away from the sled. Then he called to Ferrier, pointing with a flashlight. "Here. See?"

In the starlight, the trail of the sleds was all shadow. And here, one set of tracks had left the rest. Ferrier spotted something and switched on his flashlight, shone it on the ground. Dark red against the snow, a spatter of blood. Grimly, he looked up at Pete, down again at the snow. *God. Jablowsky. Not again. Please.* Panic was clawing at him, the hair on the back of his neck was standing upright. For a moment, he almost turned around and ran. *It's out there! Out there!*

But instead he reached for the Thompson on the upright of the sled. "I hit it once," he told Pete. "Hurt it, I'm almost sure."

Wordlessly, Pete took his rifle, chambered a round. There was nowhere to run. Only one way to face it, whatever it was. Hurt it. Kill it. Before it could get them.

They took the time to stake down the dogs, but Ferrier unhitched Robber and fastened a leash to his harness, a long leather lead. The sled tracks headed inland, up into the rocks, toward the mountain. Its path was crazy. Almost like . . ."I don't think anyone was driving," Ferrier finally said. Pete nodded. No one could have driven like that. No one would drive a sled up into these rocks.

But Robber whined and pulled on his leash. Ferrier went after him, Pete following. The dog had the scent of something up there, and now there were clouds coming in, obscuring the stars, making it harder to see. The shadows darkened and spread. Capable of hiding anything. It could be anywhere. At any moment now, it could spring . . .

Suddenly Pete held up his hand. Ferrier halted, knelt down and put his hands over Robber's muzzle. He could hear it now, the sound of dogs snarling, growling. The two men looked at each other. Robber shook his head free and made an answering growl. They were following the dog now, and the sounds of the others. They'd lost the track of the sled, back somewhere among the ice-covered rocks, and were climbing now.

Up over a ledge, and suddenly the sound of the dogs was louder. Close, very close. Ferrier could hardly hold Robber back. And then he saw, up ahead at the base of a rock, a movement. A step or two closer, and he could see the wolf-shapes, the dark, shadowy pack of them surrounding something on the ground, snarling and snapping as they fought over it.

The gorge rose in Ferrier's throat. He knew, knew what it was. Who it had been. Without thinking, he brought the Thompson up and opened fire, thinking only to exterminate the pack. The dark forms of the dogs writhed and collapsed, howling. With a shuddering gasp, he lowered the gun.

Pete stared at him for an instant, then moved closer. Not all the dogs were dead. The guide pulled out his knife, bent down, dispatched the animals with a professional hunter's efficient stroke. Somewhere, out in the dark, more dogs lived, still howling.

Certain of what he would see, Ferrier shone the flashlight down on the killing ground. Surrounded by the bodies of his dogs were Paul Jablowsky's remains, what the pack of starving carnivores had left of him, the ruined uniform, the bones. At least they hadn't eaten his dog tags. Ferrier snapped off one metal oblong and pocketed it. He swept the flashlight over the area, but there was nothing but churned-up, bloodsoaked snow.

He lifted his head. The sound of dogs howling had stopped. In a moment, Pete reappeared, his knife resheathed. "Sled . . . over there. Stuck in rocks. Three more dogs."

Ferrier nodded. He stood up. Looked around. Robber, where was Robber? Then he realized. When he'd raised the gun to fire, he must have let go of the leash. He shook his head. It was too much. One more dog.

"So," he said finally, exhaling, "I guess we found him." He started to shiver, suddenly very cold. Panic screamed at the back of his mind. It was starting again. The thing that had killed Jablowsky was out there in the dark. The darkness surrounded them, the looming black forms of the rocks and cliffs on all side. He was afraid now to switch off the flashlight.

"Better go back," Pete suggested finally.

Without answering him, Ferrier started to pick his way down out of the rocks, letting the flashlight beam guide him. He could feel the menace now, at his back, watching him. One hand for the flashlight, the other for the Thompson.

"What do you think?" he asked Pete when they finally made it back to their sleds. "What was it?"

But the guide said nothing. Ferrier could barely make out that he was shaking his head.

They unstaked their dogs and drove wearily back to the campsite where the rest of the patrol was waiting for them. The ice stretched ahead forever, and the mountains were looming black forms, even darker. *It can see in the dark,* Ferrier kept telling himself. *It can see in the dark.*

There was no light ahead, not anywhere. Nowhere to run to, nowhere to hide.

Chapter Eighteen

It was a fortunate thing. Wolff had gone south as quickly as he could, barely stopping to rest. He'd come down to the southern tip of Hochstetter Foreland when he spotted the American patrol crossing the mouth of Ardencaple Fjord from Kuhn Island. They were miles away, at a distance where the broad, flat stretch of the ice made size and scale deceiving. He could see them at first as only a movement against the island's stark mass. They came on so slowly it almost seemed like some kind of trick photography. Hours passed before he could make out the shape of individual sled teams, strung out in a line. He strained his eyes to make out — yes, there must be eight of them.

At that point he retreated inland. He had no fear that the Americans would be able to spot him in the winter darkness, but the dogs were a different matter, their sense of smell at least as sharp as his own. It would be the dogs, again, that would complicate his operation, and he meant to make no move until they were safely upwind of him.

He crouched down, watching from the distance of his hiding place, relieved to have this unexpected chance for some rest. He wondered whether the enemy was headed north to seek out and destroy the German weather station or take revenge for the killing of their two men. But it didn't matter. They were here; they were his, now.

The weight of the rifle pressed on his back, and he lifted it off, looked down the sights at the approaching line of dogsleds. Out there on the open ice, the Americans were perfect targets. From up here, it would be simple to pick them off one at a time as soon as they came into range. But the prospect held no appeal for him. He carried the weapon in case of an emergency, but he had no serious intention of using it. He wanted more from the Americans than their deaths.

Wolff finally allowed himself to feel the hunger that had begun to accumulate in the days since he'd fed on Dienst, and his teeth showed in a predatory smile. It was going to be a good hunt. A very good hunt.

Slowly the dogsleds crawled across the distant stretch of ice below him, from the far shore of Kuhn Island to the southernmost tip of Hochstetter Foreland. There was a hunter's station there, he'd spotted it in passing. Now, with the moon setting, he supposed the Americans would stop there for the night. He would meet them.

Cautiously, when they'd finally passed, he followed the tracks of their sleds in the direction of the hut. There was no urgency in his hunger — not yet. And the warning twinge in his knee as he climbed down from the heights was more than enough to remind him of the consequences of carelessness. With eight of the enemy, and their dogs, he couldn't afford it, not this time. He had no intention of failing again.

He'd learned a great deal, the last time, about the dogs, how to approach them. Slowly, at a distance. Get them accustomed to his scent. He didn't intend, that first night, to come up to the shack at all. It would take a while to get the dogs used to his presence.

But his resolve almost broke when he finally caught sight of the cabin and saw — they'd posted *sentries* outside. The opportunity was almost too much to resist. The man outside — visibly freezing, stamping his feet, rubbing his hands together — was entirely too preoccupied with his misery to be keeping any kind of watch. It would be the work of seconds to move in around the back of the hut, to take him. Bloodlust caused a spasm in Wolff's throat. He would have done it, except for the dogs. One of them, sensing something, stirred in its dugout den and whined anxiously. Wolff froze motionless, stifled his desire, and in a moment the beast settled back down. There was something, he felt, vaguely familiar about that particular dog.

He took another step closer. He had time. It would be a least a week before they could reach the weather station, and his hunger could wait. One more day.

The opportunity wasn't that long in coming. The dogs, agitated by his presence, had given the Americans a hard time all the next day. Some of the drivers were less skilled than the others. One, Wolff noted, was starting to fall behind the rest. Some of his dogs seemed to be limping a little.

As the moon set and the darkness grew more profound, the driver was soon out of sight of the sled ahead of him. Wolff spotted a high ridge of pressure ice ahead, circled around overland and waited there for his victim. As the sled came closer the dogs caught his scent, lunging against their traces. The driver had been fighting them all day. He cursed, using his whip, completely oblivious to any possible danger. Wolff's prey was blind in the dark. A quick rush from behind, and he had him.

The American was large and well-fed. Wolff struck him once to stun him and stop him from crying out or going for a weapon. He had to get him away from the dogs before he could feed, and so he carried the soldier into the rocks, climbing high where the team couldn't follow, dragging the loaded sled.

His hunger was honed sharp by anticipation. He was safe enough up here in the rocks to savor it. By that time the man was starting to recover his consciousness, so Wolff waited, running his fingertips along the blade of his knife, up to the point. Waited until his victim's eyes had opened and focused on his own, seeing at last what he was, knowing what was happening to him. Then, as the shock hit and the panic, the heart racing under the adrenaline surge, he forced the neck slowly back, stretching the throat, bracing hard to keep the man pinned down to the rock. He plunged the knife deep into the throat, exulting in the fierce hot burst of blood, rich in terror. It was a strong heart. Every beat brought a new rush of blood, surging, pulsing with life. Bloodlust crimsoned his vision, rang in his ears with the rhythm of the heartbeat. For an instant, he could have drained the blood of a whole world.

But as always, the heart faltered and failed, the pressure dropped away, the flow ebbed. Wolff let the body fall, trembling in reaction, then suddenly alert again, cursing his treacherous nature, scenting the dogs, hearing them howling nearby. But it was only the dead driver's team, hung up on their sled in the rocks and fighting to break free of their harness. They had scented the blood, he supposed. Beneath their domestic exteriors, they were wolves.

He retreated, climbing higher up along the ridges of bare rock to leave as faint a trail as possible, just in case the Americans sent a search party back to hunt for the missing soldier. Briefly, he considered waiting to ambush them there in the rocks, but decided against it. For the moment, the edge of his hunger had been dulled.

On the map, it might have seemed half the distance to cut across the headland as it was to go around the coast, but the straight line would have given no hint of the difficulties of the terrain. It was slow going, and hard. The only advantage of the route was that the Americans would certainly never come this way. When Wolff finally made it to the end of the highest ridge he could look down and see the warm light of their camp below, the small cluster of tents, the sleds, and the dogs staked out to den in the snow.

It was frustrating. Under normal circumstances it would be only a slight problem to eliminate a dozen armed men. It was the damnable dogs that made the difference. Wolff was still carrying his rifle to remind him that there was a different way. Not his way, though. For a while, he briefly considered the notion of shooting the dogs, but it was hardly practical with almost a hundred of the animals to deal with.

Still, if he could get rid of them, it would leave the men on foot and almost helpless. It was worth considering, at least.

After a while a movement down on the ice caught his eye. A pair of sleds rounded the point, the dogs picking up speed slightly as they came in sight of the light of the camp. This must be the search party back from looking for the missing man. Wolff frowned, wondering if they'd managed to discover the body.

Then the dogs in the camp caught the scent of the new arrivals and started to howl. Wolff began to climb down from the height of the bluff, taking advantage of the opportunity to get in as close as possible to the tents under cover of the commotion.

The captain pulled Ferrier impatiently into the tent. "Well? Jablowsky? Did you find him?"

"Dead," he mumbled. His face felt frozen stiff; he could hardly talk.

"What do you mean?"

"Killed."

"You're sure? You found the body this time?"

As proof, Ferrier slowly pulled off his glove; took the soft gray metal tag from an inside pocket — Jablowsky's dogtag — and handed it over. "We didn't bring him . . . his own dogs had gotten to him. The body was way up in the rocks, but they must've broken loose and gone up there after him. Some of them dragged the sled up in the rocks."

McCluskey blanched. Then, "The bastards," he whispered. "The Nazi *bastards*."

Ferrier looked up, but he was too weary to be surprised at the captain's reaction. He already knew how McCluskey thought. Nothing he could say would make any difference.

As if to prove it, McCluskey ducked out of the tent to issue more orders about sentries and doubling the watch, the goddamn Nazis were out there for sure. Ferrier just wanted to sleep. He crawled out, went to the tent he shared with Pete and

Andy Reasoner. Thank God it was already set up, that somebody was taking care of his dogs and Pete's — somebody who'd spent the last couple hours inside a warm tent instead of backtracking for miles and climbing halfway up a mountain in the dark.

Pete was already inside, eating a plate of hot beans. Ferrier took another plate from Reasoner, who handed it to him with a worried look on his face. All he really wanted was to unroll his sleeping bag and crawl inside, to get warm. But a few minutes later the cold shock of the tent flap opening roused him, and Martino came in and dragged him out of the bag. "Let me take a look at you. Come on, sit up, dammit."

He kept talking as he examined Ferrier and Pete. Doc didn't like the look of Ferrier's face, insisted on checking his hands and feet. "Goddamn. That's gonna hurt like a son of a bitch, thawing you out."

Ferrier shook his head. He knew it, and really would just as soon stay frozen. Feet'd freeze up again next time he went out, anyway. His hands were worse. They ached and throbbed, black on the tips, with oozing cracks where they'd repeatedly been frostbitten and thawed, but both men had seen the like often enough in the Arctic.

Martino shook his head. "Listen, I told the captain, there's no way the two of you are in any condition to stand watch tonight. So you eat, then get some rest. You shouldn't be out here in the first place, after what you went through before. Told him that, too."

He hesitated. "Sarge, uh — are you sure it was the krauts that killed Jablowsky? It couldn't have been . . . an accident? He got lost in the dark, his dogs ran away from him — something like that? I mean, is this like what happened to Blackburn and the other guide?"

Ferrier shook his head dully. He *knew* what had gotten Jablowsky, what was going to get all of them, no matter how many sentries the captain posted. It could see in the dark.

But it wasn't something he could say out loud. Suddenly he

thought he understood Pete, who had bolted his own food and was now a silent lump under the furs, not speaking, never saying a word.

Finally he shook his head. "We never found Blackburn's body," he mumbled. "And Jablowsky—the dogs got at him. There wasn't really enough left . . ."

"Yeah," said Doc glumly. Then, "What the hell is into those damn dogs, anyway?"

"They know," said Ferrier, looking up. "They always know when something's out there."

"Yeah." The medic looked worried. Finally he crawled out of the tent. Ferrier settled back into his sleeping bag. He felt warmer now, with the hot food inside him. But every time he tried to close his eyes, the image came: red eyes, fangs, blood. Jablowsky's savaged body. White bone of the skull and dark, torn flesh. The dogs had gone for the face first, easiest to get at, unprotected by thick Arctic clothes. Though how much, he wondered, had really been the work of the dogs?

Dying was one thing, but not like that. Not like that.

Dreams of Lars's eyes, blinking. Lars, in his dreams, staring at him. Calling out for help, his mouth forming the words but his throat torn out, unable to speak.

Ferrier wanted the reassuring shape of the Thompson in his hands. The thing could be shot. It could be hurt. Killed, maybe. It was their only hope, to kill it.

Outside, a dog whined. Feet stomped on the snow. Someone coughed. *It's out there. Out there.*

He didn't know how long he waited. Hours—it seemed like hours. Every minute marked off by his heartbeat. Every single sound outside the tent. At least he could rest inside the warm sleeping bag, even if he couldn't sleep. At least he didn't have to go out there, didn't have to go out and face it again. Not tonight.

It was almost a relief when the dogs all started yapping and howling at once. Under the noise he recognized Reasoner's voice calling out, "Captain? *Captain!*"

Ferrier snatched up the Thompson from under the groundsheet, heart racing. Pete turned around to face him. His dark eyes were full of terrible knowing.

It had struck again.

Chapter Nineteen

If he were the captain, what would he do?

It wasn't an easy question. Two men lost. Five of them left, plus the guide. Six men against — what?

They'd searched, of course, for Martino, but it was impossible, even when the moon came up. Their enemy had staged a clever diversion, cutting loose a dozen of the dogs. They were still running all over the place. With the tracks of all the teams and the sleds and seven men, no one could make anything out, not even the guide. In the middle of all the confusion, Doc Martino had simply vanished.

"Was this how it was, when Blackburn..." Ned Court whispered, out of McCluskey's hearing.

Ferrier nodded.

Landry joined them. "Listen, Sarge. I remember what you said, before. About it maybe being a bear, some kind of animal. But, I mean, it couldn't be a bear. The dogs woulda gone *crazy*."

"Yeah. You're right."

What could he tell them? What would they believe? "The dogs did go kinda crazy, that first time. Like it could've been a bear. But maybe not. I don't know."

"So it's gotta be the krauts." Landry was definite. Court looked doubtfully at Ferrier.

"It could be," he admitted uncomfortably. "I saw... some-

163

thing, but it was dark." He hesitated. "Thing is, I got the feeling somehow that it . . . they could see me, even in the dark."

Landry nodded vigorously. He was well-read. They'd seen all his magazines back at the base: *Astounding. Amazing.* "They could be using some kind of infrared lens—let you see in the dark."

Ferrier hadn't thought of that kind of thing. "Infrared? Say you had . . . something like that, would it look like your eyes were red, then?"

Landry frowned. "I don't know. Maybe, yeah. Why? You see something like that?"

But just then the captain yelled at them to get their butts moving. They were going on.

Ferrier glanced over at Pete, wrestling the last of his dogs into harness. Could the captain be right, after all? Could it really be krauts out here? Some kind of German commandos like the British ones? If only he could be *sure*.

The dogs were a problem. They'd managed to recapture a couple of the loose animals, but the rest of them were still running around at the edge of the camp, driving the other dogs into a frenzy. Ferrier remembered Blackburn's and Lars's loose dogs and knew these'd be a problem, coming into camp, stealing food, fighting with the teams. And under cover of the noise . . .

He made up his mind and went up to McCluskey. "Captain?"

McCluskey turned. His face looked haggard, and his eyes were bloodshot. Ferrier didn't want to think about what he probably looked like, himself. "Captain, I think we ought to shoot the rest of those dogs. They're going to keep following us, they're going to come into the camp at night. The dogs are our best alarm, if something's . . . getting close to us."

McCluskey thought for an instant, then nodded. "You're right, Sergeant. Do it."

A moment later gunshots rang off the mountains, across the ice. A couple of the more distant dogs managed to get away, but

Ferrier ordered the men to keep alert for them and shoot them if they got in range.

A few minutes later, the drivers were cracking their whips and the teams were moving. Going north.

Some of the other men wondered aloud if McCluskey was crazy, but Ferrier didn't really know what else they could do. Go back? Whatever was out there could just follow them, pick them off one by one, no matter which way they went. Might as well go on, find the krauts if they could. God, if it was only true, if it was just the Germans.

The moon was only slightly shrouded by the clouds, and the going was easy. They'd loaded Martino's supplies onto the other sleds, dividing up the weight so the dogs wouldn't have trouble hauling it. It felt safer, somehow, when they were all moving out in the open, and they were careful to keep together. Nobody wanted to be a straggler and end up like Jablowsky. Nobody wanted to think what was going to happen when they finally had to stop and make camp again.

They'd covered a good distance when Pete suddenly held up his hand as a signal for them to stop. "What is it?" the captain demanded.

"Something . . . under snow."

The shape of the drift revealed what it had buried—a sled, buried up to the handles on the uprights. They cleared away the snow with cautious curiosity, until they'd uncovered the frame. Ferrier recognized it. "Lars," he said flatly, shuddering. This was their camp, then. The place where it had all happened.

The blizzard had scattered the debris of the campsite. Some of it had probably blown halfway to Iceland, Ferrier thought. He stood staring at the coastline, trying to orient himself, to remember that last night before it had all gone crazy. The drifts had altered everything, burying the rocks and ice formations. "I think," he said finally, "I think it must have been up here."

Pete walked next to him, the captain on the other side, the rest of them following, weapons ready. "The tracks led up this way. About . . . I'm not sure, five hundred yards? There were rocks."

There were a lot of rocks, most of them buried under the snow. One group of boulders after the other, they dug and probed, but it was soon clear they weren't going to find Lars's body. If it was even still there.

"Bear take it," Pete suggested.

"Scavengers," the captain agreed.

Ferrier said nothing, standing by the rocks. He was almost sure this was the right place, where he'd seen Lars. But they believed him, at least. The captain and all the rest of them, they believed he'd followed the tracks out here, searched for Lars, seen the body. If nothing else.

The moon was low in the sky by then and somebody muttered something about making camp, but none of them argued when McCluskey said they were going to move out again. Especially not Ferrier. This place was haunted. He could feel it in the back of his neck. Maybe they all could. He only wanted to get out of here.

Driving by starlight, they kept the tired dogs moving. There was a hunter's shack somewhere ahead, four solid walls to put between themselves and the dark. Nobody wanted to spend another night in the tents.

Only Ferrier, and maybe Pete, doubted whether it would really make a difference, tents or cabin. The captain thought it was krauts. Landry did. Ferrier wanted to believe it, the infrared lenses and all of it. If it was only krauts, they might have a chance. But the feeling was back, the feeling that had followed him all the way down the coast, ever since the night that Blackburn disappeared. Something was out there, something was following them.

There was an even worse possibility. It had occurred to him back there when they were looking for Lars's body, back in the rocks where he'd once *seen*, for one instant, the Greenlander guide staring at him, eyes wide with horror while something bent over him with his blood running down its face. Suppose a scavenger hadn't taken the body, that nothing had? Suppose—

It was Lars? Transformed to something that walked in the dark. Something that *couldn't* be killed. Something that had waited there for them, was following them now . . .

Terror prickled like ice down his spine. No. No, that was crazy. Let it be Nazis. Let it be nothing but the Nazis.

The patrol finally came to the hunter's shack on the map and gratefully unloaded the sleds. By the time Ferrier came inside, the stove was already going and starting to take the frigid edge off the air inside.

The captain was facing a mutiny. His face was red. "I gave an *order*, soldier!"

Court, Reasoner and Landry were all three standing their ground, insisting, "No way, Captain. No way we're gonna stand watch out there to get picked off like Doc, one at a time. If those krauts got some kind of secret weapon that lets them see in the dark, we'd be sitting ducks!"

"Who the hell said anything about secret weapons?" Mc-Cluskey demanded, but Ferrier could tell his heart wasn't really in it. The captain was having his own doubts. Two men could stand watch, in pairs, he suggested, but the men were having none of it, and Ferrier backed them up. As long as they were inside, maybe it couldn't get at them. Maybe. Archie Blackburn had gone outside, to see what was bothering the dogs.

"We could keep a watch inside, Captain," he suggested. "Somebody should stay awake, listen for a sign of trouble. Don't forget, the dogs are outside. They can tell if something's up a lot sooner than we can."

It was a compromise. One man at a time would keep watch, staying awake *inside* the shack, fully dressed, with his weapon ready. And God help that man if he fell asleep. "You can take the first watch, Sergeant."

"Yes, sir." Ferrier knew he couldn't sleep, anyway. The others stowed themselves in their sleeping bags. They were soldiers, and it was one of the first things a soldier learns, to sleep—anywhere, anytime — because he never knows when he'll get another chance. Ferrier remembered a guy in basic who said the Army was paying scientists to breed a soldier who never needed to sleep. But that had been a long time ago and another world, where there was day and night and things weren't always out there in the dark.

If it was only Germans. He closed his eyes for a second. Could it have really been a German soldier he'd seen bending down over Lars — a Nazi wearing red lenses? Had he really seen the blood running down his face, the fangs?

Maybe he was losing his mind again. How long could he go — two, three days with no sleep? His eyes burned, his head felt like a radio full of static. If he could make himself believe it was Germans, maybe he could sleep.

Someone snored, the sound breaking off abruptly as if another man had kicked him. The dark form over there in the corner, that was Pete. Could the guide sleep? When Ferrier went over to wake him to take the next shift, the Greenlander sat up silently, pulled on his boots and took his rifle. Ferrier took his place, crawling into his own sleeping bag. He had to close his eyes, couldn't keep them open any longer, no matter what he saw in his dreams. It was out there. *But we're safe in here,* he told himself desperately. *Safe inside.*

His thoughts blurred, drifted. Black shapes running across the ice, under the full white moon . . .

A dog whined outside, and he snapped back to consciousness, heart racing.

But nothing happened, Pete was keeping watch. Ferrier drifted back into nightmare, an uneasy sleep full of blood, where red-eyed wolves tore his face, red-eyed wolves with white fangs, howling —

"Captain! Captain, wake up!"

Ferrier started awake. And it was the dogs howling, the dogs going wild outside. "Don't go out there!" he screamed.

The captain shot him a glare. "No," he ordered, "we all go out together."

There was only one way out of the shack, one door. They'd have to rush through, one man at a time, while the rest of them covered him.

The noise from outside was getting louder. "Maybe the dogs got them," Court said nervously.

"Quiet, dammit," from the captain.

At his signal, Ferrier eased open the door. It was dark out there. The black shadow-shapes of dogs were everywhere, running, fighting in the snow. "The dogs are loose," he whispered. "Looks like all of them."

"Bastards cut their tethers," said McCluskey through clenched teeth.

"If we go out shooting . . ."

Every man knew what he meant. If they went out shooting, there was no telling how many dogs they'd kill. And they couldn't see the enemy.

"Bastards," the captain said again. "Okay. Nobody fire till you can see what you're shooting at. Go!"

Ferrier rushed out the door, low, hit the ground, rolled. He lay on the snow, gasping, heart pounding, halfway expecting shots to be coming at him. He swept an arc in front of him with the Thompson, ready to fire, but there was nothing, just the dogs running, out onto the ice. Another man came through the door behind him. A minute later they were all outside, staring into the dark, trying to spot some sign of their enemy.

Ferrier waited. The signal came from McCluskey. Get up. Fan out. Keep the guy next to you in sight.

Ferrier got slowly to his feet. He felt exposed, a target. *It can see in the dark.* He glanced to either side of him — Court on his right, Reasoner on his left, McCluskey beyond him, a vague shadow in the darkness. The Thompson in his hands — his only real protection.

The shack was at the top of the beach. Below, the slope was covered with scree and broken ice running down to the shore. There was no cover, either for them or for the enemy. Above them was the mountain, twin peaks with a saddle between them, packed with thick snow. The dogs had run off in all directions.

They fanned out, each man as far as possible from the next on either side without losing sight of him, their line stretching down to the shore ice, searching for tracks, sweeping the ground with their flashlights, for any sign of their enemy.

"Keep your eyes peeled," McCluskey ordered.

A fugitive dog ran out onto the ice, and someone fired reflexively. Their nerves were all on edge. "Hold your fire, dammit," McCluskey yelled.

Suddenly the ice brightened. Ferrier spun around to see flare of orange as the dry wood of the shack caught fire. Something moved against the flames, and Reasoner fired, some of the others. Then they ran, desperate to save everything they had. All their supplies were inside — food, sleeping bags, all of it — and the cabin was already burning. Ferrier tripped, fell hard to his knees on the jagged ice, picked himself up. Too late, too late. There was an explosion from inside the shack, and a gust of flame shot out the open door. A couple of men had reached it before Ferrier, had been trying to decide whether they could run in and try to salvage anything. The blast drove them back.

Ferrier came up, recognized Reasoner and Court. He turned around as someone came running up behind him, but it was Landry. "Where's the captain?" he yelled. "Where's Pete?"

"Here," shouted the guide from the other side of the burning building.

From the captain, nothing.

Then the five of them stood and watched helplessly as the cabin burned, taking with it almost everything they needed to survive.

Chapter Twenty

He had them now.

Wolff smiled with satisfaction, watching the four Americans and their guide stand impotently around the burning hut in the distance. *You can run, but you can't hide,* he told them silently.

Their officer lay at his feet, furious and terrified all at once. Wolff had tied him with lengths of harness leather. Another large man. The apoplectic sort, with high blood pressure, from the looks of him. He was struggling behind his gag to say something. Wolff loosened it. The American gasped. "Nazi bastard!"

Ignoring the rest of the invective, Wolff glanced back in the direction of the fire, but the rest of them were still there, watching their supplies go up in smoke.

He tied the gag tight again. In this emptiness, the sound of screams could carry a long way. "I think your men aren't coming to look for you, Captain," he said in English. "This is good. We will have a long time together, you and I."

He pulled out his knife and tested its point on his thumb, glancing down at his victim. There was something different in his eyes — recognition. The scent of terror intensified.

"Yes," he said softly, "I think you're ready for me now. I think we can begin."

The American captain whimpered.

* * *

He was in command now.

The last time, everyone else had died. But the men didn't need to be reminded of that right now. Ferrier gathered them around the smoldering fire. "The way I see it, we've got a few choices left."

He ignored the look on Ned Court's face — *Oh, yeah?* — and went on, "We could try to make it back, all the way to the base."

"How?" Court demanded. "We got no supplies left! You're talking at least a hundred miles!"

Ferrier had worked this out with Pete and taken inventory of their resources. "We've got the sleds, still. The tents — they were packed on the sleds. Our guns. We can hunt for meat. Pete says there's hunting around here."

"What about the dogs?"

"The dogs'll get hungry. They'll be back. We ought to be able to catch as many as we need to haul what's left, anyway.

"Or we could winter up here. We could go back to the last hut. Or there's the one just north of here, closer, maybe a little bigger. It'd be the same thing — we'd have to hunt for meat. And there's the dogs, again. More meat. We skin them, use the hides, too. The Greenlanders do it."

"And what's going to keep the krauts from burning down that place, too?" Reasoner burst out.

Ferrier shook his head. "Same thing that isn't going to keep them from picking us off, one by one, the way they've been doing. You got an idea? I tell you the truth — we try to go all the way back, I don't think any of us will make it. But if that's what you want to try, okay."

They looked at each other glumly — at the smoking wreck of the shack, at the snow-covered ground. None of them mentioned the captain or volunteered to go out and search for him. But they were all thinking: First Jablowsky, then Doc Martino, then the captain. Who was going to be next?

Ferrier surprised them. "We've got one more choice. There's that German weather station supposed to be someplace north of here. They'll have supplies, and a radio."

None of the three men said anything. They only stared. Now the Sarge had gone nuts, as bad as the captain! "We don't even know exactly where this damn weather station *is!*" Landry argued. "Or how far away. We only got five men, most of our ammo just went up in smoke. How the hell are we supposed to take on a kraut base?"

"The way they've done us," Reasoner suggested. "Ambush. Wait outside, pick them off one at a time."

"Or," said Court, "we could surrender."

It was a possibility. Even as prisoners, they'd be inside out of the cold, the krauts would have to feed them. It might come to that, if they could find any krauts to surrender *to*. Ferrier didn't argue with the notion that their enemy was some kind of German commando. It was easier that way, even if common sense kept saying that if it was a kraut out there, he could pick them off right now. Standing around the fire, they were perfect targets. Just a few quick shots and that would be the end of it.

But the enemy obviously wasn't going to make it that easy for them. Near the shore, he could see the gray wolflike shapes of a couple of dogs lurking. He noticed that Pete had seen them, too.

"Pete, you get down there and see how many of those dogs you can catch hold of. The rest of you, I want everything from these sleds. We'll see just what we have left. I want to save whatever we've got—harness leather, everything. Oh, and Reasoner—you take the first watch. Take cover away from the fire."

The Americans had packed all their remaining equipment onto one sled, with nine recaptured dogs to haul it. Wolff had watched the process without much surprise, but that changed when he saw they were still headed north, in the eventual direction of Weather Station Flieger.

Well, he meant to kill them all, anyway. This was just another reason.

He glanced back at the bloodstained snow, at the mutilated body of the American officer. He'd intended to enjoy himself as he hadn't been able to do since the occasion of the late, unlamented Sturmbannführer Scholz. But the fact was, he'd gone too far.

Wolff was not, at the moment, proud of himself. It was part of his nature to savor pain. Pain, terror, despair—they all sharpened his bloodlust. Scholz's pain had been profoundly satisfying, as vengeance always was. But the American officer had done nothing to deserve what had happened to him. The man had only been doing his duty, and he'd posed no particular threat.

There should be limits. It was a lesson his father had tried to teach him when he was very young and his lusts only human, since the first time he was aroused by the sight of a serf being whipped for some transgression. As a nobleman, it was his right to punish his servants as he saw fit. He'd done so—ordered a young maid stripped and flogged, then taken her still bleeding, his own sexual excitement heightened by her pain. He repeated the experience with a page boy a week or so later.

The next day he found himself summoned to his father's room. The lord did not dispute his son's right to do as he had done, nor did he deny the pleasure that such acts could bring. "But the essence of power, my son, is control. Control over yourself. If you fail in this, your lusts will end up ruling you. And the greater the power, the more danger you face."

As if he had known, Wolff thought now. But at the time, being young, he'd spurned his father's advice, had only been more discreet in pursuit of his pleasures. Later, of course, he had learned. His needs were different now, the temptations so much greater.

But that particular choice was well behind him. And the American was dead.

The others were driving north now again, slowly as they must with five men and only one sled. It would be no trouble following them. There was plenty of time. After the officer, he was sated. It would be a while before he felt the urge to feed again.

At a distance, the gray shapes of dogs waited, drawn to the scent of blood. As Wolff left the place, they slowly crept forward, cautiously, on their bellies.

The Americans were never going to reach the next cabin at this rate, and they could hardly go much faster, not with only one sled. None of them wanted to spend another night in the tents. But the weather was getting worse.

Ferrier knew how close he had come to dying the last time out. Exhaustion, hunger, exposure could kill a man. A single mistake, even something as small as not having dry socks. And all their spare clothes had gone up in the fire, their sleeping bags, their provisions. The tents, the Primus stoves, and their fuel had been left stowed on the sleds, but personal gear and food was always taken inside, out of the way of the dogs, who'd eat almost anything.

Now he had to decide whether to call a halt. As tired and hungry as the men were, they were just as afraid of what was following them. Ferrier knew how they felt. He'd seen what none the rest of them had seen.

He called Pete over. "What do you think? Is it a storm?"

"Some storm."

"I mean, a big one. Will we still be able to go on?"

"Maybe not."

Ferrier bit his lower lip, felt the sting as the wind hit it, turned the moisture to ice. Their beards were all ice-crusted, the moisture of their breath frozen even in their eyelashes. This was nothing new. But if they had to spend more than a day or so waiting out a blizzard in the tents, with no sleeping bags, they were probably dead. If they had to kill the dogs, it was the same thing in the end. He pulled his collar up higher and glanced at the sky again. If the weather got much worse, they might drive right past the hunter's shack without seeing it.

The responsibility was his. And it was probably no use, no matter what he did. He spun around suddenly, seeing nothing.

But it was out there and it wasn't going to let up until they were all dead.

German soldiers would have finished the engagement by now. They wouldn't want to be out here in the storm any more than he did. A single man with a rifle would have had a thousand chances to finish them off. Court had mentioned surrender. If only they could. If only there was an enemy they could surrender to, an enemy they could *see*.

They drove into the lee of a cliff that gave at least a little shelter from the wind. He called for another halt. Checking quickly — yes, the other four were still there. It hadn't gotten them yet. "Pete, that shack up ahead. Just how far away is it now? Are you sure you can spot it in this weather? Otherwise, we're going to have to stop here."

"Maybe better stop."

From Pete, that was decisive. Ferrier nodded. "Okay, we'll pitch the tents here. Hope this weather breaks soon. That shack can't be more than a day's drive away."

The dogs were fractious when they staked them out, but there was nothing to do about it, nothing to feed them. Pete was alert with his rifle to shoot any of the others that came around hoping for food, but something seemed to be spooking them, keeping them at a distance. Ferrier was afraid he knew what it was.

He and Court were in one three-man tent, Pete, Reasoner and Landry in the other. The men worked slowly with numbed hands setting them up, banking up snow against the canvas walls for insulation. No telling how long they were going to be here.

"How about maybe bringing a couple of the dogs into the tent with us?" Court asked him.

The huskies weren't house pets. They'd been bred outside to make them tough. But their body warmth might be welcome, and there sure wasn't much of anything they could steal. "Okay, but if they make trouble, you're the one has to take them back out."

It might have been a good idea, but it didn't work out. The dogs wouldn't settle, and one of them damn near upset the Primus. Cursing, Court hauled the animals back outside to stake them where they could burrow into the snow with the others, while Ferrier covered him with the Thompson. Then they both had to start the process of getting warm all over again.

Ferrier had a couple of strips of jerky in his pocket, and he dropped one into the pot of snow melting over the stove. It might make something they could pretend was soup. He didn't like the look of Court's feet. He made him take off his socks, hang, them up next to the stove to try to get them dry. In fact, he figured Court might have to lose a couple of those toes. If not worse. He missed Martino and wondered if the Germans had a doctor or a medic at their weather station.

Maybe war didn't belong here in the Arctic. Men should be trying to help each other survive out here, not kill each other.

The wind outside had hit a high, screaming pitch. Ferrier hoped it wouldn't tear the snow cover off the tents, but they were in a pretty sheltered spot. He hated to think of how bad it would have been out on the open ice.

But it bothered him that he couldn't hear much of anything over the sound of the wind. Not the dogs. Not the runaway animals skulking outside. Maybe they'd all gone to ground in this weather.

"At least the krauts won't be out in this either, right?" Court grinned weakly.

"Yeah, that's right," he agreed without enthusiasm. They shared out the jerky broth, chewing the shreds of meat slowly to make them last. Ferrier thought he ought to get some rest. Sleep if he could. If this didn't blow over soon, they'd have to think about killing one of the sled dogs for meat.

The wind seemed to be dying down. They were lucky. Maybe. Ferrier got on all his clothes, braced himself against the cold, and crawled outside. The other tent was buried under a mound of snow.

And the smaller mounds where the dogs still slept, protected against the blowing wind . . .

Ferrier stared. He ran shouting to where they'd staked the dogs, groping in the drifts for their leads. There was nothing. Nothing but the snow and the severed ropes and harness.

Ferrier sagged in despair. Now they were all dead. The dogs were gone. Someone had cut them loose during the storm.

"Damn you!" he screamed out into the faceless night. "Damn you to hell!"

He was never sure afterward that he hadn't heard a faint laugh in reply.

Chapter Twenty-one

Wolff watched the storm gather and strike, saw the Americans making camp. He took shelter himself close at hand. They were determined, he had to give them credit for it, pressing on under these conditions. He wondered what they thought they were going to accomplish, heading north. By now, in their condition, they were hardly much of a threat to the weather station.

He had no sense of urgency, no hunger at the moment. It would be good to wait, good to draw out the hunt. His days in the Arctic were numbered. The solstice had passed, already the sun had reversed itself. In the south it would be cutting a higher arc across the sky. But he had well over a month before it would begin to touch the darkness at this latitude. Plenty of time for the Americans.

Somewhere in the remote distance was Europe, was the war. Wolff imagined armies like huge beasts savaging each other's throats. All that blood spilled—and when it was over, what? How many of those men fighting took any joy from the deaths of their enemies?

Ordinary men didn't know what it was to kill. Not even a man like Oberführer Kessler of the SS, whose crimes were on an industrial scale. Death—should be something intimate, close. Wolff meant to experience Kessler's death very intimately indeed, to repay him for his insults at Tromsø. When he was finished here.

But now on Greenland the storm was like a curtain, shutting off the rest of the world. He doubted that the Americans would venture out under these conditions, and even if they did, they couldn't get far. Especially without their dogs.

Under the cover of the wind, he crept into the camp. The dogs were buried deep under the drifts with only a small opening in the snow so they could breathe. They sensed his presence, they stirred and whimpered, but his scent was no longer strange to them. When the nearest animal finally shook itself free to confront the intruder, Wolff met its eyes. One predator faced another, and the dog whined, backing to the end of its tether. Wolff's knife flashed, cut it free, and the husky fled.

One by one, he slashed the lines and sent the dogs running from the camp. Then he returned to his own den to wait. After a time the storm seemed to be abating. While Wolff watched, a figure broke through the snow covering one of the tents and crawled outside. The man held up a gloved hand to protect his face and looked around the camp, then, with a despairing cry, he ran toward the place where they had staked the dogs, digging into the snow to try to find them.

Then he straightened and screamed out into the dark, "Damn you. Damn you to hell!"

Wolff couldn't help laughing out loud.

The rest of the Americans ran out to join him, and all five men stood staring at the evidence, the cut lines. Some of them cursed, and their voices cracked on the words. Some said nothing. But the man who had damned Wolff started to give orders, and after a few minutes they were all at work packing up their tents onto a single sled. Four of them took harness lines and wrapped them around their waists while the fifth man shoved from behind. With an effort, they hauled the sled free of the drifts and down toward the shore and the open ice.

At a safe distance, Wolff followed, fascinated. The man at the back of the sled had the hardest job. The four doing the pulling couldn't generate the speed of the dogs, and none of the men, obviously, could ride along on the runners. Then he frowned. Hanging from the upright at the rear was a machine-pistol — he recognized it as a Thompson submachine gun.

This, he thought, was possibly the soldier who'd shot him, the one who'd gotten away after he'd killed the first guide. He had no particular animosity toward the man; he'd only been doing his duty, after all, and trying to save himself. Wolff knew it had been his own carelessness that had gotten him shot. He didn't care to repeat the experience, though. He could wait.

The Americans weren't making very good time. Some of them were limping badly. Without the dogs, the sled was slowing them down, but it was still the only way to haul their tents and supplies. After a while they paused to rest, and then another man took the position at the rear. Wolff watched him intently. This one seemed more exhausted, less alert. Wolff came up more closely behind him. This would be tricky. On the other hand, it made an interesting challenge.

The poor visibility, with the wind still blowing, with the clouds, was to his advantage. After a while he noticed that when the sled came to a patch of smoother ice the soldier would let go of the uprights and let the others pull for a few moments. More and more, he would fall behind the sled, then have to hurry a few meters to catch up.

There was an iceberg up ahead. Wolff waited for the right moment, then rushed his victim, grabbed him up and pulled him back behind the berg, quickly rendering him unconscious. An instant later, one of the men in front noticed the difference, spun around. "Landry! Goddammit, Landry!"

The leader tore clumsily at the line connecting him to the sled, finally got free, ran back with his machine gun. He stood, staring out into the darkness, then fired his weapon wildly, spraying bullets on the ice, sending shards of it into the air. The leader grabbed him, wrestled the gun away.

There was an argument, whether to go after the man named Landry or abandon him to their unseen enemy, who always managed to disappear without a trace. In another moment the figures of the armed Americans appeared, coming around the iceberg, searching through the curtain of blowing snow for any sign of their missing comrade. The leader had a flashlight. He paused beneath the iceberg. But Wolff had carried his unconscious victim to a shelf of ice over the searcher's head, was lying on top of him, dressed in white, motionless, invisible. The Americans had come from both directions around the berg, had met now halfway around the other side, and found nothing. Wolff heard their voices finally recede, still quarreling.

Wolff turned to his victim at last and released the grip on his throat. He put the tip of his knife into it and fed. He was quickly sated. When he was done, he left the body and followed after the four who were left.

They went on for about another kilometer, then halted again. Wolff could see the reason, the lead of open water, black in contrast with the ice. After another brief argument, two of the Americans began to put up their tent while the guide went, out alone onto the ice, following the open water to a place where a seal might emerge for air. The fourth man, the leader, stood covering him.

Wolff watched, intrigued again by the way the Greenlander could stand so still, almost as if he didn't feel the cold. The Americans obviously did. After a while the guard traded places with one of the other men, taking shifts. With the other two warming themselves in the tent, the sentry was the vulnerable one, but Wolff's hunger was dormant.

He watched, instead, wondering if the patient figure out on the ice would catch the seal. It had been more than an hour, and he was still standing there. Suddenly there was a shot, a cry. The seal had appeared in the water, but the hunter had been too slow, too late, too cold after all that waiting. He'd failed.

The leader went out to him, there were a few words, then the guide followed him back to the tents.

Wolff thought he recalled that a hunter's station wasn't too far from here, the same place he'd first encountered the three-man American patrol. A dogsled with a fresh team could have made it in little more than an hour, over good ice. But here there was open water blocking the way, and broken pressure ridges closer to the shore.

Wolff loped ahead and found the station. The cabin was half-buried in drifts. Wolff hesitated. He didn't want to leave any tracks in the unmarked snow. Then he had an idea. There was plenty of time before the Americans could reach this place. Starting from behind the hut, he tunneled through the packed drifts up to the rear wall. It was nothing to dislodge a board and make a gap so he could squeeze inside.

The interior was disordered, US military equipment lying abandoned on the floor and the bed. A sleeping bag, a blanket, half-eaten rations, everything frozen. More food stored near the stove. The Americans could survive here for quite some while — if they ever did get here.

They were no use to him frozen to death. There were tools in the hut, and Wolff took some time to improve his access, cutting a trap door below the table against the rear wall. Then he backed out through the tunnel the way he'd come.

By the time he'd finished and made his way back to the shore, he could see the Americans in the far distance, hauling their sled over the broken shore ice. Two men pulled and one followed behind. Wolff scowled until he noticed the form of the fourth man on the sled, obviously not fit to walk. It was no wonder the remaining three were having such a hard time of it, dragging his weight.

It was painful to watch their slow progress, their struggles. Poor mortals, succumbing slowly and inevitably to hunger, exhaustion, and the bitter, relentless cold, their tissues freezing, blackening, decaying. There were times when the disadvantages of his condition had made Wolff bitter, but now, watching the three men hobbling across the ice, damnation seemed worth the pains.

As he watched, the sled halted and the one riding on it stood up and begin to limp along behind, clinging to the upright handhold when he started to fall. There was a point when death could be a mercy, and Wolff had extended such mercy many times. Though he could enjoy inflicting pain under the right circumstances, there was no purpose in suffering for its own sake, no use in keeping mortals clinging to life.

Now the pressure ridges were so bad the Americans were having to lift the sled and carry it bodily over the buckled slabs of ice. The man with the frozen feet wasn't much use in this task, and the others were too involved in the effort to look back at him.

Wolff saw an opportunity. But before he could approach too closely, the guide called out to the others. He'd seen the hunter's station up ahead. The Americans cried out aloud in joy and relief, abandoning the burden of the sled, and started to run up the shore toward the shelter. The two Americans half carried the frostbitten one.

Wolff was perversely pleased and almost proud of them. A short time later he saw the smudge of smoke rising up into the darkness of the sky and he settled down to wait, knowing that this was as far as they could go.

He'd spent a great deal of time waiting lately. It tended to make him contemplative, thinking of his nature and his past, events beyond changing.

A time later he was alerted by the cabin door opening, the Americans coming back down to the shore to retrieve their equipment from the sled. Three of them. Wolff looked up, back to the hut. Where the crippled one stayed behind, alone.

This was an opportunity. He slipped into his snow tunnel and carefully put his eye to a crack in the wall. The soldier lay on a low bed. His teeth were clenched, his face was contorted with the pain of thawing flesh. He was alone now, he didn't have to pretend to be bearing it with stoic fortitude. Most important, his weapon was out of reach.

Caught up in his misery, he didn't notice the faint rasp of wood as the trap door opened. Wolff slipped through, then rushed. The soldier heard him then, saw him too late, was still flinging himself awkwardly at his gun when he was seized.

Wolff disabled him quickly, dragged him out through the opening in the wall and replaced the trap door. He'd intended this death to be merciful — easier, at least, than the slow process of gangrene in frozen hands and feet. But the American wept and begged until the end, preferring his suffering.

Chapter Twenty-two

To reach the hunter's shack. It had all come down to that. They were beyond terror. The only thing left was survival—food, shelter.

Now Landry had disappeared. Four of them left. Matt Ferrier had almost stopped trying to fight it. It was almost . . .

You turn around. Another man missing—Jablowsky . . . Landry . . . who next? *Not me. Not me this time.* You're ashamed of thinking that. And at the same time, you're thinking—*Maybe he was the lucky one. How much longer to go on?*

But they'd made it. Now, with the fire going in the stove, real food in their bellies for the first time in days, they were all four undergoing the pangs of thawing frostbite. It was nothing new to any of them, they were all experienced Arctic men. Court was worst off, he could barely walk the last couple of days. They'd even tried carrying him for a while. Ferrier was hurting, too, but he couldn't make himself worry about losing a few toes. Not now.

They had to go back and get the gear they'd left on the sled. Not right at first. But after they'd rested a while. It was hard, hard to go back out into that cold. Just the three of them, taking their guns with them, leaving Court safe back at the hut. "Don't be crazy," Ferrier told him when he reached for his boots.

Already the wind had been trying to bury the sled. The three men got their stuff in their arms, climbed back up to the cabin, back out of the cold and the wind, dumping their snowy loads on the floor. It was a couple minutes before they noticed that Court was gone.

"Court? Ned?"

"Maybe he went out to the latrine?"

They looked, everywhere outside the hut, all the way back down to the shore, but they found nothing. The cabin was surrounded by drifts, there were no tracks, only the ones that led down to the sled.

"Damn! Why the *hell* would he go out, by himself? He *knew* better than that!"

But no one could answer the question. Court had just simply vanished, the way Landry had, and Martino, the captain, Jablowsky.

And whatever had got them was outside their door. Soon, it would get one more of them. And then one more. There were times when Ferrier wondered what it would be like, seeing that face again, those eyes. But the raw edge of his fear had worn away. He was numb to it now. Their enemy belonged to the darkness. There was no escaping it, no safety.

Still, a man can't just give up, give in to it. Ferrier had volunteered for the first watch, sitting on a crude wooden chair, still feeling the pain of his frostbite thawing. The Thompson across his lap, remembering again how he'd shot it once. One chance was all he wanted. Kill it before it killed all the rest of them.

But he'd been too long struggling across the ice at the very limits of exhaustion. Too long without food. Now, in the relative warmth of the cabin, his vision blurred, his eyes closed . . .

And he jerked awake in a panic. What was that? A sound? He stood up, paced the length of the hut, opened the door to scoop up a handful of snow and rub his face with it — anything to make himself stay awake. The last time, it had burned down the cabin. What if it burned this one while they were asleep inside?

Just one chance. All he asked for. Just to get off one good burst.

Eventually he woke Reasoner and settled down in his place, glad for the fading warmth of the other man's body. Finally to close his eyes.

Pete woke him hours later. The aroma of coffee filled the hut. The Greenlanders couldn't get enough of the stuff. Ferrier was still weary to the bone, but hungry, too. There was a sack of flour and some lard left of the provision in the hut. Ferrier was no cook, but he did his best.

"So what now, Sarge?" Reasoner asked finally, when there were no more crumbs. "Do we just . . . wait here? Or what?"

Ferrier shook his head. They had supplies to last them a couple of days or so. A week, maybe, on starvation rations. No, there was only one way to survive wintering up here, and that was to hunt. Pete was still sure he could get a seal, if that lead was still open.

But Reasoner had his own ideas. "What about that kraut weather station? Didn't the captain say it had to be somewhere around here? North and west?"

Ferrier groaned inwardly. What did "somewhere around here" mean on Greenland's uninhabited east coast? The weather station could be another twenty, fifty miles away. Or more. To think that so many men had died trying to find that weather station, and this was as far as they'd got.

Pete stood up. He'd been checking over his rifle while he stood watch. Now he started to put on his high, moss-stuffed boots. "Got to eat. Got to get seal."

Slowly, Ferrier reached for his own gear. "We'll cover you."

Reasoner moaned, but followed him. They took up their post at the edge of the ice while Pete went out to where the lead of open water had been. It had frozen over, but the Greenlander turned back and gave a signal of success — there was a seal's breathing hole in the new ice. All he had to do was wait. Unless he froze to death first.

Ferrier stamped his feet to keep the circulation going. He didn't want them to freeze again, not so soon. How Pete could stand it, he didn't know.

Reasoner couldn't keep still. Ferrier remembered how Lars had said that any movement out on the ice scared the seals away — that they could hear the slightest sound from up on the surface. It was strange — Pete never mentioned Lars, never talked about his cousin.

"You don't think he's really going to catch anything out there, do you?" Reasoner complained, turning around so his back was to the wind.

"Look alert!" Ferrier snapped. "Yeah, I saw Lars catch a seal that way — the other guide, remember? Standing out there on the ice like that for hours."

Reasoner shivered. "What a life. Shit, I'd hate to be a seal, swimming around in that water, looking for some crack in the ice so I could breathe."

Ferrier glanced out at Pete, back behind them. He had the Thompson, Reasoner his rifle. They were covering Pete, covering each other. Their enemy was waiting for them to get careless, waiting for a chance. He flexed his hands, trying to keep them warm.

When the shot came, his heart lurched, but it was Pete, waving to them and struggling at the same time with something in the water. "C'mon!" Ferrier yelled, and ran to help him with the seal before it slid back beneath the ice.

Together, they hauled the bleeding creature through the hole in the ice and laid it down. Pete had his knife out, slashed down through the belly, spilling guts. The smell of the blood was sharp in the cold air. Pete pulled out something dark and slippery, sliced quickly with his knife, and Ferrier crammed the hot, bloody strip of liver into his mouth, chewing, swallowing, reaching for more.

They finished all the liver there on the ice, the three of them, gorging like the dogs, then dragged the rest of the carcass back up to the cabin. Pete cut out the intestines, left them on the rocks just below the hut. "Dogs," he explained briefly.

Ferrier nodded. There was nothing for the dogs to eat out there, nothing—except the bodies of dead men. The scent of the fresh blood ought to draw them. Was that . . .

He brought up the Thompson, held his fire. Was that something moving way out on the ice? Whatever it might have been, it was gone, now. Frowning, he asked Pete, "Think those guts might draw a bear, too?"

"Maybe a bear."

They brought the seal inside and Pete knelt with his knife. "Need woman to do this," he complained, peeling off the skin.

"Yeah, women—that's what we need," Reasoner agreed, but his real interest was on the meat. "We're gonna cook it, aren't we, Sarge?" he asked dubiously, though out there on the ice he'd bolted the hot raw liver just like the other two.

On the floor, the seal soon lay gutted and dismembered. Pete chewed on a piece of fat. Ferrier got up and put more snow on the stove to melt. There wasn't nearly enough coal to last them through the winter, he noticed. No more than a week's supply, using it at this rate. Not enough gas for the Primus stoves, either. Maybe they could burn blubber or seal oil, the way the Eskimos did it. He supposed Pete would know about that kind of thing.

Suddenly the Greenlander, cleaning his knife, stiffened. "Hear that," he whispered.

Ferrier picked up the Thompson, holding his breath.

Yes, outside. A noise. A snarl, a growl—dogs!

They peered through the door cautiously. Two thin wolflike animals facing each other, snatching and tearing at the lengths of gut. Another two skulking up behind, bellies low, ears down. Ferrier thought he'd seen hungry dogs before, but these would be dangerous.

He quickly grabbed up some scraps from the seal carcass and approached the dogs with it, calling them. The two lower-ranking animals ran up, thin and wild, snatched the gobbets out of the air as he tossed them.

The first dog snapped as he slipped a line around its neck. There was a wolf-look in its eyes, and he recalled uneasily that it had probably eaten human flesh. But he cursed and hit it across the nose, and it subsided sullenly, accepting his mastery. For the moment, anyway. Soon there was nothing left of the heap of guts, not even a stain of blood or shit in the snow.

Back in business, he thought involuntarily, thinking of the hard, weary slog hauling the sled across the ice. Even four dogs would have made a difference, those last grueling miles.

Four dogs, the seal—enough meat to last the three of them out the winter? If they shot a bear—that was maybe a thousand pounds of it.

But dogs could pull the sled.

He shook his head. Pull the sled where? Going back all that way to the base—the three of them would never make it, not with their enemy out there. It was crazy. They wouldn't be another day out on the trail before one of them was dead. It could pick them off whenever it wanted—it had already proved that much. But in the back of his mind was still the German weather station. Somewhere around here. And it had to be closer than Clavering Island.

"Now what do we do, Sarge?"

Ferrier shook his head. To go on. To go back. To stay here—they had food now, they had shelter. Would they be safe?

"We stay here, kill dogs now—they eat more," Pete advised.

Ferrier looked at the animals, already settling into the snow. The old routine. Probably tomorrow they'd be ready to run. Four dogs could pull a sled, loaded light. He couldn't decide, couldn't decide. Because no matter what they did, no matter what they did . . .

A sudden gust whipped snow into his face. He looked up at the sky and shivered. If there was another storm, it'd leave them only one choice. All he could think was, better trapped here than out there on the ice.

"We'll wait till tomorrow," he said finally. "Wait till tomorrow and see."

* * *

He stirred in his bed, stretched aching muscles. God, he was tired. All that way across the pressure ridges, the broken ice. Hauling and shoving that damn sled. Finally a chance to sleep . . .

Suddenly Ferrier's breath caught in his chest, frozen there by a surge of panic. Sleep — how long had he been asleep? Who was on watch?

In the guttering light of the candle, he saw Reasoner, there in the chair, his head lolling back. Fallen asleep on guard. Ferrier opened his mouth to cuss him out, but . . .

He stood up slowly, approached the chair where Reasoner still sat, eyes staring open forever.

Ferrier's glance went at once to his throat. With the stub of the candle, he lit a lamp and saw the thin line of blood that had run from the small cut down into his shirt. The stain was still bright. The blood, when he touched it with his finger, was sticky. The cut itself was less than an inch wide, and the skin around it was bruised. One small cut. No pair of puncture wounds — but the rest of the blood — where was the rest of the blood?

It had come in the night, in the dark, while they slept. There was no safe place. In here or out on the ice, it was going to get them one by one, one after the other.

The blood — the blood was still wet.

"Pete!" he called finally with a cracking voice, and the guide woke up, saw, moaned something in his own language — a curse, a prayer.

Ferrier grabbed his arm. "Take the dogs," he whispered urgently, knowing it could hear them. "Go back. As far, as fast as you can. Maybe one of us . . . one of us can make it."

Pete stared at him a moment, then nodded, still without a word. Quickly, he packed his supplies, including the carcass of the seal.

When the guide had driven off and the sound of the dogs'

cries had died away, Ferrier finished his own preparations.

He stepped out alone into the darkness of the Arctic night. He could drag more than he could carry across the ice, and so all his gear, no more than a hundred pounds, was on the small sled behind him. He'd made it himself, along the lines of a child's toboggan, from some of the furniture inside the hut. He'd discovered the trap door in the process, but it hardly seemed to matter now. The Thompson hung from its strap around his neck.

It could only follow one of them at a time. The other one might . . . maybe . . . make it. It was the only chance he could think of, for either of them, Pete and him. If they stayed together, they were both dead. Nothing could stop it, nothing. It could see in the dark, come in through the walls.

He strapped on his skis and pushed off with the poles. Hard to get started, dragging his load, but easier once he was moving, once he was on to smoother ice. If his enemy was following him — well, then maybe Pete would have a chance to get away. Otherwise . . .

The German station was around here someplace. North and west of the hunter's shack, the captain had said, that's where the radio signals were coming from. Somewhere north and west.

As long as he kept going, he'd be warm enough. Through the darkness. The sound of his skis gliding over the snow. The sound of his breath, freezing in the air in front of him, freezing on his beard and eyelashes. The submachine gun, its metal parts too cold to touch with ungloved hands, slung around his neck so he could reach it in seconds — if he had the seconds to react. Then he'd know for sure if it could be killed. Or else the last thing he'd see would be the glow of its eyes.

Either way, it'd be over with.

On and on and on. What was it waiting for? Didn't it ever get cold, ever get tired? Ever get hungry?

Ferrier forced himself to halt. Alone now. Had to take care of himself. Get warm, get food. Stuff he'd learned years ago, when he was just a kid in the woods. No dogs to take care of, no tangled harness. It was easier like this, in a way. Put up the tent, get the stove going, snow to melt. Water more important even than food. Leftover rations from the hut. Not enough to last him more than a couple of days.

He crawled into the sleeping bag that had been Blackburn's, the Thompson close at hand, protected from the moisture of the air inside the tent. Not making any mistakes.

No chance that he'd be able to close his eyes. Not now, knowing it could be right outside the tent, just inches away. Waiting to make its move. Waiting. But he could rest, lie down and rest and get warm for a while.

Then boots back on, gear packed up, moving again, hauling his stuff across the ice, across the snow. Kraut weather station out here somewhere. Yeah, right. See any krauts, Captain? See any goddamn Nazis yet? See anything out here but ice and snow and the mountains?

Talking to himself. He'd never felt so much alone. Every sound he made was magnified. The crack of the snow under his skis. The rasp of his lungs. His heartbeat, sounding in his ears like a drum.

Whatever was following him made no noise. If it was out here. If anything was. For the first time, he had real doubts. Where *was* it? Why didn't it come, get it over with? Or was he crazy, after all?

No. *Something* had killed Andy Reasoner. Left him still sitting upright with a single hole in his throat and hardly a drop of blood spilled on the floor. Ferrier was remembering Lars, his life's blood running down the monster's face. Ferrier's hands went reflexively to the Thompson. *Coming for me, next. My blood it wants*.

Unless it had gone after Pete.

Yeah, that was possible. It'd gone after Pete, and now he was alone out here, alone on the ice. He laughed out loud, and the sound made a strange echo. Then the German weather base was his only hope. Somewhere along these hundreds of miles of coast . . .

Got to keep going, then. Got to find it. Just like the captain wanted. Gotta follow orders.

He caught himself laughing again, and knew he had to stop and rest. The tent, too hard to get up. Oh, the hell with it. Just crawl into the sleeping bag. Just rest for a while. Little bit. Little bit of rest . . .

He knew he shouldn't sleep. There was a reason. It was out there, out there in the dark. Bending over him, eyes glowing . . .

Bending over him. Hands on his shoulders, shaking him. Slapping his face.

"Soldier. Soldier. You have to wake up."

Haff to vake up. Strange accent. German accent. German.

Ferrier fluttered his eyes open, straining to see in the dark. The figure bent over him, ghostly pale. He screamed, struck out wildly, reaching for the Thompson. His arms were pinned, and he couldn't move.

Then, slowly, his eyes focused, and he saw the pale features, human features, the white hooded parka. No fangs, no glowing eyes. Only, just visible under the parka, the collar tabs of the Nazi uniform, the double SS runes.

He sobbed aloud in relief.

Chapter Twenty-three

Wolff found his captive amusing. The naked, grateful relief on the man's face when he saw he'd been captured by a human enemy and not — whatever he might have feared.

It had been a good chase. And a long one. Wolff had been sated and sated again with his victims' blood, but he knew that within a week his hunger would begin to make its demands again, and this American was the last of them.

Incredibly, the man had gone on without dogs, on foot, with only the supplies he could drag behind him. To attack the weather station? Alone? All the way across Dove Bay? He couldn't possibly have made it. The attempt was insane.

And yet it was almost the first thing he'd said, once Wolff had him inside the small tent, fed, and halfway thawed.

"You're from that weather station, aren't you?"

"So. You were coming to attack us?"

A nod of acknowledgment.

"Well, then. I suppose I can take you there. Although I cannot let you take your weapon with you. What is it they say — For you the war is over?"

The American accepted the joke at his expense, though without laughing. "Then it is around here, somewhere close?"

Wolff shook his head. "For you, in your condition — five, six days away."

The American stared at nothing, silent. He knew he'd almost died, frozen to death. A man would naturally resent being rescued by his enemy, saved from the inevitable consequence of his own stupidity.

"Come," said Wolff, urging the rest of the food on him, "you must eat, become strong. We have a long journey ahead of us. Eat, then sleep." He saw the expression on the soldier's face and felt a private amusement. "Do not worry. With me on guard, there is no danger. No danger at all."

Reluctantly, the American finally did sleep, and Wolff considered the situation. His work was done, the enemy patrol destroyed, but there was no telling how long until Kessler would be able to take him off Greenland. And so to satisfy Kessler, the weather station would have to keep transmitting its reports. Its personnel would have to remain alive.

And so would the American. Wolff scowled, searching through the soldier's supplies, but there was very little more food. It was too far for the man to travel without food. Wolff stood up, taking his rifle — glad now that he'd carried it for so long. There were seals in the ocean and musk oxen up in the mountains. And bears, although he would prefer not to kill a bear. It was January, and northern Greenland was still locked in its winter night. He had plenty of time yet. And the American had time, for a while.

The distant report of a shot woke Ferrier, echoing off the mountains and across the miles of ice. He started, then remembered.

It had been the krauts. The captain had been right all along.

But Ferrier still couldn't quite understand it. What had he seen, then, the monster bending down over Lars? That face, the blood running down, the eyes? Had he really been out his mind?

Maybe so. Maybe so.

Who else could it have been but Wolff, following them up the Foreland, picking them all off one by one? It was war, he had to remember that. They were the enemy. Okay. But Wolff had a gun, why hadn't he used it? Ferrier shook his head. And now, why was he still alive? No matter how smooth Wolff talked, he didn't trust him. Not that it made much difference. Without the German, he was dead, and he knew it.

He wondered about the shot, wondered about Pete, whether he was dead, whether he'd gotten away. Maybe Wolff was out hunting. He hoped so.

Wolff came back with the carcass of a seal, invited Ferrier to help him cut it up, handing him a knife as if there was no chance in the world that his prisoner would turn on him. Ferrier would have been half ashamed to, war or no war. He hated feeling grateful to Wolff for saving him. This situation reminded him of the grave behind the hunter's station at Sandodden, the cross the Germans had put there.

Ferrier cut out the liver, sliced a piece, offered it raw to Wolff, who shook his head, a strange cold smile on his face, very polite. "No, thank you. Go ahead, eat it. You need it more than I do."

When he was finished, they packed the meat onto Ferrier's crude little handmade sled, along with the rest of his gear, the tent, the stove, the sleeping bag. It was almost too heavy to drag then, almost as bad as the dogsled had been, but Wolff took the other side of the line and got it moving.

They set off together. With the load, at Ferrier's pace, they didn't make much distance each day—no more than fifteen miles at the most. One day after the next.

"Where are we?" Ferrier asked once.

"This is Dove Bay."

"We're going all the way across?" He lifted his head to stare into the distance, despite the vicious wind. The German nodded, smiling that frigid, secret smile of his, and Ferrier knew that Wolff was right, he'd never have made it, not across this stretch, not by himself.

The only thing was, the only question—how had *Wolff* made it? All alone? All this way?

Wolff was a mystery. He never seemed to eat, or sleep, never got cold or tired. The white coverall was too lightweight for Arctic wear. Where were Wolff's tent, sleeping bag, provisions?

The two of them would put up Ferrier's tent when they stopped, usually far out on the frozen bay, in the lee of an island. They'd hack away enough of the frozen seal meat to thaw over the flame of the Primus. Wolff never took a share. When Ferrier lay down, Wolff was sitting there, watching, his rifle casually across his lap.

Ferrier didn't ask if he slept. Didn't want to know the answer. Somehow, he knew all Nazis weren't like Wolff. There was something about him, something he didn't want to get too close to. Something he was afraid he'd met once, in a bad dream.

But when they were awake, they crossed the bay, slowly, two men on foot dragging a load that grew lighter and lighter as the seal was consumed. And finally the western shore of the bay began to draw closer. He could make out the fjords and the mountains looming high and dark on the horizon, black rock and bright ice in the moonlight.

Almost there, almost there, he told himself, forcing himself forward, one step, another. *Almost there, please.*

They were coming up to the foot of a headland, a sheer bluff rising up out of the bay, coming close to the shoreline where there was a narrow beach.

"Are you ready to stop now?"

Ferrier looked at Wolff in despair. Weren't they almost at the weather station? It couldn't be so far that they had to rest again. They were almost at the foot of the headland, already across the bay.

"How much farther is it? he asked, willing to go on, another hour or more if that was what it took.

"Oh, not so far. Not so far at all. But you see . . ." There was a change in the tone of Wolff's voice—". . . the location of the station is top secret. To be kept from the enemy at all costs, you understand. So I'm afraid that this is as far as you can go."

He knew before he could turn around, before he was pinned, bent slowly back, gasping for the breath being forced out of his lungs. The eyes glowed red, as he'd always known they would. Eyes that could see in the dark.

The tip of the knife pricked at his throat. "It was a long chase, wasn't it? A good chase. You ran well."

He didn't fight. It was finally over.

And the knife went in, and the cold mouth to the cut, where his heart pumped out his life's blood. The pressure, the suction on his throat. One heartbeat, another, and he knew he'd been right all along, not crazy after all, not . . .

Only the fangs. He'd been wrong about the fangs.

All the rest . . .

The blood . . .

The dark . . .

Chapter Twenty-four

For weeks Weather Group Flieger had lived around the radio. Any station, German or enemy, any language, as long as someone in the group could make out the news of the war.

It was impossible not to curse the censorship practiced by both sides. The German broadcasts proclaimed victory after victory: the German armies were pushing the enemy back all along the western front, back from the borders of Germany, driving deep into Belgium, straight toward the captured port of Antwerp. The more ardent patriots among the weather group had an avid gleam in their eyes, and they spoke eagerly in terms of blitzkrieg and another Dunkerque. But the entire group felt particular pride whenever a broadcast mentioned the weather conditions that prevented the Allied air forces from getting off the ground. This was their own contribution to the victory, making their sacrifice worth while. The Führer himself, they had been told, would be conferring honors on every man of Weather Group Flieger at the successful conclusion of the war.

Of course the Allies denied it all. It was clear that they'd been caught with their pants down and were ashamed to admit it. But in the meantime, Patton was rumored to be praying for the clouds to lift.

This Christmas was one of the strangest that Martin Dietrich had ever known. The last, he fervently hoped, he would spend away from home without his family. All of the men were at least a little bit drunk, with brandy and the hope of victory and the end of the war all contributing to a general feeling of comradeship and goodwill, despite thoughts of home and lost friends. They sang the old songs to the music of Handel and Bach—German songs they'd all known since their childhoods. It was permissible to shed tears under such circumstances then.

There was Christmas music on the radio, too, as well as news of the war, although the Allied stations had too many of those American crooners for Dietrich's taste. There was no suggestion from anyone these days that it was treasonable to listen to enemy broadcasts, and a general relief, even among the most ardent Nazis, that Hauptsturmführer Wolff hadn't returned for the holiday, even though he had never explicitly forbidden what they were doing. It was Wolff's very presence that was forbidding—of everything.

Only Wederling and Richard Mundt had seen him leave, one night right after Dienst had been lost outside in the storm. "He took his pack, his rifle. Nothing else."

"He couldn't have survived out there."

Dietrich hated to admit, even to himself, how much he sometimes hoped that Wolff might have been lost. At least he wasn't around to ruin their Christmas.

They celebrated on New Year's Day, too, when the Luftwaffe took advantage of the good weather to launch a massive strike on the Allied airfields. There was an address by the Führer:

> Our people are resolved to fight the war to victory under any and all circumstances. The world must know that this state will never capitulate. I promise solemnly to the Almighty that we shall fulfill our duty faithfully and unshakably in the New Year, too, in the firm belief that the hour will strike when victory will ultimately come to him who is most worthy of it, *the Greater German Reich!*

In the glow of recent victory, the men of the weather group

stood together at attention, listening, and if any man dissented, he kept it to himself.

But after the holidays the news from the front began to deteriorate. The Americans encircled at Bastogne were finally relieved. The German offensive bogged down. Some units were even said to be retreating — if you could believe the Allied press.

"The *Jewish* press," Mundt said significantly.

"Uncivilized young lout," Pflieger muttered to himself.

Dietrich lay in his bunk, pretending to be asleep so he wouldn't have to intervene in another dispute. It was the same thing, day after day, the same petty quarrels and irritations. If this kept up, he was going to start to envy Hans Ziegler, Klostermann's navigator, who spent most of his time staring at the ceiling, feeding his self-pity.

But it was Ziegler's voice he heard next, high-pitched to whining. "Don't you know — Germany's already *lost the war?* All of this is for nothing, *nothing!* We're stranded! They're going to leave us up here! Like that ship, crushed in the ice! We're all going to die!"

Appalled, Dietrich rolled over and opened his eyes. This wasn't just another complaint. He couldn't let Ziegler go on.

But the demented navigator had already pushed his way to the door, flung it open, and disappeared into the frigid darkness.

"Shit," Busch was muttering, pulling on his boots, "shit, he's finally done it."

But by the time he had on his coat, Richard Mundt was standing in front of the door, blocking it. "Let him go. Let the traitor go. We don't need defeatists around here. He's useless anyway, eating up our rations."

Mundt was a fine, strapping, square-headed product of the Hitler Youth fitness camps, and he outweighed Busch by thirty kilos. But the pilot confronted him with clenched fists. "Get out of my way."

Mundt shoved him back.

Dietrich saw Klostermann coming to support Busch, Manstein and Wederling to back up Mundt, and he bellowed, *"Ach-*

tung!" bringing all the combatants up short. "Turn off that radio! Everyone to your post — now! Mundt, get away from that door."

He took a breath. No one moved, except Mundt, who slowly took a step away from the door. "There will be no brawling. I won't have it! We still have our duty here, and by God, you'll remember it, every man here!"

Mundt looked sullen, Busch barely containing his anger. Privately, Dietrich almost agreed with Mundt — it might be better just to let Ziegler go. The man *was* entirely useless; his presence had been a morale problem since the moment the seaplane had landed, and now this last outburst had created a discipline problem, too. Defeatism was a major offense. God knew he sometimes felt that way himself, probably most of the men did. But you kept those opinions to yourself. You did your duty.

"Busch, go on after him," he ordered reluctantly. Sometimes he wished he could censor all the news of the war, but then he supposed he'd have a real mutiny on his hands. The door slammed shut behind Busch, and Dietrich looked back at his bunk, but instead he went out to the stove and poured the dregs of Köbler's coffee into his mug, glaring the rest of the on-duty members of the weather team into pretending urgent attention to some task. His head ached. He pulled out a cigarette.

An hour later, Busch returned to the station, white with the snow clinging to him. "I couldn't find him. I checked the sheds, I called him, but — no answer."

Dietrich went over to the door, glanced out into the snow blowing through the icy darkness, and shut it again. "It's no use," he said firmly. "In these conditions, dressed the way he was — it's too late by now."

Busch looked like he was going to say something, but Klostermann took him aside. They spoke vehemently for a short while, then Busch retreated.

Dietrich sat down at the table to make a note of the incident for his report. Inwardly, he was thinking that Wolff might have been able to find Ziegler — if he'd been here. He didn't know why he had to keep thinking of Wolff. The SS officer had been gone almost a month this time, alone out somewhere in the Arctic wilderness. It was impossible to imagine how he survived, but Dietrich wasn't about to assume him dead, not again. The rules that applied to ordinary men quite obviously had nothing to do with Wolff.

Mundt came and sat down at the radio, began to get ready for the regular transmission. The radioman looked subdued. The weather report went out and the usual reply was received—no news again. Then Manstein looked at him with a question, "Ah, Herr Hauptmann?"

"Oh, go ahead," Dietrich said irritably, and men started to gather around the set again to hear about the war.

Dietrich went back to his bunk, but he still couldn't help hearing a report about the new Russian winter offensive. *The beginning of the end,* he thought glumly. As if it hadn't already begun. Then he laughed to himself. There was a defeatist idea for certain.

What he needed was some uninterrupted sleep for a change. Dietrich swore to himself that he'd shoot the next man who made a disturbance to wake him up.

"Herr Hauptmann? Herr Hauptmann?"

Dietrich stiffened as a hand touched his shoulder. *Now what?* He turned and opened his eyes to see Wederling standing over him, looking nervous. And standing behind him was—Wolff.

So he was back again. Just when things were getting worse. How appropriate.

Wolff made a slight bow as Dietrich got to his feet, pulling himself into as much order as possible. The last few times Wolff had returned from one of his mysterious absences, he'd seemed slightly worn, exhausted. Now, despite the ragged condition of his white coverall (those stains—were they blood?) he appeared full of energy and deadly cheer.

"Sorry to disturb you, Hauptmann Dietrich. But I would like to report that the enemy dogsled patrols no longer pose a danger to this base." His voice hardened. "Since there appears to have been some doubt as to the authenticity of my previous report, I've left more of the evidence lying at the base of the cliff."

With that, he took out an object that every man in the hut recognized, the light gray metal tags jangling as he dropped the chain into Dietrich's hands. An American soldier's ID.

The room was silent. Dietrich felt the chill of the metal in his fist, and it suddenly occurred to him that even in war there were acts of murder.

Which reminded him, somehow. "Hauptsturmführer, on your way here, did you happen to encounter Leutnant Ziegler? I'm afraid he might have been lost outside—"

Wolff frowned. "Ziegler? The seaplane navigator? What the devil was he doing, roaming around outside? I gave strict orders—"

Dietrich said, "Polar madness. He went off his head, ran out the door, not wearing even a coat. This was . . ." He glanced at his watch. How long had he slept? "Last night."

Wolff looked irritable. "Then he probably didn't survive. No use looking for him, now."

"No," Dietrich agreed.

Wolff turned to the radio, a rare enthusiasm in his eyes. "So. What news of the offensive? It should be well underway by now! Are the Americans back to the beaches yet?"

No one wanted to answer. Finally Dietrich shook his head. "The attack failed," he said bluntly. "Initial progress was good, the Panzers almost reached the Meuse. But then . . ." He shrugged. But then the Germans had run out of fuel, ammunition, men. As always.

"So," said Wolff after a moment. His face was hard and stiff again. "I suppose there is no news of the fighting in the Carpathians, east of Budapest? Do the Germans still control the area?"

Dietrich had no idea. There wasn't much news from that front. "I don't know," he admitted.

"So," Wolff said again, in a lower tone, almost a hiss. "I must send a message now." Mundt still the operator on duty, sent out the transmission as soon as Wolff had it encrypted.

"You will wait for a reply."

There was no disputing an order from that source. As Mundt sat at attention with his headphones on, the rest of the men sullenly wandered away from the radio on their own business.

Suddenly Dietrich realized—Klostermann wasn't in the hut. Fear ran through his belly. What was Erich doing now? It had something to do with Wolff, of that he was sure.

He glanced at his watch. At Wolff. Wolff's silent impatience as he stood over the radio. How long was he going to wait? What kind of message had he sent? To whom? What reply was he waiting for?

Klostermann was so sure that Wolff was some kind of spy. Dietrich wished he'd leave his suspicions alone. Wolff was dangerous. He remembered poor Weber. Killed for just opening his mouth. None of them had dared to say a word against it. He hadn't.

Another look at his watch. Another cigarette.

Wolff said abruptly to Mundt, "You will give me my reply the moment I return."

Mundt's hand shot out in a Hitler salute. "Of course, Hauptsturmführer!"

Dietrich watched Wolff leave, then went chill with apprehension—Erich was still out there. If Wolff encountered him—damn it, where had he gone?

The door blew open again. Klostermann looked grim as he came into the room. "I found them both."

"Both?"

"Ziegler and the Ami, at the bottom of the cliff. Both of them dead."

Chapter Twenty-five

The news came as a shock. Not that Wolff had expected great gains, but Hitler's counteroffensive had been a complete failure! Nothing gained, not an inch of ground. Damn the Germans!

Outside in the fresh air, he regained a little of his perspective on the situation. He had to face it — from the very beginning he'd known that he was involved in a desperate gamble, that the Germans were likely to lose the war. So the title to his lands was worthless. Still, he hadn't really lost anything — only what might have been. It had been a gamble on his part, too.

But now it was finished. He'd sent his message to Kessler, telling him the enemy dogsled patrol had been wiped out, the danger to the weather station eliminated. Now, though, he was anxious for reassurance. Why was it taking so long to get a reply? He needed to know how much longer the station's operation would be necessary, now that the counteroffensive had failed. It was still dark, but by the middle of next month conditions would have changed. He couldn't remain in the Arctic once the sun returned.

Kessler had been vague about the arrangements for taking him off Greenland — the time, the place. Now Wolff suddenly contemplated treachery. He'd assumed that the Germans would need to keep the weather station transmitting. The safety of its personnel was his guarantee. And he knew that the

German record was good. Weather team after team, evacuated safely — from Greenland, from Spitzbergen, even from the territorial waters of the Soviets. Only the *Wuppertal* lost, far out in the polar icecap, with its radio disabled.

But now, when defeat was staring them in the face, it occurred to him that perhaps the Germans would consider Weather Group Flieger expendable. And if they were, then how much more expendable was he? He had sufficient acquaintance with Nazi ruthlessness to know they were capable of abandoning their own men. But what was worse was his slow realization that treachery wasn't the only problem he had to fear. What if the German navy and air force were destroyed? What if they were simply incapable of effecting the rescue? Dietrich might surrender, eventually; he could contact the Americans by radio. But Wolff was well aware that no such option was open to him.

He'd disposed of the enemy patrols. But unless he was taken off Greenland, there would soon be no weather team left alive to evacuate. Even more pressing, in six weeks at the most, the sunrise would return.

He stared into the southeast as if he could already feel the sun. Then he turned abruptly back to the base. Kessler *had* to have answered by now.

"Ziegler and the Ami? Together?"

"Well, not exactly," Klostermann admitted. "Ziegler was right below the point, the Ami was down near the beach. His throat was cut."

Dietrich slid the ID tags along their chain, then read: FERRIER, MATTHEW D. Service number, blood type. Religion: C. This was the enemy. Killing him wasn't murder.

"What about Ziegler?"

Klostermann shook his head.

"Did it look like he fell off the cliff?"

"Or was pushed?"

Dietrich reluctantly counted the deaths. The American—Wolff had admitted this killing. Weber, the first man to die. But Wolff had executed him openly. Then there was Schaus, lost while out hunting. Could the Amis have killed him? A bear? An accident? The Arctic didn't forgive mistakes. Dienst had made a fatal mistake, letting go of the guide ropes in the storm.

But it was Wolff who had gone out after Dienst. Wolff who had encountered the hunting party while they were searching for Schaus. Now this fourth death. Fifth, if he counted the American. And Wolff, in some way or another, involved in every one.

The door opened without warning, and Dietrich instinctively closed his hand around the ID tags, seeing Wolff coming in to confront the radio operator. "Any message?" he demanded.

Mundt stiffened to attention. "No, Hauptsturmführer! That is . . . I'm sorry, but no messages have been received since you left," he stammered at the sight of Wolff's face.

"I'll send another, then."

"Yes. Of course."

Something had Wolff worried. Even afraid. Dietrich wasn't sure he wanted to know what it was. But he knew Ziegler's fate was his responsibility. All the men in the room had heard Klostermann, knew what he suspected.

He went closer to the radio, waited until Wolff was finished with his transmission. The metal tags were still in his hand. He opened it, displaying them. "We found your American."

Wolff stared at him coldly. "So this time there is no doubt?"

"No doubt at all. Congratulations. I suppose it was necessary to kill this man?"

Wolff looked back at the radio. "To ensure the security of this base, yes."

"Leutnant Ziegler's body was also found. At the base of the cliff, not too far from your American."

The surprise on Wolff's face *appeared* genuine. "Ziegler? The one you said was missing?"

"That's right. He ran out of the hut. In the dark, we couldn't follow his tracks."

Busch spoke up, "They seemed to be headed east. I went as far as I could, but there was no sign of him."

"And did you climb down, then?"

Busch shook his head. "You can't climb down the cliff face at that point. I would have had to go back, down the path."

"Where was he found, on this side of the headland or around the point?"

"Closer to the point," Klostermann admitted grudgingly.

"Then that would be almost a kilometer from where I left the American." Wolff looked closely at Klostermann. "So you went so far? What did you hope to find? This Ziegler's body, then?"

Klostermann tried to meet his eyes, blinked, looked quickly away. "Possibly, yes."

"Well, then, you found what you were looking for." Wolff turned back to Dietrich. In a more normal tone, he said, "Of course, if I'd known you had a missing man, I would have searched for him myself. But as it happened, I crossed from the south shore. From that distance, I doubt if I would have seen your body. Perhaps he was even around the other side of the point?"

It could have been, Dietrich admitted. He hadn't seen the body, himself.

"We can carry him up," Busch said. "For a decent burial."

"Yes. Of course," Dietrich said. "Take two more men."

Landfried, the medic, volunteered, and Rohde. Klostermann went to show them the way.

Wolff went into the bunk room to the bed permanently reserved for him, took off his boots and began to strip off his white uniform. He scowled at it a moment, then tossed it at Köbler. "Wash and mend these," he ordered shortly.

He lay back, pretending to rest. He'd have to remain in this place at least until he heard back from Kessler. He supposed that the men here wouldn't be sorry to see him go, even if they had to stay behind on Greenland themselves. They'd certainly be very sorry if the SS took too long getting him off.

A while later, the four Germans came back. Wolff pretended no notice as the medic reported to Dietrich, "As far as I can tell, Herr Hauptmann, he died from the fall. I mean, there were no obvious bullet wounds, knife wounds. I suppose he must have run out, not seen the edge of the cliff . . ."

"We brought the American up, too," Busch added, not looking toward the bunk where Wolff lay.

The rest of them were all silent in respect, or pretended respect, for the dead. They started to make plans to bury the remains — to cover them with rocks, since digging graves was out of the question in the hard-frozen ground. The carpenter made a couple of crosses, carving the names and dates into the wood. Wolff wandered from the bunk room and stood over him a moment, watching the work. He appreciated a skilled pair of hands.

He picked up the American's cross, saw the name in Gothic letters: FERRIER. Wolff knew he would remember that chase for a long time — especially whenever there was a twinge in his knee. The upright piece was long and sharpened at the end to be driven into the ground, or the rocks in this case. The cross — the stake. Wolff stared at it, pensive, until he realized the carpenter was starting to get nervous. Quickly, he handed the cross back.

It took a long while for the Germans to bury the bodies, hacking rocks free from the ice and piling them up over the frozen, distorted corpses. Wolff didn't volunteer to assist in the task. When the work was finally done, with all the Germans assembled at attention beside the graves, Dietrich read from the burial service, holding a flashlight to make out the words while the wind tore at the pages of the prayer book. Wolff attended, for form's sake, standing off to the side behind the rest. The crosses had been driven into the mounds, and next to them were three others: ERNST WEBER, ADOLPH SCHAUS, BERTHOLD DIENST.

Wolff stiffened at the sight of the names: Weber's in particular. Here was an act of defiance. Yes—one man, then another casting a quick, nervous glance back at him. The pilot, Klostermann.

Wolff felt a surge of irritation, facing this evidence of his failure. The flying boat's crew was supposed to be his, in exchange for the safety of the weather group. But seeing the names on the crosses—of all the dead, only Ziegler had been part of that crew, and Ziegler had gone mad and killed himself. Even dying, he'd been no use to anyone.

One by one, Wolff considered the Germans, thinking of them as victims now. Some, like the carpenter, were simple hardworking peasants. He had no particular interest in causing them pain. Others—he looked hard at the arrogant young lout of a radioman who so admired the SS uniform—would be more challenging kills. But Klostermann: his suspicions were too dangerous. He would be the next one to die. Yes, and he would learn what kind of being he had dared to interfere with. He would regret, oh, how he would regret . . .

Wolff felt bloodlust building, and he shut his eyes, holding himself steady. Not here and now. Not yet. Fortunately, he'd just fed, and the sensation subsided quickly enough, by the time Dietrich had finished the last prayer.

Then the Germans all hurried back into the weather station, eager to get out of the cold. Wolff watched them, reluctant to shut himself up inside with them, hating the effort it took to suppress his real nature. It had been a long, long time since he was merely human.

But the radio was in there, and it was almost twenty-four hours now since he'd sent the message to Kessler. He had to have a reply!

He glanced up into the sky. It looked like there was another storm on the way.

This was the Arctic at its worst: deadly cold, lead black skies, heavy with storms. Even in the weather station's relatively sheltered location, the winds cut with the sting of a lash. The snow piled up until the men could no longer see over the top of it, where they'd been forced to dig between the cabin and the outbuildings. The snow at least was insulation. Ironically, now, in the deepest part of winter, the hut was warmer than in November, when the drafts had seeped through every separate crack.

The gravemounds were invisible, buried deep.

It had blown for three days and nights, relentless, merciless. Snow, snow blowing so thick a man couldn't breathe outside in it, clinging to his face, to his beard. Even Wolff was trapped inside, pacing the floor like a caged beast, feeling the hunger beginning to work within him, control on the edge of the breaking point.

The storm had affected radio reception. The technicians, Manstein and Mundt, had worked for hours, pale with fatigue, but the airwaves were filled with a blank gray hissing sound, like the wind-driven snow. "I'm sorry, Hauptsturmführer, but — I can try again, later, when the storm dies down."

"Yes. Of course," Wolff snapped, heading for his bed, forcing himself to lie there. The air in the cabin was thick and blue-gray with cigarette smoke. Some of the men lay as he did, waiting for the storm to abate. Others played cards, read the same tattered books over and over again. The meteorologist, Pflieger, fussed over his instruments, fretted about the upper atmosphere readings he was unable to take, mumbling constantly, "No use, no use."

Klostermann was watching Wolff, whenever he thought he was unobserved. Wolff fought his urge to kill.

Everyone was watching, listening for the sound of the radio.

When it finally came, faint but distinct through his headset, Manstein gasped out loud as he hurried to take down the Morse signal. Dietrich and Pflieger stepped up to the set, everyone else in the room holding his breath.

But Manstein turned in Wolff's direction with an expression

of intense relief. "Hauptsturmführer, your message. For your eyes only."

Dietrich stepped back, and Wolff took the paper with admirable control, though he was seething with impatience. From Kessler, it had to be!

He hated to decode it here in the cabin, with all of them watching, but he had no real choice. At least none of them watched overtly while he took out the code pad and made out the message; at least they had respect for security.

Then he cursed to himself as he saw what Kessler had sent: "NOT POSSIBLE NOW TO ARRANGE EVACUATION. MAINTAIN YOUR PRESENT POSITION UNTIL FURTHER NOTICE. KESSLER."

His fist crumpled the paper into a ball. He hesitated an instant, than shoved it into his pocket with the code pad. He stood, remembered himself, and snatched up the white coat, cleaned and mended by the station's cook as he'd ordered. He went to the door, which was blocked as usual by the accumulated drift, and forced it open. He had to get away, to keep from killing someone, not out of hunger but out of rage.

The air outside was cold, fresh, stinging his face. He took deep breaths of it to try to calm himself. He had been betrayed. He knew it now.

So this was what Kessler's sworn word had come to. Abandoning him here. Abandoning the weather group, with him. Kessler would know, he had to know what would happen once the Americans were all dead, if he were left here. They were all expendable.

The dugout path ended at the antenna tower, near the place where he'd found Dienst's body. Beyond, the snow was waist-deep, with drifts higher than his head. He thought of the snowshoes the American had used—better than skis under these conditions. If only he hadn't left them with the body.

Wolff pulled out the crumpled paper, read the decrypted message over again. *Not possible now to arrange evacuation.*

Not possible now. Not now. He'd done what he was sent here

for, completed his mission, kept his word. And now this. He had no idea whether Kessler had intended this outcome from the beginning or if the pressures of the growing defeat had made his rescue impossible. He didn't care. Kessler had given his sworn word. Nothing else mattered.

Maintain your present position until further notice. Until further notice. Wolff crumpled the message again. Further notice. He supposed there was still some time. More than a month before the sun rose again. He could last that long. If Kessler really meant what he'd said. If the SS still meant to take him off Greenland, before it was too late.

Wolff stared at the message in his hand. How to get rid of it? He had no matches. Finally he climbed halfway up the antenna tower, tearing the paper into tiny scraps and letting the wind carry them off into nowhere.

He went back inside the station, into the warm, cigarette-thick atmosphere and its scents of crowded humanity. As quickly as he could, he encrypted a reply to Kessler's message and handed it to the operator for transmission: "CANNOT GUARANTEE THE SAFETY OF THE WEATHER STATION IF EVACUATION IS DELAYED: WOLFF."

So. Kessler had been warned. The consequences would be on his head.

Chapter Twenty-six

The storm finally passed, leaving clear, bitter cold in its wake. The moon shone like ice. Dietrich tried to resume the usual routine, more for the sake of discipline and morale than any other reason, but there was no hope in it. With Wolff constantly at the station, only Doctor Pflieger dared to mutter to himself that it was all no use, all no good anymore. But the weight of defeat was on all of them. Now that the storm was gone, the news coming in over the radio just continued to confirm what they already knew.

But then the war, which had remained a remote event since they had come to Greenland, suddenly came much closer. Manstein looked up from the message he had just transcribed. "Herr Hauptmann!"

Dietrich could tell from his tone that the news wasn't going to be good.

"This message, it's in clear—in English. They . . . mean us."

Dietrich picked up the paper. It read: "YOU KRAUTS, WE KNOW YOU'RE HERE ON GREENLAND. ENJOY THE WEATHER UP THERE WHILE YOU CAN. IT WON'T BE LONG."

"Herr Hauptmann?"

Dietrich crumpled the paper. "It means nothing. They don't know *where* we are on Greenland. How could they? This is just a provocation, that's all." He turned to Wolff for confirmation. "It means nothing, does it?"

Wolff held out his hand for the message, unfolded it, then tossed it into the stove. "No, they know nothing. The patrols they sent out to locate this base . . . never returned."

Dietrich was still sufficiently concerned that he reported the incident through Tromsø, asking if the station perhaps ought to be evacuated in light of the enemy threats. The response from the Reich Meteorological Service was vague. It was doubtful that the resources necessary to evacuate Weather Group Flieger would be available before April, at the earliest.

He read the reply and followed Wolff's example by throwing it on the fire, saying nothing. There was no use worrying the men.

But another message came from the Amis the next day. And the next. Each one threatening the German weather base.

Keeping it from the men was impossible. They all knew. And they all, except for Klostermann, kept looking to Wolff to meet this new threat.

Wolff took advantage of the opportunity to get out of the cabin and conduct what he called regular patrols of the region around the station. However much he hated it, it was still necessary to keep up the pretense of being a German officer. At least until he heard from Kessler again, he needed access to the radio.

He kept hoping that Klostermann might take the opportunity to follow him, to spy on his alleged spying activities, but some instinct in the pilot must have warned him. Wolff could never find the opportunity to take him, alone and unobserved. His hunger had once again reached the point where it was a constant struggle to keep it under control. One wrong move from Klostermann, one unguarded moment—but there were always too many men inside the weather hut, there was always someone awake and on duty.

Instead he encountered Köbler, hurrying to the storage shack for supplies. Wolff slipped inside behind him. The cook looked back, saw him, and uttered a choked gasp of shock and surprise as the door slammed shut, leaving him in the dark.

The scent of the man's fear made Wolff tremble slightly with the force of his need. The knife was in his hand. But he hesitated. This killing hadn't been planned. Would the Germans accept another mysterious disappearance? They'd seen the American's body, the knife wound in the throat; they knew how he killed. If they saw the body, he wouldn't be able to explain this death away as enemy action or an animal attack. For a moment—while the cook begged and whimpered that he'd done nothing wrong, nothing, oh, please, Hauptsturmführer— Wolff damned Klostermann and his suspicious interference. Perhaps it might be better to let Köbler go and wait for the opportunity to take the pilot. But his hunger decided otherwise, roused to the breaking point by the nearness of the heartbeat racing with fear.

Glancing around the storeroom, he saw the bottles of brandy on a shelf. Cheap stuff, only good enough to warm a soldier's belly. But some soldiers were weak, especially a cook, with regular access to the stores. Wolff took down a bottle and pulled out the cork. "Relax. Wouldn't you like a drink, Köbler?" he invited.

"N . . . no, please," the cook stammered, but Wolff had him by the collar, was forcing open his mouth, pouring in the thick, near-frozen liquor until the man choked on it. Then he let the bottle fall, filling the enclosed space with the ripe aroma.

Good enough. Now, get it over with.

Tearing open Köbler's coat and the uniform beneath it, he drove the thin blade of his knife into the man's chest, just pricking the heart enough to make the blood spurt hard from the wound. He fed quickly, holding his bloodlust in control, finally feeling the need fade. Then it was over, almost too soon, but perhaps just as well. Someone might come looking for the missing cook.

He wiped the gore from his face and refastened the dead man's clothes. In a moment a dark spot of blood seeped through the uniform. Pulling out his Walther, the metal cold even to his touch, he fired at the mark. Then he kicked open the door and was finished reholstering the weapon when they ran out to see what had happened.

The Germans surrounded him, staring in shocked disbelief at the sight of the body lying sprawled on the storehouse floor. Dietrich turned on him furiously, but Wolff met his eyes and the captain choked off his protest.

"It was sabotage. You can see the evidence, there."

Dietrich regained his voice. "A bottle of *brandy?* You could shoot a man for that?"

"Theft is theft," Wolff snapped, his voice as hard as that of any genuine SS officer. "The man was drunk on duty. And when I confronted him, he cursed the Führer for abandoning him here. I believe you know the penalty for that."

Breathing hard, Dietrich shook his head, clenched his fists. For a moment Wolff thought he was going to protest, to do something, and he braced himself. But a moment later Dietrich turned away, back to the cabin. Reluctantly, the rest of the Germans followed him. Klostermann looked back once, the hate naked and open on his face.

But they did nothing. In the end, the SS uniform had stopped them again.

The last man went back inside, and Wolff flung his head back in relief. He hadn't dared walk away; turn his back on them. They'd accepted the killing for the moment, while they were still in shock, but he knew he hadn't really gotten away with this one. He should have waited for a better opportunity, should have had better control of his damnable needs.

He clenched his fists, cursing Oberführer Kessler. His time was running short. He didn't want to go back there into the station where the Germans might be waiting for him, but he knew there was no other choice, not as long as he needed the radio to contact Kessler.

Greenland had become a trap.

* * *

There was another funeral, this time only a grave dug out of the snow. It was all they could do for poor Köbler. Later, in the spring, they could make him a better resting place. If they were still on Greenland when the snow melted.

Wederling would tell stories from his time on the eastern front, about the bodies emerging from the melting snow when spring came in Russia, how you might almost think they'd died yesterday. "You'd see just a hand at first —" he began, but Dietrich snapped at him to be quiet. That kind of thing wasn't what they needed right now.

Wolff didn't attend the burial. A couple of the men whispered to each other that he didn't dare show his face.

When the service had been read and the cross pushed down into the mound of snow, Klostermann took the opportunity to pull Dietrich aside. "We've got to do something."

The captain went to his pocket for a cigarette, pulled off his gloves to light it. The orange tip glowed in the gray darkness. "What can we do?"

"Stop him! Kill him, if we have to."

"For what? Executing a traitor? The SS shoot or hang a hundred men a day back at home."

"And whose word to do we have for that? Think of it! Listen, what if it was really something else. What if Köbler found him doing . . . something he didn't want us to know about? The brandy, the treason business — that's just an excuse!"

Dietrich shook his head. "You're imagining things."

"Well, what about those messages we've been getting from the Amis? How do you think they know about us, where to find us? What do you think Wolff's been sending out in those secret transmissions of his? Think about it! The threats didn't start coming in until after he got back. And where *was* he all that time?"

Dietrich took a long drag on his cigarette. It always came back to that. Where did Wolff go? How did he survive? "You haven't got proof. Listen, I have a family at home. When I get back, I want them to be there waiting for me. I don't want to have the neighbors telling me the Gestapo came in the night and took them off to some KZ in Poland."

"He's sabotaging the station," Klostermann insisted. "He's killing us off, one by one." He paused. "Just think of Köbler's family. Of Weber's. Think about what happens when they never come home."

Dietrich turned pale, saying nothing, and Klostermann said quickly, "I'm sorry, Martin, I didn't . . ."

But Dietrich flung the butt of his cigarette down into the snow, where it hissed briefly as the orange light died. He went back to the cabin without another word, without looking back.

Chapter Twenty-seven

A wolf in a trap would chew off its own paw to escape, but Wolff wasn't as desperate as that.

The situation: he needed to get off Greenland as soon as possible, at least before sunrise at the end of February. He had to contact Kessler by radio to arrange the pickup. Until then, at least, he had to leave the weather group transmitting as proof that they were still alive.

But they were already too suspicious. He didn't know how much longer he could keep concealing what he was, and then they would turn on him. He had to get away from the station, and that meant a radio of his own.

He knew he had to have help. Manstein was the better of the radio technicians, of the survivors, but Wolff wasn't sure if he could trust him. Mundt was a better choice — young, an ardent Nazi and accustomed to taking orders. Mundt should have been in the SS. Well, now he'd have his chance, or close to it.

He made his approach at the end of the radioman's duty shift. "Mundt, I'd like to talk to you alone. A matter of security. I believe I can trust *you*."

Apprehension was replaced by immediate pride. Mundt stiffened to attention and stuck his arm out in a salute. "Of course, Hauptsturmführer!"

"Good. Get your coat. We'll go outside."

They stepped away from the hut for privacy, and Wolff kept his voice low. "You understand that I was sent here to preserve the security of this base. My orders came from the highest authority. You know what that means."

"Yes, Hauptsturmführer!"

"Good. And you know that traitors can be anywhere. You remember July 20th."

The mention of the assassination attempt on Hitler was enough to convince Mundt. His face glowed with patriotic fervor.

"Then you understand that from time to time I have to send and receive certain transmissions that may have to be kept secret from the other members of the weather group, even from your commanding officer."

"You don't suspect Hauptmann Dietrich?"

"The lesson of July 20th is that we must suspect *everyone*. Always."

"You can count on me," Mundt declared. "Any transmission of yours will be secure!"

"Of course. But think, you aren't always on duty."

"Well, I'm sure that Otto—"

Wolff interrupted impatiently. "I believe you have plenty of spare parts for all the radio equipment, isn't this so?"

"Yes, we do."

"Then would it be possible for you to assemble a radio set? A transmitter-receiver?"

Mundt frowned. "Well, I think so. But we do have a spare set already. Don't you remember? We took all the equipment out of the flying boat?"

Wolff briefly shut his eyes. He hadn't remembered. The solution to his problem, there all this time! "It's operable? Would it have enough power to reach, say, Tromsø?"

"Well, you'd need an antenna . . ."

"Mundt, for security reasons, I need this radio. And probably your help getting it operating."

"Of course, Hauptsturmführer!"

It might work. It might very well work. And if it did, then his most immediate problem would be solved!

"Martin, there's a problem."

Dietrich looked up from the typewriter. His fingers were covered with ink, and he wiped them on a rag. "If this is another one of your crazy notions about Wolff—"

Klostermann said in a low voice, "I noticed he's been spending a lot of time lately with Mundt, the radioman. I started to wonder what they were doing, and I remembered the set from my ship. I went to check the storeroom. It's missing."

Dietrich frowned. "You're sure?" And where was Wolff now? Gone again, on one of his mysterious errands. For that matter, where was Mundt?

"Has anyone else used it? I mean, have you authorized anyone?"

"No. I haven't."

"I didn't want to question Mundt until . . ."

"No," Dietrich agreed. He thought for a moment. Manstein was on duty now. He'd always been a loyal Nazi. But no admirer of Wolff, not since Köbler's killing, at least.

He called Busch over to relieve Manstein at the set. "Manstein, have you or anyone been using the radio set we took from Hauptmann Klostermann's seaplane? For any reason?"

"No, Herr Hauptmann. I thought we might use it for spare parts, maybe, but it hasn't been necessary. Why? Is something wrong with it? Do you want me to try to fix it?"

"It's missing."

Manstein looked blank. "I didn't know."

"Tell me, could someone use that set? To send a message?"

"Well, yes. I suppose he could. I don't know about the condition of the battery, though."

225

"One more thing. Have you seen Mundt since you've come on duty?"

"Well . . . I think he could be in his bunk."

"Check," Dietrich ordered.

Klostermann was back in a moment. "He's asleep."

"All right." Dietrich turned to the senior radioman. "I want you to check the rest of your supplies, see what else is missing besides the radio. Wire, tools, that kind of thing."

Manstein saluted, and Dietrich went to his bag for his sidearm, a Luger. He checked the action, methodically loaded the weapon. He should have done this a long time ago, he thought. The rest of the men in the room stared at him. Manstein came up, looking shaken. "Herr Hauptmann, tools are missing, yes, and wire, cable, all kinds of stuff."

Dietrich nodded, standing up; the gun in his hand.

"What is it? What's going on?" Doctor Pflieger demanded, his voice pitched high.

"Sabotage," Dietrich said shortly.

Manstein stared at him. "But, Herr Hauptmann, you don't mean that Richard—"

"He'll have a chance to explain himself." Dietrich strode into the bunkroom. He hadn't decided to do this, he was simply acting under an imperative that was revealing itself to him, moment by moment. There were two or three men asleep, but Dietrich went directly to Mundt's bunk, tore off his blanket with one hand, the other holding the gun.

Mundt came awake with a furious yell, was halfway to his feet when he saw who it was, and the gun pointed at him. He froze with his mouth open and no sound coming out.

"Stand up," Dietrich said coldly. "You're under arrest."

Astonishment, shock, guilt—Mundt's face struggled not to show his reaction. Then his jaw clamped down, his face went stiff, and he stood to rigid attention, staring straight forward at the wall.

Dietrich cursed inwardly, recognizing the attitude: remain silent, give nothing away. "Gefreiter Mundt, you are charged with treason: sabotage, theft of vital military supplies, conspiracy with an enemy of the Reich."

Mundt blinked once, but otherwise looked ahead, admitting nothing.

Dietrich raised the gun, put it to the side of Mundt's head. He was astonished at how steady his hand was, how steady and cold his voice was. "You know the penalty. If you have nothing to say in your defense—"

"For God's sake, Richard, Wolff is a spy!" Manstein pleaded. "We've found tools and equipment missing, the radio from the flying boat! Why did you do it? He's killed Köbler, Weber, God knows how many of the rest of them! He's probably the one who told the Amis our location! And you were involved!"

Dietrich noted distantly that Klostermann's conspiracy theory seemed to have spread at least as far as Manstein. None of the other men in the room seemed to dispute it. His hand never moved. He continued to hold the gun to Mundt's head as the radioman's eyes went to Manstein, back to him, to the rest of the men standing silent and staring in the doorway. Mundt's breathing was coming harder now. He swallowed, wet his lips.

"I . . ." Mundt turned his eyes—not his head—back to Dietrich, whose expression was hard, unmoving. He blinked rapidly. "He said . . . he told me . . . it was a matter of security. Anyone might be a traitor. He said to tell no one . . ."

His head turned now to Manstein, to Wederling, Rohde, pleading to be understood. "You don't really think . . . Weber was a defeatist! You all heard what he said!"

It was Klostermann who replied, "Who else but a spy would want a secret transmitter? What else is it but sabotage to steal equipment from the station? How else do you think the Amis knew to send those threats?"

Mundt started to shake his head, stopped when he felt the hard cold pressure of the gun. Slowly, Dietrich pulled it back away.

"I didn't know. I swear. He told me . . . I was the only one he could trust. I thought . . . I was obeying orders."

"Who is your commanding officer?" Dietrich demanded pitilessly, speaking for the first time since Mundt started to confess.

"He's SS," Mundt said weakly. "I thought . . ."

Dietrich lowered his gun, allowing himself to feel relief. He would never know, now, if he could have pulled the trigger. He was afraid he might have done it. He hoped he would never have another opportunity to find out.

But he had his evidence. At last. "So you admit that you conspired with SS Hauptsturmführer Wolff to steal the spare radio, along with other equipment vital to the operation of this station?"

Mundt nodded wordlessly, stunned by the shock of discovering what he'd done. All his life he'd trained, worked to defend the Reich. He would have given his life for his Führer. And now he was the traitor, he was the one conspiring with the enemy.

Even as he pressed his advantage, apart of Dietrich still felt sorry for Mundt. Now that he no longer needed the witnesses, he ordered them out of the bunkroom, all except Manstein and Klostermann. "Tell me, Gefreiter, how familiar is Hauptsturmführer Wolff with radio equipment?"

"I . . . don't know. I don't think—"

Dietrich looked to Manstein. "Could he set up that radio? Get it working?"

"I don't think so. He never seemed familiar with the equipment, the technical details. Whenever he sent something out, he always had us handle the transmission."

"Then he'd need help." To Mundt, "Did he ask you for help setting up the radio?"

228

"He said, if he needed, he might ask me."

Dietrich looked hard at Mundt, standing there miserably, opening and closing his big, capable hands. It would be the word of a frightened nineteen-year-old technician against a man wearing the uniform of an officer in the SS. A confession coerced at gunpoint. He knew, with a sure certainly, that Mundt was telling the truth. But how far could he count on him?

"What if he came back here and asked you to go with him?"

"But—"

"We need evidence that he's actually using the radio to contact the enemy. He can't be transmitting from here. We have to find out where he took it. We need you to lead us there. Your cooperation is essential, you see. It would help prove that your intentions weren't treasonable, that he was only using you."

"Yes!" With a choking voice, Mundt grasped at the chance held out to him, the only hope he could see for redemption.

"Good. For now, you'll resume your usual duties. I want everything to appear normal when Wolff comes back again. If he asks you to go with him, agree. Exactly as you would have done. Do you understand? I don't want any heroics, any stupid moves. Just go with him, find out where he goes."

He went to issue orders to the rest of them: ignore Wolff as usual, pretend nothing was wrong. He turned to find Klostermann looking at him with a peculiar expression.

"You don't think it would be better just to arrest him the minute he comes back?"

Dietrich shook his head. Somehow he couldn't see Wolff submitting to arrest. "I'm sure Mundt was telling the truth, but still, all of this doesn't quite add up. Why would Wolff steal a radio *now* if he'd been in contact with the enemy all this time?"

"His own transmitter broke down."

"Maybe."

"He *did* steal the radio. And the other things. There's no doubt. What else do we need?"

"Remember, I've queried his credentials with Berlin twice. His mission here was authorized *at the highest level*. Think what that means. Look, it's only a spare radio from a wrecked aircraft, a few tools, some meters of wire. He might even have sufficient reason for taking it—secret orders—I don't know. If we were in Germany, I'd have enough evidence to press charges, at least an investigation. But here—don't you see, I can't just arrest him. He's dangerous. Too dangerous for us to take a chance. For what I need to do I need more proof. There can't be the slightest doubt. For all our sakes."

Chapter Twenty-eight

Wolff seethed with frustration. He'd been born in a day when it could take a fast messenger on horseback ten days to ride from Belgrade to Vienna. Now there was radio communication in no time at all, across impassable distances. If only the damnable equipment would *work!*

He sat on the floor of the primitive hunter's shelter and glared at the dials and gauges and switches. He was using the right frequency, he was sure of that much, but all he could bring in was static. Mundt had said something about the antenna.

Wolff stood up angrily, brushing the dirt off his clothes. This was clearly job for a craftsman—technician, someone who concerned himself with this sort of thing. He would have to bring Mundt, after all.

He considered the difficulties as he strapped on his snowshoes. The dead American's little sled had been quite useful hauling the radio and its battery to his shelter. It would have helped to have another pair of snowshoes, but he supposed skis would have to do for Mundt. The Germans selected for duty in the Arctic were all supposed to be competent on skis.

If Mundt could get the radio working, get him in contact with Kessler, then he could abandon Weather Station Flieger while he waited for evacuation from Greenland. No more being watched every moment, waiting for an opportunity to make his kills unobserved, rushing through the business like he had with that cook. The thought of getting the radioman out here where no one could interfere was another incentive. Mundt was young and healthy, with a fine, strong heart. His blood would sustain him while he was waiting to hear from Kessler.

As always now, the Germans went silent and looked away when he arrived back at the weather station. They resented Köbler's execution. He knew it had been a mistake, had known it from the moment he wiped the blood from his face. His hunger overriding his judgment again.

Dietrich especially seemed cold, formal and distant. "I see that you're back again, Hauptsturmführer."

Wolff bowed coldly. "As you know, there's a problem with the security of the base, enemy threats coming in over the radio. I'm attempting to deal with it."

"Of course."

"And have there been more messages from the Americans while I was gone?"

"They say they hope we have better air-raid shelters than they had in Berlin. Have you seen Berlin lately, Hauptsturmführer?"

"Defeatist talk only serves the enemy," Wolff snapped in his SS voice. Not for the first time, he observed that the station's commander smoked too much. The man was under some strain. Well, Dietrich should be pleased when he was relieved of his presence.

Mundt was on duty at the radio, more pale and quiet than normal. Wolff frowned. He wondered if there were something wrong.

He had written a brief note: *"When you get off duty, meet me at the head of the path down to the beach. Wear your outdoor gear and bring your skis. Remember, you are doing this for the Führer himself. Heil Hitler! Wolff"*

He handed it to Mundt saying briefly, "A transmission." Soon afterward he left the cabin again, without a word to anyone. On the way, he met Klostermann coming from the latrine with his copilot Busch, and he cursed the lost opportunity. But their time would come. Wolff had no intention of prolonging Mundt's suffering much more than necessary, but Klostermann — that was another matter entirely. It was personal now between him and the seaplane pilot. Klostermann was going to be sorry one day that he'd been so unwise in his choice of enemies.

Wolff heard the sound of someone approaching, and he cautiously stepped back from the head of the path, where he had told Mundt to meet him. The boy was carrying his skis and poles, following orders. Good.

He came out of the darkness of a shadow into the moonlight, startling Mundt. "Hauptsturmführer?"

"I'm here."

"Your note. Do you want me to set up the radio for you, then?"

Wolff frowned again. Mundt sounded nervous — why? "Is there some problem? Some more equipment that you need?"

"No, it's . . . how far away do we have to go? I'll need to be back to go on duty again at 1800 hours."

"Don't worry," Wolff assured him. "It will be on my authority. Now, get your skis on. We'll be going overland."

Mundt looked very dubious and unhappy. He made no comment about Wolff's snowshoes, although his skis tended to sink under him in the deep loose drifts. At this rate, they were certainly going to be hours reaching the shelter, not to mention how long it would take to get the radio working. Wolff supposed he was going to have to invoke the name of the Führer again to keep the radioman long enough to get the set operational.

Damn! Mundt did it again — slowed down, glancing back. "Is something wrong?" Wolff demanded

"No," he said quickly. Too quickly. Wolff caught the fear scent then.

He stopped, turned the full force of his eyes on Mundt. "What is it? Tell me. Now."

"They know! They found out about the missing equipment! The captain made me tell him—"

"About me? *You told him about me?*"

Mundt stammered, "They said . . . you were a spy!"

But Wolff ignored him, spinning around, cursing the bright moonlight. Yes, there they were, dropping down behind the peak of a drift. *Following* him!

A shot rang out, another, and as Wolff started for cover he felt the searing pang of a bullet striking him just below the right shoulder—too close, too close!

Mundt had dropped to the ground, and Wolff grabbed him, dragged him bodily to his feet, holding him as a shield. "Throw down your guns," he shouted, "or the boy dies!"

To emphasize the threat, he wrenched Mundt's neck until he cried out in pain. "How many of them?" he demanded in a whisper, fighting for control. The blood loss, the pain in his shoulder were maddening. He could feel every pulse of Mundt's heart, pounding in terror against his own body, he could almost taste the sweat, the scent of the fear soaking though his skin.

"I don't know!" Mundt gasped, utterly sincere in his fright and pain. "They never told me they were going to follow us, I didn't know, I swear it, oh please, *don't!*"

"Let him go, Wolff!"

Dietrich. Wolff cursed aloud. There was a dark stain spreading on his white parka—his own blood. He couldn't let Mundt go now. Not alive. To discourage them, he fumbled one-handed for the Walther and fired off a shot, but the little automatic had no range, and his pursuers had rifles. And at least one of them was a good enough shot to have hit him in this light.

He pulled Mundt up closer against him, took a step backward, and stumbled over his damnable skis! He pulled them both down, harshly ordering, "Get them off! Now!"

Mundt fumbled with the bindings, gasping for breath. As soon as he kicked off the second ski, Wolff pulled him up again, but Mundt spun suddenly, driving an elbow into Wolff's chest where the dark stain marked him vulnerable. Wolff's breath exploded in a groan of pain and he felt something crack inside. His grip weakened. Mundt struck again.

The young German outweighed him by twenty kilos and was easily the fittest man on the base, besides being trained to kill in combat. Wolff folded. Mundt broke free and started to run back toward Dietrich and the others. Beyond, they were emerging from cover, shouting for Mundt to run. One of them raised his weapon, and Wolff desperately rolled to free the Walther, fired — once, twice — the rifleman's aim went wild.

Wolff's vision was washed crimson with bloodlust and pain. A dozen meters away, his prey was escaping, the blood he needed, needed now. But Mundt was foundering in the waist-deep snow. A bullet exploded in the snow less than a meter from him, but Wolff lunged, the pain clawing his ribs despite his superhuman strength. As a second shot sped over his head he brought his victim down.

Mundt rolled with the impact, ready to fight, but Wolff was beyond caring for his own pain, and he overpowered the German, striking for the throat, feeling the cartilage of the trachea collapse under his hand.

"Don't shoot!" he heard distantly from the Germans as he got his good arm under Mundt's shoulders and staggered to his feet beneath the weight of the body. Mundt's struggles were convulsive now, he was fighting to breathe through his broken throat, but his heart would beat for a while yet. Long enough, Wolff hoped, almost overwhelmed by his need for blood.

His wound wasn't life-threatening, not for one of his kind, but the blood loss would slow his healing. His body was screaming with need. And he had to fight it with every fibre of his will, to concentrate on his enemies.

They wouldn't fire, not as long as he had his hostage. He still was holding the Walther, though his arm was tiring. "Come on," he grunted, dragging Mundt's heaving body through the snow. "Come on."

In the sky, a few shreds of cloud obscured the stars and began to dim the brightness of the crescent moon.

Two more steps backward. Three more steps. "Come *on*."

Chapter Twenty-nine

"What are we going to do now?"

Dietrich stared out across the gray snowfield, illuminated by the bright thin moon. No more than five hundred meters away Wolff labored, dragging the burden of his hostage backward through the drifts. Mundt was still alive, he still seemed to be struggling, with his hands tearing at his throat, trying to break Wolff's hold.

Wederling had casually volunteered for this mission with the information that he'd once earned a marksman's award. He was now lying prone in the snow, no doubt with Wolff's figure in his sights. But for Mundt's sake they couldn't risk the shot.

"We go after him."

The Germans picked themselves up from the snow and started in pursuit. Dietrich scowled at the sky. As long as the moon was still shining they ought to be able to keep Wolff in sight. His only weapon was a handgun, and there were three of them with rifles. The snowfield here offered scant cover, except for the drifts, but Wolff was clearly heading for the slope where the terrain was more broken, a gorge running between parallel ridges down toward the fjord.

Wederling muttered an oath. "I was sure I hit him!"

"He's not human," Klostermann said through clenched teeth, awkward on his skis.

Dietrich glanced back at him, then back down at the tracks left by Wolff. "He's not on skis. I think those are snowshoes."

"Here!" exclaimed Wederling, kneeling down to a dark stain on the snow. "I *knew* I hit him!"

But Dietrich frowned at Wolff's ever more distant figure. Maybe the blood was Mundt's. It was impossible that Wolff could keep on that way if he were hit. Even on snowshoes. "Come on," he urged the others, setting off again. "He can't get far."

He couldn't. It just wasn't possible, not with him dragging another man all that way, a man the size of Mundt.

Dietrich blinked. For a moment he'd lost sight of his quarry. No, there he was, even further away now, almost into the gorge.

Damn Wolff! Klostermann and Wederling were panting behind him, leaning forward on the poles of their skis. His own breath was coming hard, taking the frigid air in burning lungs. He gasped, "We're losing him!" and tried to pick up his pace.

The darkness was gathering around them, visibility steadily diminishing as the clouds built up. But Wolff had to be tiring too. He was heading for cover, that was obvious. Probably trying to lead them into a trap. Dietrich slowed, signaled the others to spread out, be careful. Wolff was dangerous, but he couldn't get away, not with the tracks he was leaving, dragging Mundt.

He couldn't get away—but where *was* he? Damn! Gone without even a trace!

"Over here!"

Klostermann shouting from over among some rocks, waving his arms. Dietrich's heart went heavy with dread, and he saw in his mind the image of the American with the single, deep wound in his throat.

It was Mundt, sprawled among the rocks. The same single gash in his throat, the black stain of blood in the snow—it was hard to make out much more with the moon's crescent so vague and dim behind the clouds. It was clear: now that he'd reached cover, Wolff had no more need for his hostage. Dietrich reached down to close the staring eyes. It suddenly occurred to him that the advantage had shifted to the other side, that Wolff was nowhere in sight, that he was armed. Uneasily, he remembered all the American patrols Wolff claimed to have wiped out while he was alone out on the ice, all the mysterious deaths at the weather station.

He wasn't alone in his misgivings. Wederling whispered, "Herr Hauptmann, maybe we should go back. We've lost him."

Dietrich shook his head. "He can't have gone far. We can still follow his tracks. This hiding place of his can't be too far from the station."

"It can't be," Klostermann echoed, but there was doubt in his voice.

"Careful," Dietrich repeated in a whisper. He stood up on his skis. They were cumbersome here in this broken terrain. In some places the snow didn't cover the outcropping stone, in others it lay drifted meters deep. Klostermann kept stumbling, falling, foundering in the drifts. They finally took them off, carrying skis and poles with one hand, rifles with the other — awkward. And on foot they were constantly breaking through the snow, waist-deep in most places.

Wolff's trail was harder to follow now. On the snowshoes he rarely broke through the upper surface of the snow, and it was clear that he was using the exposed outcrops to confuse his pursuers. As the trail descended, the rocks rose above their heads on either side, cutting off what moonlight there still was. Dietrich paused and realized that he was afraid. He was descending into a place of shadows, deep and dark.

He no longer knew where he was, where he was going. Wolff was leading them, knowing they were behind him. Leading them into an ambush in the confined, dark space of the ravine where his handgun would have the advantage over their rifles.

Wederling had been right. He turned back to the others. "We can't follow him in here. We've got to go back." His voice was harsh with the bitterness of failure. And worse, they were going to have to backtrack, following their own trail, because Wolff had led them far astray, outrun them, outmaneuvered them, almost led them into a trap. Now they were lost in the dark, hours away from the base without any camping gear, no choice but to keep going until they got back.

The slope made it harder going, too, pushing their way through the snow, up and up. And Klostermann was stumbling now with almost every step, covered with a crust of white. Dietrich took the lead, pulling him up after, seeing the other man's face so close, visibly pale even in this light with pain and fatigue.

He called out ahead for Wederling to halt and stopped where a flat black rock cropped out from the snow, shoved Klostermann down onto it. "What is it? What's wrong?"

"Don' know. Feet. Can't . . . feel anything," he panted. "Thought I was in shape for this." Pushing him back on the rock, Dietrich started to remove his boots, despite the protests. Then he whispered an oath. Snow had drifted into the boots. It was packed there, caked, melted and refrozen. He peeled off Klostermann's damp socks, which froze stiff as soon as they were exposed to the air.

This was bad. He started to beat the socks against the rock, to knock off the frozen moisture, but it was no good. Desperately he pulled off his heavy coat, his uniform coat, the thick sweater underneath, clenching his teeth against the sting of the frigid air, but thinking all the time how much worse it must be for those frozen feet. With a knife, he ripped the sleeves off his undershirt, folded them in half, and slipped them over Klostermann's feet, folding the ends up, the best he could do, finally easing the boots back on. Best he could do.

Then, quickly as possible, back into his clothes.

"Thanks," Klostermann said weakly, with a pained grin.

Dietrich knew they should keep moving, try to get the circulation going again in Klostermann's feet, but just for a moment he sat down on the rock next to him. It was still hard to catch his breath after the climb, and he wanted a cigarette.

Suddenly he looked around, and his heart was seized with panic. Wederling. Where was he? *Where was he?*

He shouted out loud, "Wederling! Feldwebel! Where are you? Wederling?"

There was no response. Dietrich felt cold dread, and this time he knew what it was.

"What's wrong?"

"Wederling. He was ahead of us, up the slope, when we stopped. Now . . ."

He didn't want to say it. Maybe he'd fallen, maybe he'd gone too far to hear him calling. But the sense of dread only grew. "Come on. We have to find him."

He helped Klostermann to his feet, wondering how the other man could even stand. They started back up the slope. Every few minutes Dietrich would stop and call out Wederling's name again, but there was never a response.

Wolff. The American's body. Mundt. Lying there. The wound in the throat.

Then—"What's that?"

They both raised their heads. Dietrich tore back the hood of his parka so he could hear. The low, vibrating drone—a plane. He whispered a curse. *"No, God, no."*

Klostermann had heard it, too. The sound was getting louder, closer. It might be a German plane. It was possible. Let it be a German plane, please.

Their heads were back, staring into the sky, but there was nothing to see but clouds, darkness relieved only by the dim blurred light of the moon. Still the sound of the propellers kept building, echoing now off the mountains across the fjord, high, high above them. Klostermann whispered, "A Catalina," and Dietrich's heart sank as he recognized the sound and knew the other pilot was right—an American reconnaissance seaplane. It was circling, searching. And a moment later, as if they were being moved by the hand of some inimical god, the clouds shifted overhead, the thin crescent of the moon grew more bright and distinct, the shadows of the rocks standing out stark now against the light sparkling ground of the snow.

"No."

But the whispered prayers of the Germans were ignored, the sound of the engines grew even louder until they could make out the shape of the aircraft against the stars, circling over what they knew was the weather base. And louder yet, changing in tone, deepening, multiplying until it could only be one thing, and Dietrich whispered with a mouth dried in horror: *"Viermots!"* A flight of the dreaded four-engined American bombers, the long-range B-24's.

Then the pupils of his eyes contracted as the sky lit up like an instant sunrise, flares falling slowly through the air, illuminated the target. And the bombers closed in on it, the weather station—helpless, defenseless.

The earth seemed to shake as the first bombs hit, the snow on the slope above them shivered, and both of the Germans were climbing desperately then, on hands and knees in some places, anything to get to the top of the slope, to see. There was an orange glow in the east, the fire already raging with such an intensity it was obvious the enemy had used incendiaries. *No!* The mind recoiled in denial, but it was already over, the sound of the engines receding from the scene of destruction.

If Wederling were still alive, if he'd seen this, he'd already be heading back to the base. If not—Dietrich froze for a moment in agonized indecision, then turned east. The fire marked their way much more clearly than their tracks. Desperation, the need to get back, masked cold and exhaustion as long as possible. The mocking tone of the American radio messages ran constantly through Dietrich's head. This was what they'd meant. An air strike. Total destruction. Like Berlin.

But Klostermann was dropping back, starting to fall more often. Dietrich knew he had to slow down. "Go on," Klostermann urged him, his breaths rasping painfully as he stood, bent over his skis. "Go on . . . I'll make it."

But he wouldn't, Dietrich knew. Not by himself. "Come on, Erich," he urged. "We can keep going. Not so fast. Come on."

The fire licked at the sky. The weather base was burning. *Come on. Have to get back.*

Chapter Thirty

The pain receded, and Wolff's wound had started to heal. Mundt's blood had done it, but he'd been almost dead by the time Wolff got to cover, far enough ahead of his pursuit that he dared stop for long enough to take it. His hunger, though, was still alive, bloodlust stimulated but not sated by the hurried feeding. It was a dangerous condition. The Germans were still close behind him, but with the worst of the pain gone from his shoulder, he had the advantage again. Concealed among the rocks at the bottom of the gorge, he heard their voices as they discovered their dead.

He rested a while, feeling his strength return to him, waiting to see what they'd do. Then he grinned, a predator, as he heard them start to come down the slope after him, following his tracks. He hadn't believed Dietrich was such a fool.

Now he would take the offensive. At this point, the walls of the gorge were almost sheer. Unstrapping the snowshoes, Wolff sprang up, grabbing onto a ledge of rock, and began to climb to the top of the ridge. Let them try to track him now!

The Germans were having a hard time of it with their skis. Klostermann especially. Wolff watched their progress closer and closer, letting his bloodlust rise, and the urge for rest faded. His fingertips played with the cold metal edge of his knife.

He saw Dietrich stop and look around, staring wide-eyed

into the shadows surrounding him. The German captain was weary, and Wolff could scent his fear. Another twenty meters, and he'd be directly below him.

No, he was turning back. Wolff crept and climbed up along the top of the ridge, stalking the slow exhausted progress of the Germans back up the slope. Their skis were off now, they were carrying them. Awkward. And Klostermann didn't look like he could make it. Yes, he was down again. Dietrich caught up to him, pulled him to his feet, half carried him to an outcropping while calling up to Wederling that they were going to have to stop.

And Wederling, furthest up the slope, looked back down, then headed for a closer ledge to rest, sat there, laying aside his cumbersome skis. Wolff sprang from above him, knocking his victim into the soft silence of the snowbank, holding him there face down while he struggled, suffocating, half-drowning in the snow.

Quickly, but with less urgency than with Mundt, he drove his blade into the soldier's neck, pressed his mouth avidly to the spurting blood, sating himself with it, feeling the strength flowing into him, the heat, the life.

He was finished by the time he heard Dietrich suddenly calling Wederling's name, panic in his voice. Wolff grinned, and in a minute he'd buried the body in the bank beneath the shadow of the ledge. *Two down.*

He paused, turned. He heard . . . something. Distant, but coming closer. He recognized the sound of the aircraft almost at the same moment as the Germans first heard it, not understanding at first, not until he heard the approach of the bombers and saw the flares drop to mark their target.

No!

But there was nothing he could do against the destruction from the air. He was as helpless as the two Germans.

He followed them back toward the flames where the weather station had been, keeping out of sight, cursing the Americans.

The devastation was appalling. By the time the Germans arrived, the fire was already dying down, extinguished in part by the melted snow. The antenna tower had been reduced to a few carbonized stubs. A foul black pall of smoke lay over everything, but beneath it Wolff could smell the distasteful odor of burned human flesh.

Dietrich and Klostermann were searching the ruins for survivors or the bodies of the dead. It was the dead they found—charred, contorted figures with the flesh of their faces seared away to the bone, mouths open in grotesque screams. Dietrich's face was black with smoke, and streaked with tears, as he found one more body, then another.

Wolff came on one dead man sprawled in the snow not too far from the ruin of the tower, this one not visibly burned, but there was a dark splattered stain of blood in the snow and one arm torn almost completely away by a cannon shell, evidence that the enemy had strafed the area, too. He turned the corpse over for a look at its face and recognized the weather technician named Rohde.

They're all dead. Wolff realized that he was stranded here on the uninhabited east coast of Greenland, with only two living human beings. Impelled by a sudden sense of panic, he searched the area with a new urgency, straining all his senses for the scent, the sound of a living man. There was no one.

Two survivors. Two of them left out of fifteen men. And one of them, Klostermann, with frostbite. Thoughts of vengeance had disappeared, driven out by the imperatives of survival.

They'd recovered three of the bodies, laid them out side by side. Rohde's was a fourth. Wolff supposed the other two were still inside the burning wreckage of the cabin. They'd have to wait till the flames died down to dig them out. Well, there was no time for that nonsense.

He picked up Rohde's corpse. Dietrich heard the sound of his footsteps on the snow, looked up, and a disbelieving rage mixed with the grief on his face. "You!"

Wolff saw him reaching for the Luger under his coat, and he tossed down the corpse, sprang, pinned his wrist in a cold unbreakable grip. Dietrich winced with the pain as the automatic fell to the snow.

"Before you do something you might regret," Wolff said coldly, "perhaps we'd better discuss how matters stand, considering that we may have a mutual interest in survival now."

"Damn you!" Dietrich gasped as the pressure of Wolff's hold increased.

Wolff laughed shortly. "Oh, I assure you, that matter is already taken care of." Seeing Klostermann on the ground edging cautiously toward a nearby rifle, he added, "Don't move. I can break his neck as easily as I can break his arm."

Klostermann's hand fell, he looked from the gun back up to Wolff. "Good. All right, I think we have to clear up a few misunderstandings before we can proceed.

"In the first place," he nodded toward Rohde's body, "you might have been thinking that I killed that man. I didn't. As you can see, he was hit by one of the planes, strafing the ground. The Amis seem to have been thorough."

"Thanks to you!" Dietrich said through clenched teeth.

Wolff shook his head. "No. I had nothing to do with this. It's time for the truth, I think. I took the radio and equipment, just as you learned from Gefreiter Mundt. And I did kill the rest of your men, all but your navigator, Ziegler. He seems to have managed to fall off the cliff by himself."

They were staring at him. He met Dietrich's eyes. "Do you think I can let go now?"

The captain nodded slowly, then rubbed his wrist as Wolff released it. He made no move to pick up his Luger from the snow. "Why?" he asked finally.

"I had my own reasons for killing your men. We may discuss them some other time, but they have nothing to do with the present situation. As for the radio, I was attempting to reach my contact in the SS. My presence here was exactly for the reasons you were told—to eliminate the American dogsled patrols, to make sure your Führer got the right weather information to plan his great counteroffensive. The original plan to was take me off Greenland once this mission was accomplished, but more than one plan has gone wrong this winter, isn't it so?"

Dietrich shook his head, not quite grasping it all. He stared at the burning wreckage of his base. "Then how did the Amis know we were here?"

"How they found this place? I don't really know. Perhaps they homed in on your transmissions. But I didn't contact them. You have my word."

Dietrich stared at him in disbelief, and Wolff went on impatiently, "The point is, I do have that radio. The three of us are stranded here together, whether we like it or not. And he . . ." pointing to Klostermann, "isn't likely to last very long in his condition unless something is done. So for the moment I suggest we concentrate on our mutual survival."

Dietrich looked down at Klostermann with a twinge of distress. "It's his feet. Snow got into his boots."

Wolff exhaled impatiently and looked once more around the compound area, cursing the bombers for their excessive zeal in destruction. Klostermann needed shelter, and the only structure remotely intact was the balloon shed. The cabin was still blazing, the storehouse was a red-hot glowing heap of scrap—there'd been fuel stored inside, and one hit had probably sent it up. For the moment the fires were giving off a welcome glow of heat, but it wouldn't last.

"I have a shelter a certain distance from here—" He scowled as Klostermann mumbled, "Knew it," "—and we can go there. It's somewhat farther than you probably think."

Dietrich's face showed his despair. "Erich can't . . . I don't know how he made it this far."

"I'll take care of that. In the meantime, you find something to melt snow in—for both of you. Take advantage of this fire. And get him up off the snow—you ought to know what to do, they trained you for this climate, didn't they?

Never mind about the dead. They don't need your help anymore."

Just in case, he gathered up the nearby weapons. "I'll be back."

There'd still been good equipment on the American soldier's handmade sled when Wolff had retrieved it to haul the radio back to his hut. He'd taken the snowshoes, but none of the rest — the tent, a good US Army Arctic sleeping bag, the little Primus stove. Priceless, life-saving things for a human in this country, and now he dug the gear out of the snow and hauled it up the steep path.

The American's clothes had been worth saving, too, he recalled, and he went behind what had been the cabin and started to dig up the graves there. The corpses were awkward and stiff, like cold iron, and it was a struggle to get the clothes off the unbending limbs, but Wolff persevered, making particularly sure to get the socks, gloves and boots. He threw the heap of clothing down in front of Dietrich, snapped, "Don't argue about it," before the German captain could open his mouth to protest his robbing the dead.

The sled was still back at his shelter, but it shouldn't be too hard to make another, good enough for the trip back up the fjord. The walls of the balloon shed were still standing. Wolff worked quickly. The result was more along the lines of a travois, but it would do.

Together, they carried Klostermann down the path, got him onto the sled, wrapped in the American sleeping bag. Wolff strapped on his snowshoes, waited while Dietrich got on his skis.

"Just where is this shelter of yours?" the German asked.

Wolff hesitated, fighting his deep-seated instinct for secrecy. "Back at the head of the fjord, near the glacier."

"That far?" Dietrich gasped.

"I found it a convenient location. I didn't care to be disturbed."

It was Wolff who pulled the sled, the snowshoes being better adapted to the task than skis, and the exhausted Dietrich could barely manage to keep up, occasionally leaning down to comfort Klostermann. "It's not much farther, Erich. We'll be there soon."

Wolff, dragging the sled, could see that Dietrich was trying to assure himself as well. He looked back once and said, "There are some rations at the shelter. Another sleeping bag."

And again when he looked to be near collapse, "You can see the glacier up ahead."

But Dietrich shook his head wearily. It all looked the same to him in the dark, an endless stretch of gray, snow and ice under his feet, ahead of him, on all sides of him.

"Come on," Wolff said sharply. "You've got to keep moving."

"You don't . . . ever get tired?"

"Rarely. I find it an advantage in these situations."

Dietrich stared at him, then kept going. Whatever else Wolff might be, he was right, they couldn't stop. The shelter was up ahead. He had to believe it.

And Wolff did bring them to it at last, his hidden place, so low and buried in the snow that it appeared to be no more than a drifted-up part of the ridge above the shoreline. Up to now he'd been careful not to leave a clear trail leading directly from the fjord, and he saw no reason to discard the practice for the sake of the Germans. It proved easier to carry Klostermann than try to help him to walk.

They had to bend over to make it through the snow tunnel and the low entrance. The darkness inside, beneath the thick blanket of snow, was almost absolute, but there were candles and a lantern—even Wolff's eyesight wasn't up to the fine work with the radio with no light at all.

The set lay out on the crude table, surrounded by tools and lengths of wire. Wolff glanced back at the moaning Klostermann in irritation. If only he had the radioman Mundt here with him, instead.

The supplies he'd brought long ago from the weather station were tossed haphazardly into a corner. "Rations over there," he told Dietrich, ignoring his look of utter disbelief as he saw his surroundings revealed in the flare of the candlelight. But the German officer clamped his jaw shut on any remark he might have been about to make.

Good, Wolff thought. "Take care of him. I'll be back later."

There might have been a question in Dietrich's eyes, but he said nothing. Wolff looked regretfully at the inoperative radio and cursed the waste of time, but there was no help for it. He needed these two alive for a while.

He went back out to get the sled and take it back to the burned-out weather base for a load of supplies.

Chapter Thirty-one

For some reason — Dietrich wasn't exactly sure why — but he believed Wolff. "I think it's time for the truth," he'd said. There were still things he wouldn't talk about — the reason he'd killed so many men. "You'll find out, one day," was all he would say, and it wasn't a threat or a warning, just — what would happen. Dietrich never asked what that would mean, if he would die too, eventually. He knew it was more than possible. But questions might lead to answers, and he'd known from the beginning from the expression on Wolff's face that they were answers he wouldn't want to hear.

For a German officer, this was no new experience.

But it was also true that Klostermann would have been dead by now if Wolff hadn't brought them here, that he himself would have had no chance for survival all alone.

He believed Wolff in part because of the radio, the intense, obsessive ferocity of his attempts to get the set operational. Dietrich helped as well as he could, crawling outside to rig up an antenna, shifting its position back and forth. Wolff cursed every hour that the radio refused to function, every hour he considered wasted on some other task, like staying alive.

Dietrich would wake, thick-headed from cold and hunger, and there Wolff would be, still bent over the set, listening, waiting, constantly adjusting the dials.

"Go out and shift the antenna," he'd snap, not even turning around.

"Don't you ever sleep?" Dietrich hadn't intended the question. He wished it unsaid the moment he heard the words.

But Wolff only turned enough to face him. "Not really, no." It was almost a challenge: *Do you want to know why?*

But Dietrich did not. He got on his outdoor gear, crawled out through the snow tunnel and spent the next several hours going back and forth adjusting the patchwork of cable they hoped would bring them into contact with rescue. The hope of rescue was what they had in common, the basis of their truce.

But Wolff's frustration could be savage. He once turned on Klostermann, lifting him up by the front of his coat, "Well, do you still believe I've been out here sending military secrets to the enemy all this time?"

Dietrich braced himself to intervene if he had to, but Wolff just as suddenly let the sick pilot go. Another thing he couldn't understand. Klostermann had been suspicious of Wolff from the beginning, had been the one to find the equipment missing. And yet Wolff, since the bombing, had been concerned for Klostermann's life, had dragged him all this way to the shelter, gone back for supplies to keep him alive. Doing this after killing so many of the other men — a thing he'd admitted almost casually, as if it didn't really matter.

Wolff had left the two of them by themselves after that long, agonizing trek from the bombed-out station. Had simply turned around and disappeared, saying nothing except that he'd be back. Dietrich had been almost too numb with exhaustion to register the shock of finding himself in such a crude and comfortless place. He couldn't believe that this was where Wolff had stayed during his long absences, but here was the stolen radio, the rest of the equipment from the weather base.

There'd been no time to speculate. Klostermann's condition was urgent. The long ride on the sled seemed to have exhausted his reserves. He was cold, certainly suffering from hypothermia, where the body simply lost its ability to regulate its core temperature. And this place of Wolff's, while sheltered from the wind, thickly insulated under its blanket of snow, was cold. Had always been cold. The crude stove looked as if it hadn't been lit in years.

Dietrich got Erich into the bed, a low shelf covered with tattered furs. He found a little wood and lit the stove, got snow to melt — always a long process — and dug through the clutter in the corner for rations. The stove's heat was meager. In his exhaustion, Dietrich came close to tears at the thought of real warmth — a deep tub of hot water, a glowing fireplace, a thick china mug of steaming coffee.

The thought of coffee made him pause once, dig into his pocket for a cigarette. There were three in the case, only three left, and he suddenly laughed in despair, knowing they were probably the last three cigarettes on the east coast of Greenland, the last in the world, as far as he was concerned. But he lit two, put one between Erich's lips and inhaled deeply on the other, cherishing even that little warmth — better than nothing, better than no warmth at all.

The cigarette helped. A little life seemed to come back into Klostermann's face, a little color, from what Dietrich could see in the candlelight. Then he fed him some sweetened warm water, as much food as Dietrich could get into him. It seemed to help.

Dietrich had known he had to do something about thawing Erich's frozen feet. Carefully, he pulled off his boots again, unwrapped them, but the sight of them, even more, the touch of the frozen flesh, brought him again to despair. This wasn't frostbite; they were the feet of a frozen corpse, as rigid, as hard, as lifeless.

He had finally, not knowing what else to do, having exhausted himself and all the possibilities he could think of, laid himself down next to Erich, body to body, wrapped in the same sleeping bags, shivering at the touch of the other man's flesh.

They'd been there together that way, asleep, when Wolff returned, arms full of salvaged supplies including the clothes taken from the bodies of dead men back at the base. All that way and back again, with no rest. To save two men who'd thought he was an enemy spy.

It was clear that Wolff resented every second he spent on their behalf, every moment that took him away from his obsession with the radio. And yet he'd done it, kept them alive. Not for charity. Not out of love for his fellow man. No one could look at Wolff and believe that.

There was a reason. And Dietrich knew he would one day discover what it was.

Eventually they got the transmitter to work — as far as they could tell. There was no way to know for sure until they received a reply. But Wolff sent out his message, saying nothing to Dietrich of what it contained. Dietrich saw how he had to write out the Morse in dots and dashes before he could transmit, he was that unsure of the code.

"I'm supposed to be an assassin, not a spy," he snapped when he saw Dietrich observing him.

An assassin. "So . . . the SS sent you here to assassinate my men?"

Wolff raised an eyebrow. "No. I told you. To kill the Americans. Your mission was considered a matter of the first priority, back when the Germans still deluded themselves that they could win." He paused, looked over at Klostermann. "Although *they* were expendable — his crew."

The pilot struggled to sit upright. For several days he'd been suffering with his thawing feet. Now his voice was thick with pain and the shock of betrayal. "You mean . . . they sent us out here, *knowing* . . ."

"That you were meant to be killed, yes. Though the Luftwaffe balked at wasting a whole crew. I recall that the argument delayed the flight." There was an edge in his tone that would have warned Dietrich off, but Klostermann was beyond caring.

"Filthy SS bastards!"

To the surprise of both of them, Wolff responded by laughing curtly. "Yes, they are, aren't they?" At the sight of their reaction, "I've done work for them for most of the war, but I'm not really a member of the SS. Oh, the rank and the uniform are legitimate — for this mission. You don't have to worry about any irregularity of that kind."

For Dietrich, this revelation made the situation easier to understand. It came to him that this was what had been different about Wolff since the bombing, the thing that made it possible to believe him: the mask of the SS Hauptsturmführer was gone.

This was the real Wolff: no less arrogant and cold than the persona of the SS officer had been, but in way of his own, an assassin, a mercenary. It shook Dietrich to realize that the deaths of Weber and Köbler for defeatism and treason had been lies, that Wolff cared no more about the Führer than he did about the Americans, or any of the rest of them. Even his voice had changed, the accent — Dietrich had never been able to quite place it — more distinct now. He suddenly doubted if Wolff was even German. Or if that was his name — did he even have a Christian name?

Wolff was sitting with the radio again, with the headset on, listening for a reply. Waiting for word of rescue — for all of them. This was one of the things that Dietrich wanted to believe.

What he couldn't understand was the urgency. And he didn't dare ask. *Wolff had his own reasons.*

Dietrich turned back to his own tasks. Erich was staring hate at Wolff who seemed to deliberately avoid noticing him. "They sent us here," he kept saying in a broken voice. "Hans was right all along. They just . . . sent us out here . . . with *him* . . ."

Dietrich didn't know how to answer him. He was afraid Erich's feet were going gangrenous. They were probably going to have to be amputated, and how could that be done here? To be killed or crippled — which was worse? In his mind, he could still see the perfect, sure beauty of the Blohm und Voss's landing back on the frozen surface of the bay. How long ago had it been? He lifted his wrist for a glance at his watch. The luminous dial showed 2:00, but he no longer knew whether it was 0200 or 1400 hours, daytime or night. How many days had they been in this place, how many nights since the bombing?

Finally he went to look for something to eat. There was almost nothing of the rations left in the hut. In another day or so, there'd be nothing at all, unless he reduced their intake to the starvation level. Wolff never seemed to eat, though Dietrich could hardly believe he was stinting himself for their sake. Maybe he had a secret food supply of his own hidden away, maybe he waited to eat until they were asleep. Dietrich didn't quite believe this, because he could never recall Wolff eating while he was at the weather station, either. He didn't know what to think.

But supplies of almost everything were short. There was no proper fuel for the stove, so that Dietrich had been forced to use the battered American Primus stove for heating and cooking. The white gas fuel burned clean, at least, but it was running out, and the little stove was inadequate to heat the shelter.

Erich was never going to recover under these conditions.

Dietrich took a breath and approached Wolff. "Supplies are running low. You said there was probably more back at the base —"

Wolff snapped irritably, "I'm not going to spend more time running errands for you two. I've only just now got this set operating."

"I could go. It shouldn't be too hard to find the way back."

But now Wolff turned on him savagely. "You're going *nowhere!*"

Dietrich took an involuntary step backward, touched by real fear. For the first time, he realized the possibility that he and Klostermann might be prisoners here, for whatever purpose Wolff had in mind — delivery to the enemy for interrogation, torture — to the Russians, maybe. It was something Erich might have imagined, that Wolff could be a Russian agent, an assassin involved in some kind of secret Stalinist plot to turn against his American allies, annex Greenland. The others, the ones who were killed, must have known, must have found out somehow . . .

He looked wildly around the cramped hut, searching for some way to escape, or a weapon. Then he saw Wolff still looking at him, watching him, and he could only think, "This is it, he knows. He'll kill me now, like he did the rest of them. Cut my throat . . ." He backed away further, ready to defend himself, even knowing somehow that it would be futile, but it would be wrong to give up without a fight.

Then Wolff seemed to pull himself back from some brink. He clenched his fists, shut his eyes, and said, "You're right, that would be a good idea, for you to go back for supplies. You'll probably have to sift through the ashes. Take the snowshoes; they're easier than skis for pulling the sled. The moon will be up in about an hour. If you can recognize the headland I don't think you could get lost, even in the dark."

Dietrich stared, still for a moment unable to believe how abruptly Wolff had changed. Slowly he got into his outdoor gear, strapped on the snowshoes. He could escape now, he knew, but that would mean leaving Erich alone with Wolff. And—where could he go?

He stepped out into the moonlight, into the still, burning cold air. "It doesn't look like there's a storm coming," Wolff advised him, "but if you run into trouble, stay at the base. Take the tent. I can find you there if necessary." Then he put a hand on Dietrich's arm and said in a different voice, "I *can* find you."

Dietrich nodded acknowledgment, not lifting his eyes. He set out on the path down to the fjord, pulling the small sled behind him. The trek was easier than he'd expected. Exhaustion and panic had made the distance seem longer the time before. He kept up a good steady pace once he mastered the snowshoes, and after a few hours he could make out the shape of the headland at the mouth of Ursa Bay. By then there was a faint reddish glow at the southern horizon, and when he checked his watch he knew for the first time in days that it was noon, not midnight. The knowledge cheered him briefly.

Then he climbed the familiar path up to what had been Weather Station Flieger and experienced the shock again of seeing the ruins, the snow all blackened with wind-blown ashes. The sight made him want to weep or rage. There were ghosts in this place.

But he had no time for mourning, and the dead were beyond help. He began a methodical search, first of the cold ashes of the storehouse, then the cabin, picking out anything that had survived the fire intact. There were tins, blackened and often strangely contorted from the fire, but he stuffed them into a sack. Tools, utensils—he collected everything, stacking the equipment near the sled. If the load was too much, he or Wolff could always come back later for the rest.

Thinking of Wolff, he searched the snow in front of the cabin for the Luger he'd dropped, but there was no sign of it. No sign, in fact, of any of their weapons. Wolff had been back to this place before him.

It was predictably difficult to find any kind of fuel that hadn't been consumed in the fire. It was light they were short of as well as heat. He began to wish Wolff had stolen a lot more supplies. At least they had the radio. The irony of the situation would have made him laugh if it weren't so desperate.

He could feel the cold slowing him down. The work was tiring, but it couldn't keep his circulation going. He considered starting a fire. There was the wood of the balloon shack. He could maybe set up the tent and build a small fire inside, take a break and get warm before he packed up the sled and started back again. He was wondering if it might be worthwhile, on another trip, to haul all that firewood back to Wolff's shelter, when he first heard the sound: the engines of an approaching aircraft.

They were coming back!

Dietrich dropped to the ground, thanking God he hadn't already lit a fire. He forced himself to remain motionless as the reconnaissance plane came over the bay, circled overhead. They wouldn't spot him if he didn't move. Or they'd think he was one of the dead. But how, *how* had they known he'd be here? Wolff? Had Wolff told them?

No. That was impossible. But—it was possible that they'd intercepted his transmissions. Now that he thought about it, that was the only answer. The Amis had probably pinpointed their location in the first place by homing in on their regular transmissions, as Wolff had suggested. And now they were still listening to see if any of the Germans had survived, had sent the reconnaissance plane to check the burned-out base for signs of life, to see if another bombing run would be necessary.

Instinctively, he held his breath as the plane circled lower. Within reach of his hand was a flattened 20mm cannon round from the strafing. With a sudden surge of guilt and shame he remembered that once, a lifetime ago, he'd been the one up in the air homing in on a target, all the times he'd gone in for one more pass, one more strafing round. Now he knew—this is what it had felt like for the ones on the ground.

Finally the plane banked and headed back out to sea, and Dietrich forced himself to move. He was stiff; the cold had seeped into him as he'd lain motionless, and now he knew he was going to have to put up the tent and build that fire.

He had a small slice of sausage with him, and he chewed it slowly as he crouched over the flames, waiting for a panful of gray snow to melt into a scant cupful of water. After he rested, he'd load up the sled and head back. Wolff was waiting for him.

Glumly, he admitted to himself that he was just as much a prisoner here as he was back at the hut. There was nowhere he could go, no way out—

Suddenly he realized. There was. There was a way out. The American plane. It had come searching for survivors. If he could contact them, if he could somehow let them know he wanted to surrender.

He almost wanted to run out the tent right then, to wave his arms and scream for the plane to come back, to see him, that he was still alive. But it was too late. Too late. He clenched his fists together and cursed the lost opportunity.

But he might get another chance. Wild, implausible schemes came into his mind: marking out a huge SOS in case the plane came back again. But he couldn't risk it. Wolff would be coming back here. He knew without a second thought that Wolff would be opposed to any contact with the Americans.

But if they were still listening for radio transmissions, there might be some hope. Quickly, he struck the tent and started to load up the sled. All he had to do was get to the transmitter.

Without Wolff finding out.

Chapter Thirty-two

Dietrich came up to the shelter, weary and hopeful, after hauling the sled back the length of the fjord. It was too bad he couldn't tell Klostermann about his plan, but he couldn't take the risk of Erich blurting something out in a moment of pain or delirium. If Wolff found out—

He paused. It was dark inside. Cold and dark. He couldn't see. He squeezed his eyes shut, then opened them again, hearing Wolff's voice. "So. You're back. Did you find any more oil?"

"Not much," he admitted. "It's back on the sled."

"Good."

Dietrich moved aside, into the hut, as Wolff came past him to go carry in the fuel. He'd done his share, Wolff could bring in the supplies — although probably he'd end up having to go back out after the food himself.

First, though, he wanted to see how Klostermann was. "Erich? Are you awake? God, it's cold in here! I'll light the stove. I brought back food—"

His eyes had adjusted enough to the dark that he could make out where the bed was. He reached down to Erich, but the bed was empty. Empty and cold. Sudden terror constricted his throat. "Erich?"

He knew. He knew what had happened. While he was gone. Wolff. *Oh my God, Erich.*

Then suddenly he felt—more than heard—Wolff behind him, spun around in raw panic, instinctively throwing up his hands to protect himself. But Wolff said flatly, "He's dead."

Dietrich's chest ached with the force of his heartbeat. He could taste the fear in his mouth. But Wolff was turning away, as if Erich's death was nothing, and some of Dietrich's fear turned cold and hard. He couldn't let it go, not again, not this time.

"You killed him."

"He was dying."

He didn't even bother to deny it. Tears of rage stung Dietrich's eyes, and he went on recklessly, "I suppose I'm next? When are you going to kill me, then?"

There was a silence in the darkness of the hut, broken only by the harsh rasp of his breathing. He'd done it, he'd said it, and now he would die. He waited for it, waited for Wolff to strike back.

"If we don't get taken off here soon, you'll be next. You have, maybe, two weeks."

However much he'd expected it, the flat, unemotional reply left Dietrich unable for a moment to draw breath. He couldn't speak. Two weeks. Wolff would kill him in two weeks. The way he'd killed the others, cutting his throat. Erich lay somewhere out there with his throat cut, he knew. Like Wederling, like Köbler, like Mundt . . .

"Why not now? Why not do it now and get it over with?"

Wolff took a step, reached out, grabbed hold of the front of his coat and pulled him close, so close he could feel the physical coldness of him. Dietrich flinched, closed his eyes. *He's going to do it! He's going to kill me now! No! I didn't mean it!*

Wolff's voice cut like a whip. "I'll kill you if and when I choose, for whatever reason I choose. Do *not* try to make me give a reason!" He let him go, flung him back against the low plank bed. "If you want to live, then I suggest that you pray, Hauptmann Dietrich. I suggest that you pray very hard for the SS to hear my message and respond. I can wait as long as two weeks. I intend to wait as long as I can. But time is running out."

And when Dietrich said nothing, "Perhaps I should make a few more suggestions, as long as we're discussing this matter. It might have occurred to you to try to leave this place. I advise you not to bother to try it. I doubt if you have an accurate assessment of my abilities, even yet. Wherever you go, no matter how far, no matter how fast, I can find you. I *will* find you.

"Oh, and one more thing. If you try to kill me, Dietrich, you'd better hope you succeed the first time. You won't get a second chance. And I'm not easy to kill. Perhaps you've already learned that.

"And I remind you of this, too — there is more than one way for you to die.

"Now, you'd better go out and bring in the rest of the supplies."

But Dietrich couldn't move. He could only sit there on the piled-up furs of the bed, trying to comprehend his situation, trying to grasp it. Two weeks. Wolff meant to kill him in two weeks. Unless somehow, in that time, the SS managed to take them off Greenland. And that was almost certainly impossible. With a pang of memory, he envisioned Klostermann's flying boat making its approach, the visible skill of the hand on the controls averting disaster almost by a miracle. How could an aircraft land here now? Or take off again?

But Wolff seemed so certain. Perhaps the SS had access to some kind of experimental machine. There were several kinds of secret aircraft in development, Dietrich knew. Was it possible?

He could see it again in his mind: the dark shape of the American Catalina outlined against the bright glow of the moon. The possibility of rescue. If he could signal it. If it could land. The Amis were humane enemies. They might rescue him if they could. He had a brother-in-law in a prison camp somewhere in the US. At least, the family said, Klaus would still be alive at the end of the war. A better chance than he had now, here with Wolff.

If only he'd lit that fire when he first thought of it.

On the other side of the hut was the radio, Wolff sitting impatiently with the headphones on. The transmitter. If the Amis were still listening . . .

It was his only hope. Not much of one, but it was the only hope he had left.

After a moment more, he got up from the bed, went out to bring in the rest of the supplies. He had two weeks.

Wolff wasn't human. Dietrich had slowly, reluctantly come to that conclusion, watching him, day after day at the radio—listening mostly, sometimes repeating his transmission. He should have realized it a long time ago, but he supposed the mind tends naturally to reject such a conclusion, disregard the evidence, make excuses, no matter how improbable. But Wolff never slept, he never ate, never had to relieve himself. Where Dietrich's breath condensed to a visible white mist in the air, Wolff's—did not.

But even Wolff couldn't sit at the receiver, listening, forever. His frustration and impatience were visible. From time to time he would get up, pace the hut, go outside for a while before returning to his vigil.

The first time he left, Dietrich couldn't make himself move. What if Wolff came back inside, caught him trying to contact the enemy?

The next time, he was ready, he took the chance. Moving quickly, he took careful note of Wolff's settings before switching the set to transmission and keying out a rapid SOS. It was all he dared, and he immediately restored the settings. But he'd done it!

The success gave him confidence. The next time he noticed Wolff's restlessness, he finally took a breath, said, "I could spell you with that, you know."

Wolff turned, shot a scowl in his direction. "What do you mean?"

Dietrich swallowed down his fear. What was it about Wolff, whenever he looked at you that way? "We're in this together, that's what you said. Neither of us get out of here if we don't hear from the SS. So how many days are there left?"

Wolff didn't answer him. But a while later he pulled off the headphones. "Listen on this frequency. Take down anything — you can do this, can't you?"

Dietrich assured him as sincerely as he could, sitting down in his place and taking over the headphones. The cold touch of them hurt his ears. Again, he was afraid to try anything at first. Wolff made him nervous. He could see in the dark. He could hear — too well to be human.

But time was running short. He sent a short SOS at first, nothing more. The next time he gave their location, adding that he wanted to surrender. It was all he dared transmit. It was easier to switch the receiver to different frequencies to see if he could hear an answer to his call for help, or even some news from the war. Anything, really, to prove that there was still a world alive out there, a place where the sun still rose and people were human.

If he could only hear from his family. Or send one last word to Amelia. What would she do if he never came back from the war? There were things he wanted to say to her.

But he still spent most of his time listening on Wolff's setting. Sometimes a signal would come through, and he'd copy it down, hand it to Wolff, wait anxiously for the news that it had been his SS contacts, that the rescue was arranged. It never was. If Wolff had heard from them at all, he kept it to himself.

As each day passed, Wolff's mood grew more terrible. He reminded Dietrich of a wild beast in a cage, a creature with the form, with the voice of a human being, but something else looking out of his eyes. And he was here inside the cage with it.

"Have you heard?" he asked when it had been ten days. "Do you really trust them to come for you?"

Wolff laughed bitterly. "Trust them? I suppose to the SS, we're all expendable, isn't that so? Or—maybe the transmissions aren't getting through. But it will be too late, soon, no matter what the reason."

Too late for you, Dietrich knew he meant. He had to know. Before it was too late. "What good does it do? What possible . . . use is it?"

"I have my reasons. You'll find out, soon enough."

He had lost hope, Dietrich realized. Wolff was getting desperate. He hadn't quite given up, but he didn't really expect any longer to hear from them. The same ones who'd sent Klostermann to his death had betrayed Wolff, too. It was a fitting sort of vengeance, he supposed, if Erich had been alive to appreciate it.

He dared to broach a dangerous topic: "The Meteorological Service, the Luftwaffe—if we could get word to them about what's happened to us, they could possibly drop supplies. I . . . don't know if you realize, just how hard it would be to land a plane here this time of year."

But Wolff wasn't listening to him anymore. In a little while he threw down the headphones again and stalked outside.

As soon as he was gone, Dietrich flung himself at the transmitter. Whenever he'd seen these moods of Wolff's before, men had died. If there was ever to be a chance for him, it would have to be now. He sent out calls for help on every channel—to the Meteorological Service, to the Americans—in German, in English. If he only knew for sure what he was up against, exactly how much time he had left, what it was that had Wolff so worried—

"What are you doing?"

A blow on the side of his head sent Dietrich off the stool and halfway across the room. Groggy, he tried to grope for the least damning excuse: that he'd only been trying to contact the Weather Service . . .

But Wolff wasn't listening. With one hand under the jaw he lifted Dietrich from the floor in choking hold. There was blood in Dietrich's mouth, and he couldn't swallow, couldn't breathe. Wolff lifted him higher, face to face, tightening the grip, and then raw screaming fear constricted Dietrich's guts at the sight of him, the dark red glowing color of his eyes.

This is what death looks like, but now, trapped by it, he couldn't look away. In his mind, he was screaming, but his voice was choked off. There was the glint of metal in the corner of his vision, a sharp pain pressing against his throat—

Then Wolff flung him down, hard, onto the floor. He struggled for breath, trying at the same time to crawl away, but Wolff was on him again, pinning him down with a strength he couldn't overcome, no matter how he fought. A paralyzing grip closed around his neck. Wolff's face was terrible. His teeth were bared, and his eyes . . .

"Damn you, Dietrich, don't make this harder than it has to be."

Wolff ripped the knife through his sleeve, tore away the fabric, cut deep across the flesh of his wrist. Blood spurted, and Wolff's mouth pressed against the wound. Dietrich struggled, but the grip on his throat and now on his arm, twisting the joint, were too much for him. His panic-stricken heart pumped the blood from his body, pulse by pulse, as Wolff sucked out his life. He knew what Wolff was now. He knew. It was too late.

Too late. Oh God, don't let this happen to me. Don't . . . please . . . no . . .

Chapter Thirty-three

He swallowed something warm, and the warmth spread through his body. It felt good.

There was a dim yellow glow in the darkness. He could see it even with his eyes closed. The effort of keeping them open was too much.

"Here. Drink this."

He was afraid of the voice, but too weak to resist. He swallowed.

He hurt. It made him dizzy whenever he moved his head, whenever he was lifted to drink.

A shadow passed in front of the light. He closed his eyes again.

"Open your eyes."

He obeyed.

"Look at me. Do you see my hand? How many fingers am I holding up?"

His head hurt when he strained to focus. The form took shape. A hand. Fingers. The image blurred, came together again. "T . . ." His tongue was clumsy. His throat hurt. "Two."

"Good."

He shifted his eyes to see the face that was speaking. The effort was painful. Pale, thin face . . . familiar . . .

Suddenly there was a sharp spasm in his guts and he retched, trying at the same time to fight it off, to escape. *Wolff. It was Wolff.*

He remembered. And he was still alive.

He remembered. What Wolff had done. What he was. The horror of it was with him constantly. When he closed his eyes, he could still see — that face, those eyes. When he opened them, Wolff was still there. He looked almost human again now, but he wasn't. Not human, not anymore. If he had ever been.

His right wrist ached. He felt a bandage around it. He rubbed it with his other hand.

He remembered. What had been done to him. What Wolff had done. What he had become. Or — had he? He wasn't even sure if he was still alive, if this wasn't some other condition, and he was damned . . .

He wept, unable to stop himself, silent tears so Wolff wouldn't hear, wouldn't see.

Wolff came across the room now, bringing food. He turned his face away, refusing it. He didn't want to go on like this.

"You need it," Wolff ordered.

He shook his head. "No. I remember. What you did. I don't want—"

"Don't want what?"

"You . . . like you . . ."

Wolff laughed shortly, as he always did, mocking him. "Don't you? To live — forever? Think about it. Don't tell me you're not afraid to die, Dietrich. I *know* better."

"Not — that way. Not like . . ."

"Don't pretend to be so noble." Then his tone changed. "But as I said, don't worry, you're safe. Your pure Aryan soul isn't in any more danger than it's ever been. The process isn't as simple as you think it is."

Dietrich felt something release inside him. He knew it was the truth. All the others — Köbler, the American. They were dead. He'd seen their bodies, frozen stiff in their graves. Simply — dead.

"You didn't kill me."

"No. Not quite. There's still some time."

Time left for what, he didn't say. But Dietrich understood now that Wolff meant to keep him alive, building up his strength, only until the next time he needed blood. Then it would happen again. And again. *God, no. Not again.* How much time left? How many times could he survive this?

"Why?"

A pause. "Because. Once you're gone, once the last of you is gone, it means it's over. Understand me. This gives me a little extra time — a week, maybe two at the most. Just in case they do happen to keep their word."

"So. I shouldn't count on . . . anything, then."

Wolff looked away for just one instant. "If it makes you feel better, the people who were responsible for this are going to pay. No matter what it takes."

It didn't. But Dietrich clung to the possibility that there was still hope, that Wolff's SS contacts might come for them after all. As long as he was alive, there was a chance, no matter how slight.

Later that day he got unsteadily to his feet, groped his way along the wall to the door of the hut. Wolff appeared to ignore him. He was seated on the stool in front of the radio, but the headphones were off and his jaw was clenched. When Dietrich opened the door, he looked up and said, with some apparent strain, "Don't forget. I'll find you."

At first he thought it must be the weather base on fire again, far off in the distance. Then Dietrich realized that the color was the sun, still below the horizon, but capable now of lighting the sky. He watched, oblivious to the biting cold, until the darkness reclaimed the sky and only the cold white light of the moon and stars remained.

When he came back inside, Wolff had resumed the headphones as if everything were normal. But Dietrich understood now just why he'd come to the Arctic in winter, and how much time he had left. How much time they both had.

Dutifully, he built back his strength, though he tried to appear weaker than he was. Wolff wasn't deceived.

"You're thinking you can kill me first, before I kill you."

Dietrich's heartbeat quickened in panic, and he had to sit down, a little harder than he wanted to.

"Haven't you heard my kind is hard to kill?"

"You're saying you're immortal."

"For most practical purposes, yes. That's what we all want, isn't it? Immortality?"

"Like you?" Dietrich flung it out in contempt. "Living on human blood? Killing other men just to survive?"

"And you claim you've never shed blood, *Hauptmann* Dietrich? Never killed? Don't delude yourself!"

"That was different, it was war. They were the enemy."

"Don't tell me. You were only doing your duty, protecting the sacred fatherland. And the enemy — tell me, Hauptmann, how can you be sure that your bombs never fell on innocent women and children? Or the workers in a factory? Were they trying to kill you?"

Dietrich was silent.

"I can tell you about killing. About your Germans doing their duty. I've been in your camps, Dietrich. The ones no one is supposed to know about. They don't just kill people in those places, they engineer it. Like a factory, like an assembly line. They were *generous* to me there. They had so many deaths they could easily spare a life or two for me. No, don't turn away. You know it's true. Admit it. And you're just as damned as I am, for being part of it."

Dietrich shook his head weakly, denying it. "It's the SS. If that kind of thing goes on. Not the Luftwaffe."

Wolff was relentless. "They die regardless. Just like you're going to die. That's the only real difference between us."

* * *

Every day, the glow on the horizon gained a little intensity. Every day, the sunrise came closer.

It hurt Wolff. He did what he could to conceal the pain, and Dietrich tried equally not to show that he saw. It gave him real hope at last. If he could only hold out, if he could only last until the sun was high enough to crest the horizon, his chance might come.

And yet at the same time he could realize what it might be like for a being like Wolff, to be trapped during the summer in the Arctic with its endless days, the land of the midnight sun. He understood Wolff's urgency now.

Dietrich hadn't dared to use the transmitter again, not even when Wolff abandoned his vigil at the radio. Then once he heard something, a voice speaking English, coming from the set. He ran to it, heard, *Hey, kraut. Where the hell are you?* But the voice dissolved in static, and he lost his nerve before he could find it again, thinking he heard a sound from outside — Wolff returning to the shelter.

Dietrich was counting the days, the intervals between the episodes of near sunrise. It had been a week since he'd first gone outside to see that color in the sky. *A week, two weeks at the most.* His life was down to its last hours now. He couldn't wait any longer. Wolff could turn on him any time.

He'd timed the exact moments of the false dawn, he knew the time the sky would start to color, how long it he would have. All he needed was a weapon. What could he use? How do you kill a vampire? A stake through his heart? Just how immortal was he?

Dietrich knew he could only try. His weapon was a piece of driftwood from the wall of the hut — a half-meter length of it had split; he broke it away. It was hidden under the furs of the plank bed, waiting.

Dawn on Greenland came just before noon. There were hours to wait. Hours to pray that Wolff could try to overcome his growing hunger for one more day. Not to provoke him, more than ever to avoid meeting his eyes.

This is your only chance, he told himself. *Your only chance.*

He'd learned to recognize the signs by now. Wolff would grow savagely restless, pacing the inside of the hut while Dietrich was careful to keep out of his way. Then, almost abruptly, he stopped moving. Sometimes he'd have to sit down or stand against a wall, bracing himself against it. His jaw, his fists, would clench. After a while, the symptoms passed away, but the intervals were getting longer.

Now Dietrich waited, sitting on the bed ostensibly preoccupied with unraveling the yarn from a worn sock, while Wolff stalked the cabin like an imprisoned beast. *Not yet. Soon. No, don't look at the watch!*

Wolff's step was starting to slow, to hesitate. He would never admit to pain, but he couldn't keep it from showing on his face, the lines of strain accentuating his normal pallor. He was limping almost imperceptibly now — there, he stopped, one shoulder against the wall, facing Dietrich.

Damn! Damn!

No, he was going to the table now, leaning forward slightly onto his hands. His head lowered, black hair falling forward into his eyes.

Dietrich marked the place on Wolff's back where his heart had to be. His hand closed around the splintered piece of driftwood. *Don't make a sound. He can hear you.* He was holding it now. He was shifting his weight to his feet. *Only one chance.*

Lunging forward, he was on his feet, rushing across the room. Wolff was only a few steps away, but his hearing alerted him, he started to spin around. He staggered slightly, and the sharp end of the wood ripped across his back. He hissed in pain, facing Dietrich with bared teeth.

Dietrich stabbed again with the stake, but Wolff grabbed hold of it. For a moment they stood deadlocked face to face, while Dietrich waited for Wolff to snatch the piece of wood away. Then he felt Wolff's grasp slip a centimeter and he realized the vampire was weakening. Slowly, he forced Wolff down, onto his knees, then to the floor. His muscles were shaking with the strain; Wolff's teeth were clenched, his eyes blinking in impotent rage.

With a final effort Dietrich wrenched the stake away, knelt over him, gasping, taking it in both hands, raising it up to chest level, the sharp end aimed at Wolff's heart. And he met Wolff's eyes.

The grimace of pain on his face was almost a grin. It seemed that it was an effort for him even to move his lips, and his voice was a thin rasp. "See, Hauptmann? No . . . difference."

Dietrich hesitated. He was breathing hard. His raised arms trembled, ready to strike. Wolff lay beneath him, helpless. *Kill him! Now! Before he can —*

Wolff twisted away, just as the stake came down, and the point raked across his ribs, then splintered on the hard-packed floor of the hut. Off-balance, Dietrich was knocked aside as Wolff struck out, and he lost his grip on the wood. Lunging back, he grabbed for it just at the same moment that Wolff did. Locked together again, they both strained to wrench the stake away from the other, Dietrich desperate, cursing himself for hesitating that one instant, that one fatal instant. But Wolff's strength was gaining as rapidly has it had ebbed only a moment ago. Dietrich fell forward as his weapon was twisted from his grip.

It was all over now. Death stared him in the face with glowing eyes. Wolff's right hand had him by the throat, the stake in the other. Dietrich shut his eyes. He'd failed, and now he was going to pay for it — the ultimate price.

Chapter Thirty-four

This time the darkness was a heavy weight lying on him. He should have died. He knew he should have died. To endure this, and then to have to go through it again — he tried to sink back into the dark, to let it take him.

It was Wolff who wouldn't allow it, who spooned warm liquids into his mouth when he was too weak to resist. Wolff, who had his own reasons, who wanted to prolong his own unnatural existence for a few more days, whatever the cost.

Dietrich knew he couldn't — couldn't possibly survive this ordeal another time. "You were lucky," Wolff told him contemptuously. "You couldn't hit hard enough. I hardly had to replace any blood."

He managed weakly to shake his head.

"No? Well, you had your chance. And you failed. You *failed*, Dietrich."

Wolff sounded angry. Over and over again in the dark, Dietrich had relived those crucial seconds when he had knelt over Wolff, stake raised, poised to drive it down into his heart — and hesitated, while a savage voice in his own mind urged him to kill. Why didn't he do it? Why couldn't he strike?

No difference, Hauptmann?

He had intended to kill Wolff. Had fought him, to kill. But then, when he was helpless — he couldn't do it. Just couldn't. Not like that.

He'd failed. He knew himself now. His weakness. Even if it meant his own life. But not like that.

"Do you know what chance you missed? What you threw away? *Life*, Dietrich!"

"You're not . . . alive," he croaked. His throat felt broken, and it hurt to talk. What was the use, anyway? But Wolff kept taunting him with it — his failure.

"Not the way you are, no. Coming one step closer to death every minute you live."

"You . . . didn't fail."

"No." A memory glowed deep in Wolff's eyes. "No, I knew I wouldn't fail."

Despite himself, Dietrich admitted to some curiosity, as morbid as it was. "How long . . . how old?"

"Two hundred years. I was still a young man, but I had always known I was the one meant to retrieve my heritage. Is my secret safe with you, Dietrich? I think so.

"You see, my family is old. We were noblemen on our estate since Magyar times — perhaps, even before that. You Germans think you understand what that means, but your nobility are all upstarts. The SS thought . . .

"No. Better not to speak of that."

Wolff seemed disoriented, as if there was too much to remember. "At first, it was a gift. Passed on — one time in each generation. It was Istvan who changed all that. Istvan, the Usurper. Killed them all, his family, his own brothers. All but one. Imre. Imre was eldest. He escaped. And Istvan took it — the castle. He was lord there, never dying, for over a hundred years.

"Imre's blood remembered. He kept one thing, when he went into exile. He kept the key."

Wolff exhaled, seemed to come back to himself. "I was born in Vienna, in exile. My father — never wanted the gift for himself, never tried to take it back, but I always knew what my heritage was, what had been stolen. I took it back. The castle, the estate, all of it. I ruled there — my title would be baron, for you Germans. For us, it was always just — lord.

"But — I came to the castle in high daylight. For the last time. His retainers saw me, they bowed down. They could see what I was. I knew the halls of the castle as if I had been born in that place. Nothing had changed. The key still fit the lock in the door.

"He lay there in the dark, the only time he was vulnerable. I could see in his eyes that he knew who I was, why I had come. And I did not fail, Dietrich. While he watched me, I took it from him — his blood, his life.

"I did not fail."

Dietrich shook his head weakly. "You killed him."

Wolff's face hardened. "It was the only way. He would never give what was his to give. His blood. Yes, I put the knife in his heart and I took it. He wouldn't share the gift, and so he died.

"And so you die. Today, tomorrow — ten years from now. Do you regret it now, Dietrich? Now that you know what you could have had? What you lost?"

Dietrich shut his eyes. "Not like that."

The sun was coming closer. The intervals of near dawn were longer every day.

The strain on Wolff was obvious. Dietrich could sit up now, propped by a heap of furs and dead men's clothes. Wolff was pacing, teeth and fists clenched, when he turned to see Dietrich watching him, in the instant before he could turn his eyes away. Dietrich flinched, seeing the narrow, sharp-bladed knife in his hand, but Wolff only used it to cut away a strip from one of the skins.

"Just a precaution. In case your nonviolent principles should fail under the temptation," he said harshly, tying Dietrich's wrists to the sides of the plank bed.

A few moments later he dropped to his knees on the packed-earth floor. His face, if it were possible, was even more pale. His hands pressed down against the earth.

A while later the weakness passed. Wolff got back up to his feet. Dietrich wondered, was he going to leave him tied this way? Or kill him now?

But in a moment Wolff came to the bed and untied the thongs, slipping them into his pocket. "Not much longer, now." He looked across the room at the radio, then turned away.

Dietrich swallowed. "It hurts, doesn't it?"

Wolff's laugh, as always, was bitter and short. "The sun hasn't even cleared the horizon yet."

Dietrich looked at him, thinking of the long summer Arctic days to come, the days when the sun never set. "And when it does come? What will you do?"

"By that time, it won't be any concern of yours," Wolff snarled. Then his face went pensive. "They found an ancestor of mine once, years and years ago. In his hiding place, in the daytime. He seemed to be dead, but the priests — they knew what he was." He laughed again, softly this time. "They laid a cross on his breast, doubtless expecting he would burst into flame. Then they put him in a coffin and wrapped it with chains. They buried him deep, under a stone slab.

"For fifty years. When he was finally released, he was raving mad, of course. With a hunger that no amount of blood could ever satisfy."

"Do you ever wish . . . you hadn't done it?"

Wolff's face changed. He raised his hand furiously, if as he was going to strike. Then abruptly he turned back to the radio.

Dietrich watched in silence, breathing hard. He knew why Wolff was keeping him alive — as long as he possibly could. He had a sudden, disturbing image of himself trussed the way a spider wraps a fly, suspended from the roofbeam of the hut, drained over and over again . . .

He turned his face away. He wanted to live. He wanted to go home.

In the pocket of his uniform, the picture. He fumbled it out.

The hut was too dark for him to make out their images. Tears stung his eyes. Amelia. Trudi. Home.

He woke to silence. Wolff was nowhere to be seen.

He struggled to his feet, head spinning. The radio was off. The headset dangled from its cord just above the floor. Only a few steps to the table — he stopped himself from falling by grabbing onto the edge, hung there a moment, panting from the effort. He switched the set back on, heard a faint sound of static, then nothing. He knew, then, that it was the end.

A moment later Wolff came back into the hut. There were harsh lines of strain on his face, of control held too long. He saw Dietrich standing by the radio, paused.

Dietrich's knees went weak. He grasped for the table, but Wolff was at his side, holding him up, helping him back to the bed.

He saw the knife in Wolff's hand. He closed his eyes. "Finish it this time," he whispered.

He felt the tip of the blade press down against his throat, the prick of pain, the warmth of his blood running down his neck, and the cold touch of Wolff's lips.

Then the mouth pulled away. "You're useless, Hauptmann, your blood is so thin, it wouldn't even sustain me for another day."

Dietrich's eyes blinked open. Though the blur, he saw Wolff, with his thin blade making a shallow cut in his own wrist. Blood welled up, black against the pallor of his skin. Then the first drop fell onto Dietrich's lips.

"No!" he cried out, too weak to resist as his head was held motionless.

The blood had the sharp taste of iron and salt, but it was cold, so cold —

1995

". . . and that was the last thing I remember." His hand went to his pocket for a cigarette, then dropped back. He kept forgetting. They didn't allow smoking in this place.

"So you don't know why he did it?"

Shaking his head. "I think . . . it would only have given him a few more days, to kill me. But, no, I don't know why."

"Then you have no idea what he planned to do next? Where he might have gone? He never said anything else?"

"There was nowhere to go. Unless — the people he was waiting for came through at the last minute. Kessler, the SS. But I don't know how they could have gotten him off. Or else — he could still be out there, somewhere. Still buried . . ."

"Captain Dietrich?"

Buried alive.

They waited patiently. He knew they pitied him. He didn't want that. He lifted his head to face them, still wanting a cigarette.

"He said something, near the end, about being buried. I got the impression he was saying he could survive the hunger — indefinitely. But not the sun. It was the sun he was most afraid of. And it was getting later in the year. As far as we were above the Arctic Circle . . ."

He stood and went to the window, blinking even behind the dark glasses at the dazzling brightness of the light reflected off a billion crystals of ice and snow. The doctors had told him his eyes might always be slightly sensitive to the light, but that was the only complication remaining, the only one. And even the Greenlanders could go snowblind on a day like this one.

"If you'd like that closed—"

"No." He'd already learned how the switch controlled the window shades. So much more to learn, so many things . . .

"No, it's fine." He came back to the chair, sat down, rubbing his right wrist. He'd cooperated with them, answering all their questions about Wolff. It meant they believed him. It meant he hadn't been suffering from some terrible, prolonged hallucination. Wolff had been real.

"You think he's out there, somewhere?" Dietrich asked.

"We'd like to find him if he is."

A few moments of silence. "I never thought—if I told about this, anyone would believe me."

"Well, it seems that during the war, a native Greenlander claimed to have had a similar experience. Records confirm he was the only survivor out of a patrol of American dogsled troops—he was their guide. He said the soldiers had been killed by a sorcerer who could fly through the night. One of them was named Ferrier.

"And the rest of your story checked out. We found the old hunter's hut, the equipment inside."

"Wolff couldn't fly. I saw him do . . . other things, but not that."

The two American officers looked at each other for a moment. "You say he swore to kill this SS Oberführer Kessler—Ulrich Kessler. Do you consider that this was a serious threat?"

"He meant it, yes. Wolff always meant what he said." Looking from one of them to the other. "Why? Is Kessler dead?"

"Kessler's been reported missing since the end of the war. He was traced to Brazil in 1958. But after then—nothing."

"What would you do, if you found him?"

"Wolff? Or Kessler?"

"Either one, I suppose."

"Kessler is still wanted as a war criminal. As for Wolff . . . it's hard to say. At least, we know how he can be killed."

"The way I told you." The mention of war criminals made him slightly anxious. It was still hard to realize the war was over, that he wasn't a prisoner.

They seemed to notice it. "We understand you'll be going back to Germany soon now."

"Yes. They say I'll have a new passport, identification, everything."

He was looking away from them again, and the silences were growing too long. They stood up. "Well, we wish you good luck."

They left him alone. He wanted a cigarette again. What kind of a world was it where people didn't smoke anymore?

He was going back to Germany soon. Not home. His home had been gone for fifty years. Amelia, Trudi.

They'd done the searching for him already. His wife had been dead for almost twenty years. Trudi was a widow, sixty-four years old, still living in Stuttgart. Trudi, sixty-four, more than twice as old as he was — as he had been.

They had her address. He thought he'd probably go there one day. Not to tell her who he was, just to see her, once.

He was back from the dead, and they didn't know what to do with him.

Back from the dead.

Absently, he rubbed the scar on his wrist. It still ached, sometimes.

They'd explained things to him, the doctors here. About the transfusions. There had been, when he was first revived, some strange compounds in his blood, similar to a natural antifreeze found in the blood of certain amphibians and fish. This was what had preserved him, kept him in a kind of half life, half death for so many years.

Nothing more than that. No other complications, they'd reassured him. And after the transfusions his blood was normal again. Human again. Mortal.

But why? What had spared him, kept him from changing completely—to what Wolff was?

In a fairy tale it might have been because his heart was pure, but he knew better than that. He knew his own faults too well. And the war, the things he'd learned about the war, his part in it . . .

Wolff had known those things, had tried to warn him. *Don't pretend to be so noble, Hauptmann.* It was Wolff who was the honest one.

But why had he done it? Was it vengeance? Malice? Or some twisted sense of mercy, a last-minute impulse to share his gift?

The best guess the doctors could come up with was that there hadn't been enough of Wolff's blood, not enough to make the crucial difference.

Whether by intent or otherwise—only Wolff knew the answer, and Wolff was . . . where? Brazil? Or still here on Greenland, still under the ice.

Wolff had time. He had forever. Buried forever . . .

Martin Dietrich stood up again, went to the window. Out beyond the shore, icebergs drifted in the current, and birds—a thousand screeching birds—rode the air, suspended between the blinding brilliant glare of sky and sea.

Slowly, he took off the dark glasses, blinking away the tears that started in his eyes as he looked out into the light of the midnight sun.

Author's Afterword

Well, no, this isn't exactly how it really happened.

Darkness On the Ice is a work of alternate history. For the sake of the story, an author may often depart somewhat from the documented record. Here I have modified certain events related to the Ardennes offensive in World War II. So to set the record straight:

The Greenland weather war was real. Between 1939 and 1945 the Germans made repeated attempts to establish weather reporting stations in the Arctic. Some of these were successful, others failed, and many were thwarted by the efforts of the Allied forces. The events as related in this novel up to the fall of 1944 conform essentially to historical fact.

Weather Group Flieger, however, and Ursa Bay are entirely my own invention. Despite at least two attempts, the Germans did not succeed in establishing a manned weather station on Greenland during the winter of 1944-45.

In making these alterations to history, I had to eliminate or displace certain other persons and events. I would like therefore to apologize:

To Doctor Wilhelm Dege and Weather Group Haudegen. In September, 1944, this group landed on the island of Nordostland near Spitzbergen, Norway, at eighty degrees of latitude. Their operation was Germany's only active manned weather station during the winter of 1944-45, and their reports materially influenced the planning for the Ardennes offensive. This group remained in the Arctic until September, 1945, the last German unit in the war to surrender.

To the Danish Sledge Patrol, which I summarily evicted from its Eskimoness headquarters and sent to languish in undeserved obscurity at Scoresbysund. This group of primarily Danish hunters, with Greenlander guides, discovered and fought two separate German weather parties during 1943 and 1944.

To the United States Army, for Captain Daniel McCluskey and his command, whom I brought in to replace them.

As for Wolff: To this date, there is no confirmed evidence for the presence of vampires on Greenland.

Lois Tilton
July, 1992

ERNEST HAYCOX
IS THE KING OF THE WEST!

Over twenty-five million copies of Ernest Haycox's rip-roaring western adventures have been sold worldwide! For the very finest in straight-shooting western excitement, look for the Pinnacle brand!

RIDERS WEST (17-123-1, $2.95)
by Ernest Haycox
Neel St. Cloud's army of professional gunslicks were fixing to turn Dan Bellew's peaceful town into an outlaw strip. With one blazing gun against a hundred, Bellew found himself fighting for his valley's life—and for his own!

MAN IN THE SADDLE (17-124-X, $2.95)
by Ernest Haycox
The combine drove Owen Merritt from his land, branding him a coward and a killer while forcing him into hiding. But they had made one drastic, fatal mistake: they had forgotten to kill him!

SADDLE AND RIDE (17-085-5, $2.95)
by Ernest Haycox
Clay Morgan had hated cattleman Ben Herendeen since boyhood. Now, with all of Morgan's friends either riding with Big Ben and his murderous vigilantes or running from them, Clay was fixing to put an end to the lifelong blood feud—one way or the other!

"MOVES STEADILY, RELENTLESSLY FORWARD WITH GRIM POWER."
—THE NEW YORK TIMES

Available wherever paperbacks are sold, or order direct from the Publisher. Send cover price plus 50¢ per copy for mailing and handling to Pinnacle Books, Dept. 687, 475 Park Avenue South, New York, N.Y. 10016. Residents of New York and Tennessee must include sales tax. DO NOT SEND CASH. For a free Zebra/Pinnacle catalog please write to the above address.

*HE'S THE LAST MAN YOU'D EVER
WANT TO MEET IN A DARK ALLEY...*

THE EXECUTIONER

By DON PENDLETON

#24: CANADIAN CRISIS	(267-X, $3.50/$4.50)
#25: COLORADO KILLZONE	(275-0, $3.50/$4.50)
#26: ACAPULCO RAMPAGE	(284-X, $3.50/$4.50)
#27: DIXIE CONVOY	(294-7, $3.50/$4.50)
#28: SAVAGE FIRE	(309-9, $3.50/$4.50)
#29: COMMAND STRIKE	(318-8, $3.50/$4.50)
#30: CLEVELAND PIPELINE	(327-7, $3.50/$4.50)
#31: ARIZONA AMBUSH	(342-0, $3.50/$4.50)
#32: TENNESSEE SMASH	(354-4, $3.50/$4.50)
#33: MONDAY'S MOB	(371-4, $3.50/$4.50)
#34: TERRIBLE TUESDAY	(382-X, $3.50/$4.50)
#35: WEDNESDAY'S WRATH	(425-7, $3.50/$4.50)
#36: THERMAL TUESDAY	(407-9, $3.50/$4.50)
#37: FRIDAY'S FEAST	(420-6, $3.50/$4.50)
#38: SATAN'S SABBATH	(444-3, $3.50/$4.50)

Available wherever paperbacks are sold, or order direct from the Publisher. Send cover price plus 50¢ per copy for mailing and handling to Pinnacle Books, Dept. 687, 475 Park Avenue South, New York, N.Y. 10016. Residents of New York and Tennessee must include sales tax. DO NOT SEND CASH. For a free Zebra/Pinnacle catalog please write to the above address.